More Precious than Diamonds

More Precious than Diamonds

Lisa J. Peck

ISBN: 1-55517-450-7

v.2

Published: Bonneville Books

Distributed by:

925 North Main, Springville, UT 84663 • 801/489-4084

CFI | Publishing and Distribution Since 1986

Cedar Fort, Incorporated

CFI Distribution • CFI Books • Council Press • Bonneville Books

Printed in the United State of America

To my B.G.

you've always been deep in my heart

and always will be

Acknowledgments

A special thank you to Jason Webb for his diamond expertise, and to my writing friends who I am always indebted to: Judy Anderson, Betty Briggs, Marilyn Chapman, Rebecca Crandell, Sherri Curtis, Shirley Hatfield, Sandy Hirsche, Linda Orvis, Rachel Nunes, and John Thornton. And also thanks to MaraDee Peck.

Prologue

His lips paled as he struggled to breathe. Everyone waited for another hoarse gasp. Instead, silence penetrated the room until Betsy flung herself over the skeletal body. She wailed, "No! Not him. Not now."

The others stared in shocked disbelief.

Chapter 1

"What have I gotten myself into?" Betsy asked the shy-looking delivery boy as he stomped the snow off his boots.

He shrugged and handed her a vibrant array of red, yellow, and white roses.

"I need you to sign here," the high school student choked.

"Of course." Betsy winked at him, pleased to note the crimson crawling over his face.

She signed, shut the door, then flipped the card open. Jeff, of course. Though she wanted to feign boredom to this new striking, yet conservative suitor, she couldn't. Was it his confident square face that drew out her desire for him? Or curiosity at the rich inner world his bronze eyes revealed that caused her heart to sizzle like grease in a hot frying pan. It couldn't possibly be because he was God loving, predictable, and strong in the Latter-day Saint faith, although those qualities had attracted her originally. Today they flashed plain and boring.

She'd scream if she had to conform herself to the white-picket-fence-life—the kind of life he led, and always would. Logic declared them an unsuitable match. So why the constant intensity pressing against her throat, choking her, as she thought of him and her together in the bonds of eternal love?

She placed the roses on her oak vanity, next to the four dozen drooping lilies Philippe had wooed her with less than a month ago. The sweet fragrance of the fresh flowers tickled her senses.

Admiring the exquisite offering, she tapped her long purple nails on the chest. The questions continued, until she reprimanded herself. Enough. She needed to prepare dinner for her brother's family. She lived in an apartment off the main house in exchange for helping her sister-in-law, Karen, with the housework and maintenance of their teenage kids—Mikey and Sam. In all, a good situation, granting her a nibble of family life—the life she knew she could stand no more—too boring.

The phone rang and Betsy sighed. She didn't feel like talking to Jeff as she surfed mixed waves directed toward him.

"Did you get them?" His deep baritone voice wrapped gently around her worries, smoothing them into silence.

"My sweets, they're fabulous. What a marvelous cure for my drab apartment."

"I aim to please." His romantic cadence hushed even more of her logical reasons of protest toward him, and replaced them with bubbling heartbeats. "One of these days you must let me see," he continued.

"Not until the art piece is complete. I must have it perfect." She examined the mural array of colors on her walls. So far she had streaks of deep purple, shocking pink, crossing-guard orange, and of course, yellow, even though the hue lacked the brilliance she required.

"I know about your perfection. Remember I went shopping with you for the perfect shade of paint. Oh, you sure tortured the poor store clerk because he couldn't get the yellow bright enough for you."

Betsy laughed. "I needed sunflower bright."

"They muttered that you were as crazy as Van Gogh."

"What if I am?"

"Then you're all the more attractive even if you still have both ears."

"Ummm."

"Talking about perfection, have you tried that Italian restaurant on Center Street?"

"Not in this life."

"I'm taking you there tonight."

"What about your son?" Betsy asked.

"He has scouts. To tell you the truth, I'm glad. He hasn't been doing much lately, except moping around."

"I'll fix that."

"I hope you can. I'll be by in a half an hour."

◇

Karen Ashforth inhaled the smell of old leather as she settled herself in the antique chair. Mr. Rawles, the head boss, had just asked her to make herself comfortable.

"Mr. Rawles," she said after he cleared his throat, "I've been studying the effectiveness of your data entry employees. I have several suggestions that will improve the morale among the co-workers, plus increase productivity."

"And I'm sure they're good. Do them."

"What?" She crossed her legs.

"You have already implemented some cost saving ideas and have more than mastered your job skills. Therefore I'm promoting you to manager of the database program. You'll do great as always."

Karen stood and shook his hand. "Thank you, sir. I've been wanting this opportunity for a long time. I will do a good job."

"I have no doubts."

◇

At times like this, meat loaf was always the answer. Quick to cook and everyone loved it; so in a sense, Betsy wasn't slacking.

Her nephew strolled in; she greeted him with a shriek. "You're wearing all black!"

Sam smiled. "Like it?"

"No. How many times have I told you it projects negativity to your soul?"

"Tttt," he said from the corner of his mouth. He opened the oven door. "Meat loaf again?"

Betsy lifted her wooden spoon high, threatening to swat. "Was that a complaint?"

He glanced up at the utensil. "Smells...like...garlic." His hands ran through his brown hair. "It's my favorite. It keeps vampires away."

"Vampires?"

"Where's Mom?"

"Work. What did you mean by—?" The doorbell drowned out her question.

Sam tossed his soccer ball in the air on his way to answer it. Seconds later, he poked his head back in. "For you. When Mom gets home, tell her I need her."

"To show off your new death look?"

"Gothic," he mumbled and left.

Betsy shook her head and rushed to the microwave to catch her reflection on the door. Jeff was early. After wrestling down a few strays, she called, "Come on back. You're early and upsetting my harmony, but I'll forgive you this once."

"Will you forgive me twice?" a woman's voice asked.

"Lydia!" Betsy yelled, flinging her arms around her friend. "Oh my solar system and bright stars. It's been years." She pulled away to eye the finger-ring size waist, the shapely hips, and the sporty jet-black hair with its splash of auburn in the front.

Lydia smiled, tucking her bangs behind her ears. "I must've surprised you if the great Betsy is at a loss for words."

"Can you blame me? It's been what? Ten years, and you show up out of the blue without warning."

"I rang earlier and left a message with Mikey."

Betsy tapped her fake nails against her cheek. "The irresponsible insect must have stung that child. But even if the hormone behavior has finally hit, neglecting to give people their messages is intolerable. I'll have to talk to her. Why don't you sit while I finish cooking dinner?" She motioned to the swinging chair. "Has it really been ten years?" Betsy asked.

"Yep. Let's see... We were last together at the New Mexico Energy Workshop. The other day I woke up and decided that the phone, letters, and email just weren't enough. So here I am."

"I'm glad you came."

Slipping onto a chair at the counter, Lydia asked, "How did you get directed to come to—Utah?"

"George was transferred here so I started investigating this place and realized Utahns needed me badly, and *voila* I'm here." Betsy spread her arms out in dramatic fashion. "Karen had some health problems. I stayed to help with the kids and housework. Besides, I've never done domestic work. Thought I'd try it."

"You, housework and kids?" Lydia laughed heartily. "Unbelievable. You must be going crazy."

"It's a slower paced life and does have bonuses." Betsy sighed. "Truly, I'm starting to grow bored. I took a vacation last November to California. Now I'm waiting to be guided to my new destination. For some reason, I have the strong inclination my future is tied up here. It makes no sense; I must trust that I'll be guided to where I need to go. I always have before. The time might be soon because Karen is doing so much better."

"I can't believe that you, Betsy girl, live in Utah, of all places."

"It's not that bad," Betsy said as she added tomato sauce to the meat.
mountains are gorgeous. Maybe that's where I'll go. I've always wanted to
learn more about nature's wonders. I could go on one of those wilderness sur-
vival trips."

She wrinkled her nose. "But isn't Utah like a conservative religious place?"

"It is. Filled to the brim with Mormons or their proper name, The Church
of Jesus Christ of Latter-day Saints."

"How are they?" Lydia asked, leaning on the counter. She rested her chin
on her hand.

"They're saints," Betsy answered. "I've got a surprise for you."

"What?"

"I'm one of them."

Lydia's elbow slid off the counter, causing her head to jerk forward. "You
gotta be kidding. Truth seeker, Betsy, a Mormon? Not possible."

"It's more than possible, my dear friend, it's a fact."

Her eyes narrowed. "Do these Mormons believe in the New Testament?"

"Yes," Betsy said. "Jesus Christ is in the name of the church."

"Betsy, it's a sexist organization! How could you? After all we have done to
open women's minds, you go and join the enemy."

"Whoa, wait a minute. I did no such thing," Betsy set the casserole dish of
spice meat on the table and placed her hands on her hips.

"Yes, you did. If you belong to a church that believes in the *Bible*, then you
believe in Paul, and Paul was one of the greatest sexists to walk the planet."

"What are you talking about?" Betsy asked.

"Aren't you familiar with the book?" Lydia asked.

"I've read some."

"A good portion of the New Testament is written by that man. Do you have
one around? I'll show you what he says."

Betsy flipped the oven on 350 degrees and left to grab a copy of the scriptures. When she returned with her new triple combination, she handed it to
Lydia.

"Why is yours so big?" Lydia asked.

"The Mormons believe three other books are scriptures as well as the
Bible."

"Good heavens," Lydia gasped. "Betsy, you really got in deep. I arrived
none too early. You finish cooking your dinner and I'll search for that
passage."

Betsy busied herself with setting out plates and cups. After that, she scurried to the cupboard to fix a quick vegetable. She decided on green beans.
They'd make a great contrast of color with the brown meat and red sauce.
Once the water boiled, the doorbell rang. She hadn't even freshened up yet.
Lydia was here and the last thing she wanted to happen was for her friend to
meet Jeff. The two of them together would be like lighting a match in a gas-
filled room.

"In here," Betsy heard Sam say. Betsy gazed around the kitchen as if the solution to stop him from entering lay in some tangible object. Her search continued when Jeff glided through the door with his attractive designer tie woven with shell pinks, dabs of grass green, and Alizarin crimson grabbing her attention. Her favorite tie. The tie he wore when they first met, right after Betsy's first sacrament. The tie she could love a man for.

"Jeff—"

"Found it!" Lydia said. "Oooh, these words make my blood boil." She rushed to Betsy, only to bump into Jeff. She looked up in a surprised jerk.

"Lydia, this is Jeff. We're going out to dinner this evening. Jeff, this is my old friend, Lydia. We go way back."

"Betsy was actually the one who introduced me to the healing methods of certain rocks and density. She saved my life," Lydia said as her eyes traveled over Jeff. Was her friend appraising him, figuring how much she'd bid?

"Rocks?" Jeff asked. The wide eyes were first directed to Lydia then drifted to Betsy.

"It's a long story." Betsy patted Jeff on the arm and spoke over Lydia's explanation. Her friend could ramble on for hours about energy density and it wouldn't do Jeff any good to learn what she once believed. It might even scare him away. "Maybe I'll tell you about it someday."

"You're not one of those Mormons, too?" Lydia asked as she continued to size him up.

"What's wrong with that?" Jeff asked. "It's the only true church on the earth. We—"

"True! You believe in supporting sexist behavior. You believe in suppressing women! What kind of truth is that?" Lydia's shrilled voice border-lined somewhere between a hysterical yell and an angry cry.

"We don't—"

"You believe in the *Bible*, right?"

"As far as it is translated correctly."

"And so you believe that Paul was an apostle, right?"

"He's a prophet."

"So you support what he says in Timothy?"

"What exactly does he say?" Betsy jumped in.

"I'll read it to you." Lydia straightened her shoulders. She cleared her throat and read: "'In like manner also that women adorn themselves in modest apparel, with pride and sobriety; not with broided hair, or gold, or pearls, or costly array.'" Lydia peered up and said in a strained tone, "It's like he thinks that women should be ashamed of themselves and aren't worthy of gold or anything nice."

"That's not what he's saying. He's talking about being prideful, not about losing your identify," Jeff said.

"Betsy, these women Paul described definitely doesn't fit you. But that's not the worst. The next paragraphs are unreal. Listen: 'Let the woman learn in silence with all subjection.' Subjection! Can you believe he said that? Can you support such philosophy, Betsy? Then he adds acid to the wound by concluding, 'But I suffer not a woman to teach, nor to use authority over the man, but to be in silence. For Adam was first formed, then Eve. And Adam was not deceived, but the woman being deceived was in transgression.'"

Lydia offered Betsy a smug look.

"It says that?" Betsy felt weak. The church was true. They believed in equality and respect for women. Why would those verses be in there? There had to be a logical explanation. She was still new, so didn't know all that doctrine yet. She'd have to study this one.

"Where is that?" Jeff asked, grabbing the scriptures from Lydia.

She pointed her red nails into the book.

"First Timothy, huh?" Jeff said.

Lydia stood up on her toes and peeked over. "It goes from the paragraph numbered nine to the end."

"Let's see if Joseph translated these verses."

"What?" Lydia asked.

"We don't believe the *Bible* was translated correctly all the time," Jeff said. "So our prophet was inspired and would change some of the things back to the way it originally was."

"Oh," Lydia said.

"Did Joseph translate it?" Betsy's throat tightened.

Jeff flipped the pages of the scripture. "The New Testament, John, Romans...ah here it is, Timothy. It has something for verse four but we're worried about verse nine, aren't we?"

The women nodded.

"Nothing." Jeff closed the *Bible*.

"Nothing!" Betsy shrieked. "Not one word of explanation?"

"Sorry, pumpkin, but you and I know we don't believe in women being dominated. Look at any recent conference report and you will see that the brethren have talked about treating women with respect and love. They even promote the equality of the sexes."

Betsy nodded. What Jeff said was truth. Perhaps that passage was translated wrong. Joseph Smith hadn't fixed everything that needed correcting. He had run out of time. It must certainly be a mistake in the scriptures, she thought, because it almost sucked her away into Satan's vortex.

"It'll be okay," Jeff said, taking Betsy in his arms. He wore dreamy cologne.

"Is dinner ready?" Mikey questioned as she walked into the room. She looked around and said, "Hi, Lydia. Been a long time."

"Sure has. You've sure grown. The last time I saw you, you were this big." She gestured her hand below her waist.

Mikey smiled, posing like a young fifteen-year-old superstar having her picture taken. "Do you like the change?" she asked in her best Marilyn Monroe voice as she flipped her brown hair onto her back.

"We need to have a talk about taking phone messages," Betsy said.

Mikey continued to beam for the imaginary photographers, moving slightly one way then to the other, as she suffered from aunt-deafness.

⋄

Karen's head throbbed as she strolled to her car. Thank heavens it was Friday and she could get some rest over the weekend. She had already taken three Tylenol to counteract the headache, but the medicine seemed to be meandering around before dissolving into working chemicals. It had been another long, good day at work.

Slipping into her car, she winced from the added pressure caused by the change of latitude. She needed to make it home, lie down, and suffer the pain properly. The discomfort originated from a mixture of stress and lack of sleep. A whiff from the cardboard pine tree scent that dangled on her rearview mirror tempted her stomach to lurch. She tugged the abomination off the mirror and tossed it to the backseat. Lying her head on the steering wheel, a light flashed in the middle of her forehead. Not a migraine, she prayed as she lowered her stiff shoulders in to release the tension, a futile effort.

Sitting up, she squinted. The low light of the sunset reflecting on the snow blinded her. She started her engine and pulled on to the main road, not noticing a car a yard away until a loud screech of tires skidded across the pavement. All she had time to do was grasp the steering wheel before the car bolted to the left as metal scrunched. Karen grabbed her head to relieve the pressure booming inside. Blackness.

◊

Jeff scrutinized Betsy's friend, after Lydia read from the *Bible* and so belligerently dismissed his explanations. What sort of woman had he tripped into battle with? She wore dark red silk, hinting at money, passion, and eccentricity. Jet black hair with a streak of red along the front, conveying a taste for the dramatic. Her knowledge of the *Bible* revealed a scholar. Her interpretation suggested that she was a woman activist with a political agenda. The wavering tone in Betsy's voice told of Lydia effectiveness and of the danger she possessed.

He felt an urge to shield Betsy from any further doubt in the church. She needed more experience with the basics and with the spirit before she took on the sensitive areas. "Betsy," he spoke with a calm tone to counteract the alarm Lydia ignited. "Are you ready to leave? I'm starved."

Betsy didn't move from the book. "Paul said some harsh things."

Jeff nodded. "That was a long time ago. Things are different now."

"So you don't believe in everything the *Bible* says then?" Lydia asked. She cast her deep mesmerizing eyelashes at Jeff.

He smiled at her lure of passion, a character trait he always liked. Such beauty and such craftiness, he thought. "I didn't say that."

"How do you explain it?" She shot back.

"Tell you what," he said. "Why don't I explain that to you later? It would take some time and I'm really hungry?"

"Want to buy some time, huh?" she arched her elegant eyebrows. He watched her. She waved her hand and said, "I'm feeling generous today. Why not? When will I see you again?"

"We'll run into each other since we're both Betsy's friends."

"I'm sure we will."

"Until then," she held out her creamy, white hand. He reached for it and shook the soft palm. "It was nice meeting you," she said.

Jeff sighed and put his arm around Betsy.

"Lydia, have you eaten?" Betsy asked. "We would love to have you join us. I'm sure Jeff wouldn't mind. It's been so long since we've seen each other, and we have a lot of catching up to do."

Jeff's arm, draped around Betsy, tensed.

"Ah, no, I'd be interfering. You two go on your date and we'll meet for lunch tomorrow."

"Sounds good," Betsy said.

"Great. And I'll sign us up for hang gliding lessons. So be prepared."

"What? Hang gliding?" Betsy asked.

"Don't tell me you haven't done it?" Lydia asked.

"Not for years."

"If you don't want to go—"

"No," Betsy yelled. "I promised myself I wouldn't slow down when I grew older and I'm not going to. Thank you, Lydia. I feel my old self returning. It's been dead too long. This is great. I'm looking forward to it. Come on Jeff, I'm in the mood to either heckle those poor musicians at the restaurant to shame or cheer them till they die of blushing. It depends, of course, how they play." She seized his hand draped around her shoulder and guided him toward the front door. She stopped and said to Lydia, "Why don't you stay and say hi to Karen and George? I'm sure they'd love to see you."

"I think I will. It's been forever, and besides, I'd like to talk to them about living among the Mormons."

"I wouldn't do that if I were you," Betsy said.

"Why not?" Lydia challenged.

"Just don't, please? For me. I'll tell you tomorrow when we're running down the mountain right before we jump into the big plush sky."

Lydia smiled and waved.

Once Betsy and Jeff made it into the hall, Jeff studied her and asked, "You're not really going to go hang gliding, are you?"

"Why not?" Betsy asked. "It sounds like the perfect way to end my melancholy."

Chapter 2

Karen leaned against the seat, eyes closed as pressure gathered like a rubber band twisted too tight. A loud pounding on the door squeezed the rubber band to the breaking point. She heard a distant, "Lady, are you all right?"

The person was a blur.

"I'm calling 911. You pulled out right in front of me."

Karen groaned. "Please," she muttered. "My head—"

"The ambulance and police will be here in no time. Do you want me to lean your seat back so you can lie down?"

Karen nodded. The strained vessels in her head felt as though they had snapped. She swallowed, her throat dry. *Patience. I must have patience.*

✧

Thick bulging folders lay in every direction, like a whirlwind had hit, dumping all the debris on his desk. George forced his eyes to his notes, avoiding the mess. Normally he would have organized the upheaval, but a threatening deadline demanded his attention.

His extension rang. He picked it up, pressing the red button. "Yeah."

"George, Pat here, I need the Mentoya file."

He grumbled as he leafed through the stacks. Sometimes it didn't pay to come to a job highly recommended, even if he was the supervisor of the chain *Milestone and Sons* in Provo. He felt more like a servant to the employees than a boss. "We need the data right now for..." "What should we do about...?" "Have you made your decision about...?"

They expect him to perform like three miracle men, George decided, gloomily. He'd meet their expectations. He always pulled through, though the stress bothered him. Like now, for instance, his stomach hurt, but he didn't have time to pop an Alka-Seltzer.

A loud knock jolted his attention. A shiny, bald head peered around the doorframe. "I'm here."

"Sorry, Patrick, I haven't found it yet."

"What's with you?" he asked, dropping into the closest chair.

George stared at his comrade. "I'm buried."

"Are things all right at home?"

"Yeah, they're fine," George grumbled.

"Karen's not—" Patrick eyes darted around as though his thoughts searched for the perfect way to phrase the question so he wouldn't offend his friend.

George put an end to Patrick's misery. "No, she's not having panic attacks anymore."

When the Ashforth family had first moved to Provo, Karen suffered severe panic attacks. Patrick had been supportive and closed-mouthed when George needed to take time off work to attend to Karen in the hospital.

"I'm glad to hear she's doing better," Patrick said. "Is she adjusting to the culture here?"

"Didn't I tell you?"

"What?" Patrick asked.

"She got baptized during Christmas."

"You're kidding?"

"Do I look like it?"

"No. That's wonderful news. She really is doing better."

"Yeah."

Patrick grinned broad. "The Lord truly does work in mysterious ways. Who would ever have believed your wife would become a Mormon?"

"Or my New-Age sister."

"When did she—"

"A month or two before my wife. I didn't know moving here would have so many consequences."

Patrick smiled and patted George's shoulder. "Only good ones. Very good ones."

"Glad you think so," George muttered. He opened the door.

As Patrick left, George quickly said, "As soon as I find the file, I'll bring it right to you."

"I'd appreciate that. Hard to believe," he said, shaking his head.

George strolled to his desk, picked up a sharp leaded pencil and flopped it back down. Hard to believe, that's what he thought too. Why did Karen have to do that?

What she believed shouldn't affect him. But it did. He remembered earlier that day at breakfast. He was running late and slamming cupboard doors. "I can't find the coffee beans," he said to his wife when she entered the room.

Her eyes avoided his. "I don't buy them anymore."

"What?" he asked. "Why not?"

"I'm a Mormon now."

"So?"

"They don't drink coffee. Don't you remember me complaining about it? You said it'd be good for me to give it up. It'd improve my health."

"What does any of this have to do with my coffee drinking? Just cause you don't drink it doesn't mean I have to give it up."

"That's true," Karen said. "But I can't buy it. If I have it in the house, it'd be too tempting. I could never resist."

"That's not fair."

"Can't you pick up a nice hot cup on the way to work?"

"I'm busy. I don't have that much time."

"George, please, help me out. It's hard enough not to have a morning cup to get me going."

He sighed at the memory as he ran his hand through his hair. The computer screen flicked to the screen saver, nagging him to return to work. Stopping by McDonald's and grabbing a cup of coffee was no big deal, but the frustration of the past couple of months had gotten to him. He'd had to tiptoe around Karen when her panic attacks struck. If he acted normal and let her fend for herself, she ran the risk of becoming overwhelmed and having a mental break down. If he were too overprotective, she'd grow angry and complain that she couldn't breathe.

Thankfully, facing her fear of Mormons had healed her.

He was glad because he didn't know how long he could have endured it. It really bothered him when she couldn't pull it together.

His door opened.

"George?"

"What?" he asked, spinning his chair around to face Lindsay, a young woman with silky short blonde hair. He'd worked with her on several assignments lately.

"I wanted to know if you've completed the report yet so I can add my finishing touches?"

"Doing it right now."

"Is there anything wrong?"

"No, why do you ask?"

"No reason."

◇

An expensive, tailored green awning trimmed the multi-windowed building. Italian words scrawled on each windowpane. *Oltavios Ristorante Italiano.*

Jeff opened the wooden door for Betsy. She paused to savor the experience. The array of soft browns, rich ambers, and deep greens instantly pleased her. Floral arrangements mixed with potted plants and facsimiles of ancient swelled jars made up the atmosphere. His arm fell gently over her shoulder.

"Charming," Betsy gasped up at him.

A satisfied twinkle flashed through Jeff's eyes. He pecked her on the nose.

Lively music saturated the air as suave musicians sprinkled the evening with delightful notes. Jeff grabbed Betsy's hand and danced a few spins as waiters and waitresses dressed in black skirts or pants with crisp white shirts filled orders.

They collapsed on the maroon cushioned bench, waiting for their names to be called. She drank in bronze eyes that smiled at her. With his dark brown, graying hair, strong jaw, and acqualine nose, she suspected passionate Italian blood flowed through Jeff's veins. "You were right about this place," Betsy said.

"Thank you." A blush spread across his face. His eyes darted over to the redwood check-in counter.

Betsy followed his gaze and spied an old rustic map hanging on the wall. The ends of the chart wrapped around scrolls. He was so fresh on the dating scene the slightest compliment made him flush. She wondered if he missed the comfort and security of his former wife.

"*Sicilia, Pompeii, Milan, Venicia, Sardinia, Corisa,*" Betsy spoke with heavy enunciation. "Such beautiful language. I love hearing Italians talk."

"Better than French men?" Jeff asked, his voice filled with mischief or a hint of annoyance. Betsy wasn't sure which.

"My good man," Betsy patted his leg, "it's not the language."

Soon after their name was called, they followed the overweight girl, wearing clothes three times too small. Betsy looked away from her, refusing to allow her to ruin the beautiful atmosphere.

Italian flags stood on several half walls, spicing the room with rich flavor. A mural of an angel drawn in style of Michelangelo, captured Betsy's attention. "Wait!"

The hostess turned around, her eyebrows knitted together.

"I must examine the mural." Betsy gestured to Jeff and the hostess. Then she hustled to the recessed wall and gazed over the circular fresco. An angel with a hammer in his hand filled the frame.

Betsy sighed. The angelic face was the greatest merit of the painting. "I love the face," she said.

"That's because you're an angel yourself," Jeff said.

Betsy squeezed his hand.

After the orders were given, Betsy closed her eyes. The musicians playing the accordion circled around their table. She swayed to the rhythm, feeling herself breaking free from the day's stress. "I soar to this music," she whispered. She opened her eyes and saw Jeff acting amused. "You know, since I've become a Mormon, I do my meditation less and less. Maybe it was because I got into so much trouble when I first started teaching your son's class."

"The ideas and your teaching methods were unique. I thought poor Sister Cox would die of shock when you tried to teach her son meditation."

Betsy laughed. "Ahh, so did I. I did fear she'd come after me with a butcher knife."

Jeff chuckled. "You gotta watch out for those momma bears. If there's one thing I've learned since being in the bishopric, it's that those are the most knee-shaking-people I have to deal with. Believe me, I've had a lot of unnerving experiences."

"I'm sure," Betsy said. "If you've crossed anyone, which you're bound to do, and they respond with the same degree as Sister Cox, it's time to ask for a release."

"Naw, I believe Heavenly Father called me, and at the right time, He'll release me."

"Pure gold. That's you." Betsy unfolded the napkin on her lap. Was he thinking of her now? His dead wife? How rough was the competition? She longed to ask him, but instead she said, "Tell me what your wife thought about you —" Betsy paused to see if he'd give her an answer.

"She liked me," he said. Betsy noticed Jeff avoided eye contact and his complexion deepened in color.

"Did she have any sort of problem with you? Oh please, tell me you aren't perfect. It'd make me feel better."

"It says more for her than me that I don't know what she didn't like." Jeff's voice shook. "She was very much a saint that way. Never heard her complain once about something I did. She was a positive person like you are, and utterly refused to think negative about another person"

Betsy flipped her fork around. Jeff must be glorifying his wife. It couldn't possibly be true that she never complained. "You were perfect, huh?"

"I didn't say that."

"It seems like she'd agree with my prediction about you being the bishop some day."

"You don't really believe in reading peoples auras?"

Betsy drummed her fingers on the table. It sounded like she had just lost a point. "Of course I do. Everyone reflects light. Some of lightness, some of darkness."

"That's true."

She stopped the drumming. "Out with it. Something's bothering you. What is it?"

He shrugged. "It's nothing."

"Please be open with me."

"I'm a little nervous about the New Age philosophies you brought into the church."

Betsy twisted her napkin. More minus points. "Why?"

"Because some of its false doctrine."

"Like what?"

"Your meditations."

"What? In church they always encourage us to meditate."

"Not in the same sense as you."

"Do you believe it's wrong for athletes to picture their routine in their mind before they perform?"

"No."

"That's meditation."

"True. What I'm worried about though is when you talk about going into other realms."

"You mean it's wrong when I search deep inside myself and realize my sins or frustrations I have so I can work on forgiving?"

"No. That's probably fine, too."

"What is it then?" Betsy asked. The waiter slid the bread, olive oil, and Balsamic vinegar onto the table.

"The leaving the body stuff."

Betsy laughed and leaned in to pat his hand. "I don't do that. Always had a funny feeling about it so I stuck to pondering my thoughts, behavior, and philosophies. I do have a confession, though, I hate being the same as everyone else, but I thought you liked that. I thought that was how I reminded you of your wife."

Jeff sighed. "That's true. It's good for me to be on my toes. A refreshing break. Although one of the differences between my wife and you is she was a long time member and never questioned anything."

"There's nothing wrong with questioning, my dear boy. That's how you strengthen your faith."

"Or fall away." Jeff yanked a corner of bread off the loaf.

"That doesn't—"

"Betsy, how many different philosophies or religions have you joined?" Jeff chased the oil with the bread.

"I found the truth."

"You're right. Stick to the basics. Faith, repentance, good works, and you'll always have the light."

"There's nothing wrong with questioning," Betsy said.

"I'd hate to have the devil put doubt in your mind."

Betsy winced. Did the devil already do that? "You're right. I just don't get why those verses are in the scriptures. Why would it have something so sexist in it? One of the problems I had with the church before I joined was that I thought men ruled. I couldn't join a church that supports that principle. It's wrong."

"Don't worry, my dear." He winked. "Christ is the biggest advocate for women."

"I don't know the Savior that well."

"You'll be pleased with the findings," Jeff said.

Betsy smiled and their meals arrived. The waiter set down a huge white bowl filled with noodles buried in Pesto sauce. Pinenuts sprinkled the top along with mozzarella cheese. Chicken Pesto. Her favorite. She took a bite then smacked her lips together, kissing her fingertips. *"Delicioso.* Do you want a bite?"

"Of course." His fork pierced several noodles.

When the couple finished half their meal, Betsy asked Jeff about his son. "Tell me why you're worried about Dud—-I mean Chad." Betsy remembered Jeff explaining about his son's name. "His real name was Dudon on his mother's insistence. But a couple of weeks ago, his friends started calling him Chad from his last name Chadwick, and the new name caught on faster than a forest fire." Jeff thought the new name was so much better and his wife wasn't around to stop him so he had asked Betsy and all of Dudon's other teachers to refer to him as Chad. Dudon was pleased with the name change and corrected anyone who goofed it up.

"I'm worried because he seems depressed."

"I don't get it. When I taught him last Sunday, he told jokes, laughed, and gave insightful comments. What possibly could've happened?"

"I think I know," Jeff whispered.

"What?"

"We were planning to take a vacation and when he flipped through the calendar and saw my big black writing in February." Jeff stirred the pasta around his plate not taking a bite.

"And?" Betsy said.

"I had labeled the day Cindy died."

"Oh." Betsy leaned back in her chair. "Poor boy. He misses his mom."

"What can I do for him?"

"It's natural for him to be sad around this time. You're probably feeling it, too."

"Me?" Jeff sat up straighter. "I'm fine."

"You don't have to do the macho thing," Betsy said. "I'd still like you if you were human. Perhaps even more."

"It's no act. God has taken the pain from me."

Betsy eyed Jeff, not believing him, but also not wanting to openly disagree. "It wouldn't be a bad idea to take your son to a counselor."

"Why would I want to do that?" Jeff asked loudly. "He's perfectly fine. There's nothing wrong with him."

"I never said there was," Betsy said, her voice decreasing in volume. "But he's been through a traumatic experience. It might give him peace of mind to talk out his pain."

"My boy's doing great. He doesn't need a shrink. I appreciate your concern."

"Jeff, there's nothing wrong with going to one of them for help. I have. They helped me understand my illogical thinking—"

"My boy doesn't need that. Sometimes you have to stop searching for ways to make your trials easier and face them head-on."

"You think I'm a coward?" The fork clanged the top of the bowl.

"I didn't exactly say that," Jeff said. "I'd rather not talk about this, okay?"

"That's fine. I need to be going anyway." Betsy stood and for the first time noticed a couple of people darting glances at them.

"Betsy, sit down."

"No. If we're not going to engage in open honest communication, I'm going. Now you're trying to control."

"Sit please," Jeff whispered, sounding like a harsh brisk wind.

"Don't worry about me. I need a walk," Betsy said.

Jeff hurried after her and grabbed her elbow. "How are you going to get home? Why don't you wait for the check to come, and I'll drive. Please. I didn't mean to get defensive."

"So you're willing to talk about going to a therapist?"

"Not really. Sorry."

"You're forgiven," Betsy said.

"I'm sorry about overreacting. You hit a raw nerve."

"I'm going to go anyway. I need the time alone. It'll do me a world of good. Trust me."

"It's so far from your house."

"No worries," Betsy said, then waved good-bye.

◊

The meat loaf was cold when George arrived home and no sign of Karen. Strange. He hung his keys on the rack and picked up the phone to call her work number. No answer. Maybe she'd gone to the store. He opened up the cupboard that competed with Old Mother Hubbard. At the same time he ─── ered only peanut butter was left, which he got out as a burst of laughter ─── the front room diverted his attention. He decided to investigate the noise ─── found Mikey, Sam, and Lydia sitting around the formal living room con─── versing.

"Lydia," he said. His lungs seemed to have constricted together, allowing rugged pronunciation.

"George." She rose from the chair.

The grandfather clock ticked in the entryway as the two stared at each other.

"Aren't you going to say how nice it is to see me?" Lydia asked with a bit of a smile.

"It's been a long time," George said flatly.

"Have I changed?" She swung around in a circle.

"Never. Age doesn't touch you."

She beamed as he looked at Sam. "Where's your mother?"

He shrugged.

George then asked Mikey. His daughter flipped her hair in a huge motion. "Pa, I haven't seen Ma. But when I do, I'll tell Ma of your intentions."

George stared at her wondering what to say. That child was always in a dream world. Looked like she was pretending to be on *Little House on the Prairie* today. "I'm going to see if her car is in the garage. You guys go ahead and eat."

"It's meat loaf again," Sam said.

Mikey wrinkled her nose, creating thousands of lines. "Gross. Aunt Betsy is trying to kill us. She's going to kill us." She fell to the floor, gagging and flopping, first in dramatic motion then gradually relaxing as though death.

Sam stepped over Mikey's dead body and motioned to Lydia to come. "If we hurry, we can have the last of the peanut butter."

"Sounds lovely," Lydia sneered.

The phone rang. Mikey popped up from the dead and raced Sam to answer. Sam won and Mikey showed her severe disappointment by jutting out her lower lip.

"Who is it?" Mikey asked before Sam had a chance to speak. "Who is it?"

"Hush," Sam said. Something in his mannerism stopped Mikey. He hung up the phone, looked at Mikey and Lydia, then said, "Dad, Mom's been in a car accident and she's in the hospital."

"What?" George asked as though he hadn't heard the information.

"Mom's at the hospital. The nurse said she's okay and is asking for you."

George stood still. His son tugged on his arm. "Dad, you've got to go to the hospital."

He nodded as Sam grabbed the keys from the rack. Once he had them dangling in his hand, he tossed them to his father.

Lydia rushed close to George and snatched the keys from his hand.

"This isn't time for games!" Sam said.

"I'm not playing them," Lydia said. "Your father is obviously in no condition to drive, so I will."

"Nonsense," George snapped. He held his palm out to Lydia. "Stop horsing around and give me the keys."

"No, seriously, you're in shock."

"Would you knock it off? Of course I can drive. Hand me the keys."

Lydia smiled and wrapped her long nails around the jagged metal. George blocked her path and seized her wrist, forcing her fingers to let go.

They hurried to the car, Lydia following. George turned to her, "Lydia, you don't need to come. We have everything under control. You're welcome to stay and wait for Betsy. Tell her where we are."

◇

Betsy had only strolled a block before grumbling at the fact she had worn high heels. Her feet would be sore tonight. She wished she was already at home soaking them. But that wasn't a reality so she'd use this uninterrupted time alone to think. And, oh, there was so much to mull over in her mind; her relationship with Jeff, to her recently ruined relationship with her ex-husband Philippe, to Lydia and her comments on the *Bible*, to this whole Mormon thing. Overwhelming.

Did she really belong to a sexist group? When she arrived home, she'd have to hit the books.

Now for Jeff, one minute she was confused about her feelings for him, the next sweet on him. Then last, mad. What was she supposed to make of all this?

◇

"Karen, are you okay?"

She nodded. The drugs helped even though they hadn't completely zapped the pain.

George grabbed her hand and kissed it. "I'm sorry about this morning."

Swaying motions in her head slowed everyone's speech patterns. "You're fine," she said drawled out. "My head still hurts."

George brushed her bangs aside and kissed her forehead.

She closed her eyes, smiling. "Thank you for coming."

"Like I wouldn't?" George said.

"I knew you would, but I'm still grateful."

"The doc said you can go home as soon as you feel up to it. The kids are waiting in the car. Would you like to go now?"

Karen nodded. "I want sleep."

"Good. That's what the doctor ordered." He grabbed her hand. "Let's get you out of here." Karen sat up and George knelt to look her in the face. "There is just one thing I probably should tell you about first."

She blinked.

"I wouldn't tell you, but you'll see as soon as we get in the car—"

"What."

"You're son's dressed a little weird."

"How weird?"

"You know the Gothic style some of the teenagers around here are into?"

"Oh, no."

"It's not so bad right now. He only has on black pants and a black tee-shirt with a silver skull on front."

"Good heavens," Karen whispered.

The drive home was quiet as though the children had been struck speechless seeing their mother's pale face, and flashing grimaces of pain. Karen felt the pressure of her husband's gaze on her but said nothing. Her stomach twisted. She was making life hard on him. It wasn't fair. He already had it tough with her mental breakdown. He earned a rest, deserved it, and she seemed to be incapable of giving it to him. Things needed to change. She reached for his elbow and fumbled for his hand. He squeezed it. We love each other, Karen concluded. He's a good man.

"Mom, are you feeling okay?" Sam asked finally from the backseat where he and his sister sat.

"My head hurts."

"Do you have a concussion or something from hitting it when you wrecked?" Mikey asked.

"No," Karen whispered. "I didn't hit my head."

"How did it happen?" Sam asked.

"I was pulling out and the guy hit me," Karen said. She rubbed at the center of her forehead.

"Jer-r-rk," Mikey said long and deliberate.

Karen sighed. That child was always acting to the point Karen doubted she knew how to be herself.

"Where's the car?" Sam asked.

"I called a tow truck. They picked it up and took it to the mechanic," George said.

"Did you get a ticket?" Mikey asked.

"Let's not bug your mom right now. She doesn't feel well. You can talk about that later," George said.

The group fell silent until they neared their walnut castle-house. "Whose car is that?" Karen asked. She still leaned against the headrest with the headache throbbing, especially when the car hit a pothole.

"Betsy has a friend visiting," George said.

"Which friend?" Karen asked in a strained tone.

"It doesn't matter. What's important is that you're fine."

"I want to know what's going on here."

"I'm sure she'll leave soon."

"It's Lydia," Sam said.

"Lydia!" Karen yelled, then winced at the pain the outburst caused her. "Not her, not now."

"When would be a good time for her to visit?" George asked.

"Never!" Karen's fists clenched.

George chuckled. "That's what I thought."

Karen tossed around the image of Lydia. She was probably in her late thirties—early forties. She had always been beautiful, never the teenager with pimples and braces. She had always applied make-up to the point where she looked fabulous. Everyone else appeared frumpy in comparison.

She took one more glance at the visiting car. She had to deal with a car wreck, her migraine, the distance in her relationship with her husband, Mikey possibly going insane, and Sam going Gothic. Now Lydia. How could she do it?

◇

Betsy had wandered for perhaps a mile when Jeff's car pulled up to the edge of the sidewalk and stopped. Betsy laughed. Her steam had faded and she welcomed the sight. She walked to the door and plopped her shoes over the edge of the window seal. "Hello," she said. "Did my strong thought patterns reach you and tell you I changed my mind?"

"No. I couldn't allow you to walk all the way home and feel good about it. I do try to be a gentleman."

Betsy smiled. "My walking home doesn't make you look like a good date, does it?"

"What would my neighbors think? Once they found out, they'd try to dissuade you from being with me. I wouldn't want that," Jeff said.

"And why not?" Betsy asked, peering into his handsome face.

"Because I enjoy dating you."

"Even after tonight?"

"Yes, especially after tonight. I realized something about you, Betsy."

"What's that?"

"You say things the way you see them without hesitation."

"Of course. If I was afraid of anything, it wouldn't be healthy. It's fine to fear, but my motto is to stamp it out the second I see it. I'd like to get over my idiosyncrasies and get on with living. I'm growing older. I have a lot of living to accomplish in a short time frame."

"What do you want to accomplish most?" Jeff asked.

Betsy stood and stretched.

"I'm sorry. Get in and let's talk," Jeff said.

"Finally, some manners. Let's see, what do I want to accomplish most?" Betsy climbed in the car and sat. She opened her purse and searched until she found her sunglasses. They swallowed her face when she slipped them on. "I want to be a truth seeker. I want to learn as much truth as I possibly can in the time I have been allotted on the earth, and I want to apply its principles. I don't care where I get the truth—I just want to own it."

"Sounds admirable," Jeff said. "It also sounds exhausting."

"I believe it's both," Betsy said, "and a whole lot more."

Jeff smiled. "I really do like your passion. Forgive me about what happened earlier. I get a little sensitive when it comes to my son."

Betsy laughed. "Your son caused our first fight too, remember?"

Jeff nodded, reaching for her hand. "Will you forgive me? I'm still new this."

Simply charming, Betsy thought.

◇

After the date, Jeff pulled up to his dark gloomy house. He banged the steering wheel. The clock in his car flipped 9:15. How had things gone wrong with him and Betsy? Why did she consistently have to add her two bits on parenting? She should stay out of it. Everything else about her seemed so right and he knew he had completely fallen in her spell. The only problem between the two of them was her child rearing advice. He and Cindy had never fought about how to raise Chad. Of course Chad was their son. Jeff climbed out of the car. He knew that wasn't the only reason Cindy and him hadn't fought over him. The other was he had never been involved. Whatever Cindy did was good enough. He'd trusted her. Or was it because he was lazy?

He hastened to the house and entered the family room that was now Chad's room. His son, leaning to the right in his chair, watched the lights of the television flicker. Jeff studied him. The boy's shoulders slouched low; his expression held no hint of emotion, good or bad.

"How was Dutch oven cooking?" he asked.

Chad slowly looked at him. "Dumb."

"Want to tell me about it?"

"Nope."

"Come on."

"You throw food in the pot and put the lid on and set it over some coals. Haven't you done that before?"

"Have. What did you make?'

"Don't know."

"What do you mean? Dinner dish or desert? Did it taste good?"

"I left early."

"How did you get home?"

"It was at the Wilson's."

The neighbor lived across the street. Chad could easily maneuver his wheelchair over and back. He had done it countless times.

Jeff stood silent, tossing over what he should do. At last, he flipped the television off.

"What did you do that for?"

"Let's talk."

"Ah, Dad, I hate lectures. I want to see the end of my show."

"What were you watching?'

"Ah...ah..."

"Chad, I'm worried about you. You seem extra depressed lately. What's the matter?"

"Nothing."

"I'm not going to leave you alone until you tell me." Jeff scooted the chair in close to Chad then sat.

His son looked at him and grunted.

"I love you. I know I'm older than most fathers and that might make it harder to relate to me but... With your mom gone, we only have each other. We wanted to have siblings for you, but your mom was too old. Now it's just you and me. So please, don't block me out."

Jeff put his hand on his son's knee and waited.

Time dragged before Chad spoke. "My hip's killing me. I hate being in this stupid wheelchair."

"It can't be fun."

"It's not."

"I don't think that's all that's bothering you." He waited, but his son's face remained hard.

"The anniversary date of when your mom passed away is coming up."

Still nothing.

"Maybe we should do something special to remember her."

He looked down.

"Would you like to visit her grave?"

Chad nodded.

"How do you think we should decorate it?"

He shrugged.

"I could buy her some roses."

"Daisies," Chad whispered. "Those were her favorite." His voice cracked as he spoke, then quickly became sobs. "Dad, I miss her. I want Mom back. I need my mom." Jeff put an arm on his boy's trembling shoulders then grabbed Chad and embraced him. When he pulled away, Jeff reached out and wiped the tears from his son's face.

Chad looked up, blinked, and wiped tears from his father's.

Chapter 3

"George, is Karen all right?" Lydia rushed into the kitchen to greet the Ashforths.

"I'm fine, thank you," Karen grumbled. "A fender bender."

"That's nice." Lydia flashed the couple one of her fantastic smiles.

Nothing had changed over the years, Karen decided, her fingers piercing her palm. "I need some sleep, George."

Her husband's face softened as he put his arm around her shoulder. "That's what the doctor ordered." He turned to Lydia and asked, "Is Betsy home yet?"

"She's upstairs changing. I came down for a drink of water."

She could've had a drink in Betsy's apartment, Karen thought, before tugging her husband's arm.

Betsy peered at the top of the stairs. "Is Mikey down there?" she called.

George yelled back, "No, why?"

"No reason in particular," Betsy said. "Just some things have been rearranged in my room and I was wondering if she rambled through my stuff again to find set pieces for those movies she always shoots in her head."

"I'll have a talk with her," George said, before guiding Karen to bed. Once she nestled under the covers, he bent and kissed her. "Good night, my love."

"Where are you going?"

"To do some work."

"Stay."

His index finger tenderly traced her face. "Sweetheart, we've been through this before. I love you, not Lydia."

"I know." She reached for George and brought his forearm to her mouth, caressing the hairs with her lips. "I've been so difficult for so long. Do you ever feel like escaping?"

"Karen, I love you and want to be with you. Get those crazy ideas out of your head." He pulled the blanket further up on her shoulder. "Now get some sleep."

"Hold me."

He slipped in bed and wrapped his arms around her. "I'm going to fall asleep and won't get my work done."

"Do you mind?"

"No, I'm grateful for the great excuse."

◊

The next morning Karen woke to her own scream. George pulled her close. "What is it?" he asked.

"A nightmare."

"Tell me."

"Lydia had a black marker. She scribbled on me. Each time the black touched me, that part of my body faded. She had almost completely erased me when Betsy yelled at her, drawing Lydia's attention away. She had managed to get Betsy's arm by the time I awoke." Karen struggled with a few breaths before adding, "She said you were next."

♦

Maybe if I open one more cupboard I'll be pleasantly surprised, George wished. He hoped Karen had felt guilty and bought fresh coffee beans, or at least weakened her resolve and given up the silly idea of banning caffeine. He opened the cabinet door, but there were no coffee beans. Actually, there was hardly anything but Puffed Rice and peanut butter.

"Karen didn't have time to go to the store yesterday," he heard his sister's voice behind him. "Remember, she worked late, then the accident happened."

George turned around with a half-cocked smile eyeing Betsy. "How—?"

"I'm your sister."

"A sister who's still brighter than the sun."

Betsy pulled her tie-dyed robe closer and smiled. George had said her clothes glowed brighter than the sun, for as long as she could remember. "Did Lydia ever leave?"

"At two." Betsy yawned. "How'd you like her five hundred dollar pantsuit?"

George whistled.

"You know Lydia has to always look her best. I remember when you two were dating. Once I came and visited you at college, you stormed around, complaining about how much time she took getting ready." Betsy sat down at the kitchen counter.

"I hated that. We'd waste half the evening with me sitting in the living room twiddling my thumbs."

"Now she's taken to keeping a plastic surgeon very rich. He probably bought a jet just from her patronage."

George shook his head. "I wonder if she keeps her plastic surgeon waiting."

"She does look dynamite... I'll have to ask for references. I'm tired of not looking my spirit's age."

"You wouldn't dare go under the knife." George joined her at the table with a bowl of Kix.

Betsy's eyebrows raised as she prepared for the duel.

"Jeff seems to be interested in you the way you are."

"I'm fighting his memories of his wife." Betsy waved her long nails in front of her face.

"Doesn't sound good."

"Yeah, well, you know, he's not all he seems to be."

"Betsy, you're making excuses because you're afraid of commitment."

"That's not true."

"Who just sent Philippe back to France?"

"Well..."

"That was a good choice, but Jeff is perfect for you. He has character, dependability, and a flush of oddness to keep you interested. But perhaps because he's perfect you plan on leaving him."

Betsy grunted.

"You can't tell me you haven't already tossed around the idea of moving."

Betsy cracked a smile. "I'll think about your insight."

◇

The phantom headache lingered with a faint pounding in Karen's head as she lay in bed late Saturday morning. She closed her eyes before answering the ringing phone.

"Karen, just the person I wanted to talk to." It was June, a friend and neighbor down the street. June had been kind enough to have her over at her house while she heard the missionary discussions. She took the lessons secretively as a Christmas present to her family. Nothing would be a better gift to them than to have their mom face her past and embrace what truly would bring her and her family eternal happiness. It was a step forward in her dream of having a forever family.

"What's up?" Karen asked her friend.

"I know this is late notice, but I'm having a scrapbook party later on this afternoon and wondered if you'd like to come?"

"What's that?"

"Bring your family pictures and we'll put photo albums together. I'll have all the supplies: paper, stickers, everything."

"I'd love to come," Karen said.

"Great! We'll do pictures until we drop."

After she hung up the phone, she dragged herself out of bed to invite Betsy. As she slugged down the hall and up the stairs, she heard New Age music bouncing from Betsy's apartment. Karen winced at the loud noise. Half drugged, she staggered to the stereo and flipped off the sound.

Betsy smiled as she rolled over in her bed to look at Karen. "Don't you love the rhythm?"

Karen mumbled, her eyes fixed on the blooming roses. "Flowers?"

"The live ones are from Jeff and the dead ones from Philippe."

"You sure make the rounds." She sat on a chair. "So how are things with you and Jeff?"

"Pretty good."

"You're not going to dump him out of boredom, are you?"

"I'm insulted you'd say such a thing," Betsy huffed.

"Your past record does point to that kind of behavior."

"Did you and George talk about me last night?"

"Not a word."

"You two definitely ride the same plane of thought."

Karen laughed. "I hope that's true concerning Lydia."

"No fears, my dear, your husband complained how annoying she was this morning."

"Good to hear," Karen said. "By the way, do you want to come to June's scrapbook party with me this afternoon?"

"Sounds fun, but I promised Lydia I'd take hang gliding lessons."

"Oh, definitely do that then." Karen picked at the lint on the couch. "How long is she staying?"

"She's waiting until she feels prompted to go. She hates having a plan."

"Great," Karen mumbled.

◊

Muscles rippled underneath his tee shirt as George tossed another shovelful of snow off the driveway. Karen looked a few feet closer at the mound of snow and saw the sleeve of his buried coat. The routine was the same every time he cleared the walks. George would declare he was going to shovel the snow and Karen would nod. He'd say it again with more conviction, almost as though he said he'd be heroic enough to lift the mountain out of their way.

Karen would thank him, kiss him, and hand him his coat. He'd glance at the coat, say he didn't need it, but put it on after she begged. Five minutes into the job, the coat would be off and the next head cold would be on the way.

She watched her husband for a few more minutes before slipping on her own coat.

Even though times like this irritated her, she had married a good man. Since George had talked so long and detailed about coffee this morning, her craving for a sip had grown to almost an acute ache. She had already rationalized that the caffeine would be medicine for the lingering effects of the migraine. Zap the pain away. But if she gulped a mouthful, it'd make withdrawal that much harder and she'd feel guilty when the bishop asked her about her resolve.

Besides, she thought, buttoning her coat, she wanted to attend the temple in a year and she needed to be worthy. She smiled at her piety. She did feel that way, but wondered if her conviction to resist caffeine would be as strong if she wasn't already late going over to June's house.

She threw her box of photos into the car and headed over to George. "I'm leaving now." She stuffed her hands into her pockets.

He leaned on his shovel. "Have fun. When are you coming back?"

"Don't know. June says it goes until we drop."

"All right. See you then." George shoveled another scoop of snow.

"Don't I get a kiss?" Karen called after him.

"Come get one."

Karen sighed and offered a quick smack. "Your lips are freezing."

George laughed as he fake-tossed snow toward Karen.

"Don't you dare." She hurried to the car.

Once on her way, she thought about the upcoming get together. June's house was decorated in a country theme, so this scrapbook event would take on a home spun feeling. That might be nice after a long week of work.

Karen didn't make it very far down the road before she slammed on breaks. The car door banged behind her as she marched up to her daughter.

Mikey wandered backwards with her hands around her eyes. Chairs, books, umbrellas, and towels were scattered across the plowed street.

"What are you doing?" Karen asked.

Mikey gave a startled scream, her hand resting on her heart. "Oh, Mom, you ruined my perfect set up for my shot. Now I have to redo it."

"Mikey," Karen said after biting her lip. "This movie thing is getting out of hand. I thought it was cute when you were younger, but now you're fifteen years old. It's time to get out of this dream world."

She watched her daughter look over the different props along the side of the road. She wasn't even listening! "Mikey, if this doesn't stop, I'm taking you to get medical help."

Mikey's chin snapped up. "Mom, I'm fine. Just trying to have fun."

Karen slipped her hands in her coat pockets. "That's good to hear. Now pack this stuff up and no more movies in the middle of the street. All right?"

Mikey nodded, chin and gaze down.

Karen quickly left her daughter as though she could leave the reality of her odd behavior. Once she got to June's house, snow brushed along Karen's shoes as she marched up the cleared walkway. Karen glanced around the block, hoping no one had seen her daughter. She shuffled her boxes to ring the doorbell. June answered, long, straight blonde hair outlining her heart-shape face. High cheekbones and thin eyebrows arched upward, drawing attention to her rich brown eyes. Full red lips gave her a beautiful and earthy style.

"Come in," she said, finishing off a chuckle, her hand setting self-consciously on her swelling stomach.

Karen gave her a curious smile as she glanced at the drapes done in blue and yellow. White frilly lace trimmed the edges, establishing a cheerful atmosphere. A vanity with Valentine crafts reminded Karen that the love holiday approached. As of yet, she hadn't seen one duck but knew they must be somewhere because that was all her daughter, Mikey, had talked about.

"Emma told us about her husband's panic when he realized he got the kids for the rest of the day." Karen heard someone say as she entered the room.

"Doesn't he ever watch the children?" one of the women asked.

"No. I have them all day every day, and it blows his mind to tend them a couple of hours. You should've seen the absolute terror on his face when I left. He kept saying, 'Don't you want to take the baby with you?'"

June laughed, her blonde hair slightly bobbing. "Men." The group offered hellos and smiles to Karen and she quickly slipped into work mode until June asked her, "Have they given you a calling yet?"

"I'm still wet from baptism—"

"It's not too early to get you involved. The Lord needs your service as much as He need ours."

"Exactly what happens? I vaguely remember when they asked Betsy to teach the eleven-year-old boys. I know you don't get to pick your job because she ranted a bit for not being able to teach the Relief Society sisters meditation."

June's eyes enlarged. "It's probably a good thing she's not in Relief Society. That'd stir up a lot of trouble. But you," June placed her cold hand on Karen's arm, "have nothing to worry about. The calling will come soon enough. Enjoy the calm before the storm."

Karen nodded, hoping her friend was wrong.

The party was set up in her kitchen. They had a counter big enough to fit their five kids plus two more. It rounded out shaped like a kidney with attached swinging chairs.

"I like those chairs," Karen said.

"They're great," June beamed. "I don't have to clean chair legs. They used to get so much gunk on them."

Sister Wilson looked at Karen and asked, "Where's Betsy?"

"She has an engagement. An old friend showed up unexpectedly last night and since she already had a date with Jeff, she arranged for hang gliding lessons today."

"Jeff who?"

"Chadwick."

The room buzzed. Ladies rapidly saying, "Ah, Betsy and Jeff would make such a cute couple. I'm glad Jeff is finally coming out of mourning."

"Was that their first date?" June asked.

Somehow the tone of her voice or the way she looked led Karen to believe something was up.

"They've been dating a month or so."

June sank in her seat, color draining from her face. The room buzzed even louder with this fresh information.

◊

When George put the shovel away, he noticed trash had blown against the house along the back wall. He picked up several math papers and a missing person's flyer before a car pulled up to the front of his house. He straightened.

It was her. She'd rented a Porsche, black. She always liked to be in sharp and snappy cars. He watched as she slipped out of her vehicle, fur boots wrapped around her legs. The boots reached her knees, but her skirt didn't come close. A fur coat complemented her upper body. George glanced away.

Although Lydia was beautiful, she was bad news, and besides, he didn't want to stir up insecure feelings in Karen. Of course... She wasn't home.

In a flash, he decided avoidance would work best. He had retreated halfway around the house, almost to the back door, when she called.

He peered behind his shoulder and watched as she jumped from one of his big footprints in the snow to the next.

She smiled as she stopped close to him. She wore deep red lipstick today.

"Doing yard work?"

"It's a never ending process," George said. "But it keeps me happy. I like working outdoors."

"You always did." She tilted her head to the side and watched him out of the corner of her eyes.

"Are you here for Betsy?"

"We have snowboarding lessons. I couldn't find a place who taught hang gliding during this season." She stepped closer to him. "You and I have a lot of catching up to do."

"No, we don't. We broke up. I found Karen, got married, and have two kids. You know all that. You and Betsy live a much more exciting life. How's your retreat business going?"

"Are you happy?" Her hazel eyes watched him.

"What kind of question is that?"

"I've been guided here, George."

"What?" He took a step back. "Don't you have a husband yet?"

"Yeah, I had the wrong one. That was a big mistake. Just got rid of him. I need someone more dependable, sweeter. You've always been so nice. I've never seen you lose your temper. Always the perfect gentleman. You gotta start thinking about yourself, George. People take advantage of niceness. Does Karen realize how lucky she is? Does she stand on her own so you two can enjoy the happiness of being soul mates?"

"That's none of your business."

"Am I not allowed to care about one of the best friends I had through college? You've been there for me so many times, I need to repay the debt. I want you to be happy. I'm worried with Karen caught up in that Mormon thing, and having those psychotic attacks, you're not getting the appreciation and support you need."

"I'm fine," George said. His pulse jabbed through his veins. He looked at the trash in his hand and tightened his grip.

"I've always appreciated and valued you, George." She smiled at him then turned around and left.

◇

"This isn't fair," Karen whispered as she climbed out of June's car Saturday afternoon to head for the house.

"Do you want me to walk you in?" June called.

"No, thanks. I can handle it from here." Karen slunk toward the door, pausing to say, "Thank you for the ride. I had a good time until the headache."

"Thank you for coming. I hope you feel better."

"It's likely to go into a full-fledged migraine."

"I hope not."

"Me, too," Karen whispered, closing the door. She grabbed her head. Then it registered that before she came in, she had seen George and Lydia alone together by the garage.

Groaning, she walked outside. It had started to snow. The cold chilled her senses, but did nothing to deaden her flared temper. She found George closing the trash lid. He jumped when he saw her.

"What are you doing here?" he asked.

"What were you doing with Lydia?" she returned.

"She cornered me, Karen. She saw me out here and attacked."

"Why would she attack you without encouragement on your part?"

"Karen, honest, she flirts with any man available. It's kinda of a power kick with her. She has to prove she's attractive."

"But she already had you once."

"She's older now. She's testing to see if her charm still works. Unfortunately for her, I've wised up. I'm not the same naive boy."

"You'd think she'd find someone else to seduce."

"Why's that?" George asked, sucking in his paunch.

"Because you're settled. Lydia shouldn't mess with families."

"She mentioned a divorce," George said.

"That explains it." Karen reached her hand toward him. "She's just looking for some reassurance because her self-esteem has received a dent. You're easy bait. She figures if she bats her eyes at you, you'll go cuckoo over her and she'll feel better again."

"What?" George asked, taking her hand "Easy bait?"

"Yes, she's thinking you're a bored family man." She looked up at him then pressed his hand and said, "Promise you love me?" She walked into George's arms. He squeezed her back tightly. She felt the thunder of his heartbeat.

"Promise me?" she asked, looking through a foggy tunnel vision.

"You're my love." He gently kissed her. "I married you."

Her heart quickened. Her husband wouldn't betray her. It was all Lydia's fault.

George squeezed her tighter and Karen moaned. He studied her. "You look sick. Do you feel okay?"

"No. Another migraine. I had to leave the scrapbook party. I need to lie down."

"Did you drive?"

Karen shrugged. "I've learned my lesson."

"What do you mean by that?" George asked. "Did you have a headache before the accident?"

Karen nodded.

"Darn it. That means the accident was your fault."

"I told the police as much."

"We're going to have to pay more for insurance."

"I'm sorry," she whispered. Both hands went to her forehead. "I'm going to throw-up." Her strength drained from her legs and her head spun.

"We need to get you to the doctor."

◊

Betsy closed the primary manual as the clock clicked toward noon. Her lesson would be a fabulous mixture of cool doctrine and insightful commentary. She had spent the morning pondering scripture passages. Chad had always responded to thoughtful, probing exploration of gospel truths. If she were going to reach him again, it must be on his terms. Betsy pushed herself off her unmade bed and put *The Book of Mormon* commentary on the ⸢...⸣ in the middle of her room. She grabbed the orange New Testament comⁱ⸢...⸣ tary and returned to her bed. Fluffing a couple of pillows, she leaned agaⁱ⸢...⸣ the bedpost and went back to work.

Time to discover the logical explanation for Apostle Paul's bias. The feelings she had for the Church, and for her Savior, burned strong enough that she didn't doubt her belief even though Paul raised questions. She needed to search for understanding of why Paul's views against women were included in the standard works.

She decided to tackle the first objection brought up. The part in Timothy where Paul said women should dress modestly, without plaited hair or gold, pearls, or costly array. Why? Wasn't it a good thing to look your best? Dress portrayed your personality. She scoured the scriptures until someone knocked on her door. No answers found yet. She glanced at the clock, impatient at being pulled away from her studies before she had found an answer. "Come in." One o'clock! How did it get so late?

Lydia glided in, dressed in shimmering golden stirrup pants with a richly textured pullover sweater of camel, blueberry, and tea rose. The waist cinched in accordion pleats, emphasized her Barbie doll form. Her full red lips wore a displeased pout when she spotted the book in Betsy's hand. "Still reading that thing, huh?"

"My dear, I get wonderful vibes from its source." Betsy put the book on top of her rainbow colored sheets.

"Even from Paul?"

"I'm studying it. You know he has written many beautiful passages about hope, charity, and having a pure heart."

"It's too bad he couldn't have applied those concepts to his attitude toward women." Lydia went to the table. She fingered *The Book of Mormon* commentary. She touched the outside of the text as though it was a rattlesnake that could awaken any moment to strike.

"I know there's a logical reason why he put it in there."

"What?"

"I haven't found it yet."

Lydia smiled. A few deep wrinkles appeared at the corners of her mouth. "Tell me when you do."

"Of course," Betsy said. "I always love to share the truth I've found with everyone."

"So true."

◊

Jeff found his son watching sports on TV in the family room, now bedroom. The lunch hour had passed and he hadn't seen his son eat a bite. "Chad, have you made up your mind about how you want to remember your mom?"

He shrugged.

"I know this is difficult. It'd be easier if you talked about it." Jeff walked over to him and patted his son's waist.

Chad screeched in pain as he moved in the tight fitting wheelchair.

"What is it?" Jeff asked, removing his hand as if it was a red coal.

"Nothing," Chad said.

"That doesn't sound like nothing. Tell me." Jeff scooted a chair up close to the wheelchair. He assumed the thinker position and watched Chad trying to vanish. "I'm here for you. You can talk to me. I love you and care about you."

Chad's burnt-almond colored eyes continued to stare at the flashing television screen.

"Do you have another bedsore?"

Chad shrugged, his long bangs moved above his brow.

"Do you?" Jeff's voice rose louder than he liked. The doctor had warned that in extreme cases bedsores turned infectious. "Do I need to look for myself?" He bit his tongue.

"It's a little red, nothing to worry about."

"Where?" Jeff asked.

"Same place."

"Your hip? Maybe we should take you to the doctor."

"Why? He'll just say to change my position a lot and to keep it clean."

"Are you using rubbing alcohol?"

Chad rolled his eyes. "Yes, Dad. It'll go away in a few days like it always does."

"Maybe I should have a look?"

"Dad!"

"Sorry. You know, I don't always know how to be a mother," he muttered.

"Mom's the only lucky one in this family."

"What do you mean by that?" Jeff leaned closer.

"Nothin'."

Jeff pointed a trembling finger at him. "I want to hear none of that kind of talk! Do you hear me boy? I thank Heavenly Father daily that you are alive. Daily. I love you too much and can't...I can't lose...." He broke into tears.

Chad put his arm around his father. "Sorry, Dad, I guess I'm bothered about Mom," he said hoarsely.

"You miss her?" Jeff asked.

Chad nodded. "Will the pain ever stop?"

◇

"How dare he jump into a serious relationship right after Cindy's death! She has only been gone for a little more than a year. Didn't he love her?" June asked, after the last lady had left the scrapbook party.

"June, calm down," her husband, Kendall, said, locking the front door. "You're making a bigger deal out of this than it is. Of course, Jeff loved your sister."

Brown angry eyes flashed on him. "Oh, I am, huh? Why do I even talk to you?"

"June."

She looked into her husband's square face. Normally he wore a broad grin, revealing large square teeth, but today his full lower lip and thin upper curled as the lines between his brow crinkled into a deep crease. He ran his hand through his short blond hair as she cried, "I'm sorry. I can't believe he'd replace her like that." She snapped her fingers.

"He hasn't replaced her. They aren't getting married."

"But they're dating, seriously."

"It means he's lonely and has found someone he can talk to. He does have a heavy burden on his shoulders. He's been left to raise a lame child on his own."

"That's what his sisters are for, or his mother, or even a psychologist. He doesn't have to turn to another woman. Especially her!" June scurried back into the kitchen, heading for the mess left on the counter from the scrapbook party.

"What's wrong with Betsy?"

"She's weird."

"She's full of life." Kendall picked up the small clippings of paper, kneading them together in a ball.

"She has purple hair!"

"She dyed it red. I saw her the other day. It was auburn-orange red. It almost looked like everyone elses. Almost."

"You're kidding me?" June said.

"Not."

"That doesn't matter. He shouldn't be dating."

"June, why not? She's a member of the church—actually seems to be on fire with the greatness of the gospel, which is something we old timers in the church should learn. If you ask me, she reminds me a lot of Cindy." Kendall threw his pile of paper in the trash under the sink.

"No way. Cindy wasn't so loud or caught up in strange stuff." She wrung the washcloth after filling it with water.

"Have you forgotten your own sister?" Kendall asked, his narrow eyebrows lifted as hazel eyes watched her.

"I haven't, and that's why I'm going to make dang sure Jeff doesn't either."

"He never will, June." Kendall grabbed her by the shoulder. She looked into his worried face. "Believe me, that will never happen."

"Yeah, but..." June glanced down. "If he marries Betsy, they'll get sealed. My sister will be eternally miserable if she has to share her man. She told me that much a thousand times."

"Jeff's so sad and so lost."

"I don't care. He can be faithful to my sister's memory." She threw the washcloth into the sink without finishing cleaning the counter.

Kendall grabbed her by the shoulder. "Come on, June, this isn't like you. I've never seen you so hard toward someone."

June rested her head on her husband's shoulder. She took several breaths before saying, "I don't want to go on with life pretending Cindy never existed."

The dam had been let down with those words. The flood of tears dampened Kendall's shirt. After the river had subsided to a stream, Kendall spoke. "Cindy will always exist."

"I know," June choked, wiping her eyes. "I just don't want her to be up in heaven thinking I'm ungrateful for all the things she did for me."

"She's not, baby, she's not." Kendall stroked her hair.

◊

"Lydia, I'm too old to snowboard!" Betsy yelled, standing in the ski rental shop Saturday afternoon. Her hands planted firmly on her hips.

"Nonsense," her friend declared, before turning her attention to the store clerk. "She'd like to rent a shocking pink snowboard and I'd like mine lime green with a dash of maroon."

"What size?" the clerk peered through long stringy hair. His face was plain with small nondescriptive eyes. Early twenties.

"We don't care, just get the right color." Lydia eyed the man with a quick flash of annoyance.

"We're not a make-up counter. I'll see what colors are in." He left to look.

"I'm ten years your senior and have bones that threaten to break," Betsy said.

"Would you stop? We both know our spirits are the same age. That's why we're such good friends even though you're a decade older than me."

"Stop rubbing in your youth. Our spirits may be the same age, but our bodies aren't."

"You've forgotten what it's like to live. I've come to save you."

"I don't know about—"

"Betsy, are you slowing down?"

"A little."

"The person you were ten years ago would be disappointed in you now." The perfectly arched eyebrow lifted.

"The person ten years ago didn't have to deal with creaky bones. It's easy to talk big when you're not in pain."

"Are you quitting on me?"

Lydia's features had turned almost child-like. A glimmer of hope sparked in the corners of her big pleading eyes. Her lips hinted at a pout.

"It was one thing to hang glide. You only have to worry about falling once. But snowboarding is one continuous round of crashes."

"Do you know how to ski?" the sales clerk asked.

"Of course she does." Lydia smacked her lips. "She and her second husband used to ski the black diamond runs in Switzerland."

"If you skied those," the man said, hair swinging as he spoke, "then you definitely can handle snowboarding. Actually its much more fun than skiing. If you try it once, you'll never go back. It gives you a sense of freedom."

"Fine, I'll try it," Betsy said. "I've never chickened out of anything before, so why start now?"

Lydia smiled, satisfied. An hour later they were at the ski lift with snowboards nestled under their arms. Their boots stomped through snow. Betsy hired an instructor, Nancy, who looked in her mid-twenties with her lo.. '-.' pulled off her face by a headband. She took one look at Betsy and laughed

"This is great. I love it. Can I take a picture?"

"Of course," Betsy said, fingering her Cat in the Hat cap.

"My grandma's going to flip when she sees a picture of someone her age actually taking snowboarding lessons." Nancy snapped the camera several times before teaching Betsy how to slide her boot onto the board.

Betsy laughed unevenly at the foot of the beginner hills when she practiced the turns. "I'll be lucky if I don't break a hip."

"You won't hurt yourself," the instructor informed, "all you need to learn is how to maintain balance and control. We're going to take it easy."

"Not too easy," Betsy said. "I want to do some flying. That's what we planned and I hate ruined agendas, especially when it's something I really want to do. Now I hired you for the whole day, and I want to be an expert by the time I'm done."

"Don't worry. If flying is what you want, it's what you'll get. Let's take the first couple of hours learning the basics."

Betsy tipped back on her snowboard and yelled, "Here weeeee goooo."

Chapter 4

"Jeff, I gotta talk to you." A stressed voice came on the other end of the phone line.

"Mmm." He nudged down farther into his blanket on his bed.

"Jeff, are you awake?"

"No."

"Then wake-up." He recognized the staccato rhythm characteristic of Betsy. It was irritatingly loud. "My symmetry isn't right. I'm all flustered inside."

"What is it?" Jeff asked before he yawned.

"It's this whole thing with Paul not respecting women. I can't find any peace."

"Betsy." Jeff sat up.

"Yes."

"Do you believe the church is true?'

"Yes."

"Do you believe in Latter-day prophets?"

"Yes."

"Then if you have a testimony, let it be."

"But, Jeff, you don't understand. I have to come to some sort of agreement with this. I mean what could possibly be wrong with women wearing braided hair and having gold in it? Does that mean we're not supposed to dress up?"

He sighed and rubbed his eyes. He'd have to help her or risk never getting any sleep. "Look up in the scriptures on costly apparel and stiff necks." Jeff waited to hear a counter argument but none came. "Why is it so quiet on your end of the line?" he asked.

"I'm jotting down your great flow of knowledge. That's an excellent idea. I can't wait to pursue it.'" She made kissing noises and hung up the phone.

Jeff flopped his head against the pillow as the smell of snow stirred his senses. The scent was faint, crisp, and fresh. Only a few people he knew had the ability to detect it. He was too tired to glance out the window to see if he was right. Betsy was pretty, true, and had dramatic features with creamy white skin and dreamy blue eyes. Her excited enthusiasm was delightful unless it was at one in the morning. But she did love the truth and always had something interesting to talk about.

♦

Betsy flipped through the pages in the scriptures quickly even with inch long nails. She never let her beauty get in the way of learning truth. Jeff's idea of looking up costly apparel seemed intriguing. She doubted she'd find anything, but people said the answers hid in the scriptures.

The first verse she found that related was Alma 1:6. In the verse it said, "he began to be lifted up in the pride of his heart, and to wear very costly apparel."

Betsy ran her hand down her pearl silk nightgown and wondered if that would count as "very costly apparel." Did she wear it because she thought she deserved it? Was she proud? Meditation on that was required.

The next verse Alma 1:32 read, wearing costly apparel led to "persecuting, lying,...and all manner of wickedness." After that she flipped to Alma 4:6-8. Those verses read much like the others but added the additional insight, "they began to be scornful, one towards another, and they began to persecute those that did not believe according to their own will and pleasure."

Betsy shut the book and closed her eyes. Costly apparel—pride—malice—persecution. An interesting train.

Was she wrong to have long fingernails and wear lots of make-up? Was it evil to be an individual? She couldn't think of anything bad. But clothes? Could a person really think himself or herself better because of what they wore?

She climbed from bed to blow out the burning vanilla scented candle. The aroma had grown too strong.

✧

Sunday morning Karen awoke to a loud buzz. She slapped at it in the shadows. The creaking stopped short like a crying baby who had found a full bottle of milk.

"What's that?" George slurred his words together in his half asleep state.

"The alarm," Karen said.

"It's the weekend." George yawned.

"Church." She stretched.

"You're not going, are you?"

"Why not?" she asked, hearing her tone peak high.

"What about your headache?"

"It's not as bad."

"What if you lose your eyesight again?"

"I took two Imetrexs. I should be getting better. My heart was racing enough from it last night. I hate that stuff. We should be over the top of the wave on this one."

"What if you aren't? You should rest."

"Betsy will be there with me. Besides, I can't miss church."

"Why not?" George asked. In the morning light Karen could see his eyes were still closed, but the wrinkles at the edge of his mouth and eyelids deepened.

"You don't understand."

"I'm worried about you."

"Then come with me." Karen scooted closer. She rested her head on his strong chest. Her hair draped across her cheek as she smelled lingering whiffs of his cologne.

"No thanks."

"Why not?" Karen asked, lifting her head to gaze into George's light blue eyes.

He avoided eye contact and said, "If you want to go to church, that's fine with me. I'm not going to tell you what religion to believe. But personally, I don't need it."

"How can you say that?" Karen asked. "God needs you."

George didn't answer.

"I've been so much happier since I've had the truth in my life. I never realized the size of the empty gap inside me." She brushed at the strands of hair that had fallen into her eye.

"You've been happy since you faced your fear of the Mormons."

"That's true. But God gave me the strength to do that."

"I'm glad for you. Really I am."

"George, how can you brush it aside without even learning about it?"

"I told you; I'm fine the way I am. I don't want to discuss it." George's intonation was short, rough, and brief like sleet tumbling on her head.

Karen pulled from his embrace. "I'm sorry I brought it up."

"Me too," George grunted.

Karen climbed out of bed to dress. Soon Betsy would knock on her door to ask if she was ready.

After Karen slipped into her royal blue floral dress, and ran her fingers through the snarls of her straight brown hair, she hurried back into her bedroom, hoping George had awakened and they could resolve their differences. He laid still except for the soft hum of snores.

Her caressing eyes glided over his rugged, firm face. She studied his features, a pleading grew inside and knotted her throat. He lay motionless, unaware of her pain, the void spreading. If love and desire could join them together, then they'd have a perfect marriage like portrayed in the fifties' TV shows. But relationships didn't work that way. At least none she'd heard about. Every couple she knew well admitted to having challenges and settling for less than satisfactory conditions. Sad.

She wondered if the cookie-cutter families she watched in sacrament meeting felt the same void, or was theirs over-flowing with warmth and kindness toward one another? Did they have the blessing of mutual respect and reverence? If George joined the church, would the crystal glittering of family life and the blessings and happiness be hers? At the very minimum, she wouldn't sit alone on the church bench.

Disappointed by George's refusal to wake-up, she returned to the bathroom counter. Her hair hung formlessly flat. She gathered it up in a twist, but the hair looked awkward and uneven. She worked curls and waves into the strands. Useless. Today her hair matched her mood perfectly, might as well give up.

She dabbed eye shadow, lipstick, and blush on her tired looking face. Closing her eyes, images of Lydia came over her—her seductive eyes lurking like a beast of prey waiting for the right moment to tempt.

A retry on the hair was required with another drop of foundation under the eyes to cover the black circles. She again set to work. Feeling like there was nothing else she could do to save her looks, she went downstairs and saw

Betsy at the breakfast table.

"You don't look so good," her sister-in-law said. Then closed her eyes. "I sense some kind of turmoil within you."

"Migraine sufferer." Karen walked slowly to the cabinet so as not to worsen the throbbing inside her head.

"I thought you had that the other night."

"And on it continues."

"Have you tried alternative medicine? I heard Ginseng's great for reducing stress."

"No thanks," Karen said. "I'm not interested in quack treatments."

"Herbs can really help. Even traditional medical societies are beginning to accept them. You know you can trust my judgment, don't you?"

"Actually, Betsy, to be truthful, you've been into some pretty strange things."

"Not of late."

"I wouldn't say that. That color breathing to help your moods and mental well being is quite hokey."

"Color does have a very profound effect, not only on your mental status but also on your psychological, although that wasn't my last phase. My last was the Mormon Church and you disapproved of it so much you joined yourself."

"If you try enough odd things, you're bound to trip over some light sooner or later," Karen muttered.

"Would it hurt you to try the herb? Give it a go before you knock it. Wouldn't it be worth it to get rid of the migraines?"

"I'd do anything to have them stop."

"So that means you will take the herb?"

"Only a couple of days to see if it'll help. Though the Imtrex works well as long as I take it early enough."

"I'm glad they work. Keep them around for backup but you don't want to use them all the time. Why even have the headaches?"

"Fine, fine. You win. Stop talking about it."

"I have some Ginseng in my room. Let me grab it."

In less than two minutes, Betsy had returned with the white plastic bottle. She gave Karen one pill than settled herself at the kitchen table, eating a multi-grain cereal with soymilk.

Karen sat down with her Sugar Smacks and shook her head. "I don't get how you can eat that junk."

"It's healthy and makes me feel better."

"But it's so disgusting."

"You get used to it with a little time."

"Like, I hope George will get used to me being a Mormon," Karen said.

Betsy stopped eating and watched her sister-in-law. "We do need to work on him."

"He doesn't want to be messed with. He doesn't even want me to go to church. I don't think he'll ever become a Mormon." Karen's spoon dangled halfway between the bowl and her mouth. A far away sad look crossed her face.

"Now, Karen don't sound so hopeless."

"But I want the forever family the missionaries talked about. If George doesn't become a Mormon, I'll never get to go to the temple and become sealed to him."

"It'll work out. I promise," Betsy said.

Karen's eyes watched her cereal spin in circles as she moved the spoon around. Betsy reached across the table and patted Karen's hand. "I have a good feeling. We'll get him yet."

"Get who?"

The two ladies glanced up and watched George, in a navy blue bathrobe, hustle into the kitchen.

Karen smiled. "Hi, honey, want some Sugar Smacks?"

He shook his head. "Who are you two trying to get?"

Karen sneaked a peek at Betsy, whose eyes widened, then back to George whose eyes had narrowed. "Betsy told me about this herb she heard of that gets rid of migraine headaches."

"Does our insurance cover it?" George asked.

"Doubt it," Karen mumbled. "You know our insurance hardly pays for anything."

"Sounds like another one of those fads," George said. "But if you think it'll help, go ahead and try." He sat at the table with a box of Shredded Wheat.

"It'll help her. You'll see," Betsy said. "When this lady told me about it at homemaking meeting the other night, I got the greatest feeling. I knew it would help Karen."

"You should check out the side effects before you try it," George warned.

Karen gave a half roll of the eyes and said, "Okay, that's probably smart."

"I had a good feeling inside." Betsy stated loudly.

"It seems hocus pocus to me," George said.

"Why? You don't think God speaks to your soul? You don't believe in having a conscience that tells you right from wrong?" Betsy questioned.

"Well I—"

"So you're telling me there's no internal monitor inside you that warns you it's wrong to, let's say, murder? Then why has society set up laws against it? Hum?" Betsy raised her eyebrows, revealing indigo blue caked on her eyelids. "I'm waiting for an answer."

"You've got a point. But what about those people who believe they're angels, and God tells them everything to do and they kill people?"

Karen bit her bottom lip. "Charissa died because of one of those people."

George glanced at his wife with a look Karen knew was a careful study of her response. "God wouldn't ask you to kill. I'm sorry I brought it up."

"You're right though," Karen said. "There are people who take it too far. We must always be careful how far we take our emotions. Charissa's death is a testimony of that."

"You don't seem as upset about that as you used to," George said.

"God will hold Charissa's mom accountable for what she did. I have ⟨ ⟩ He'll make restitution."

"That sounds healthy," George added.

"It's that kind of thing we learn in church," Betsy said.

George held his spoon in mid-air. He looked at Karen and then to Betsy. "Very funny. I don't need to be a Mormon to learn healthy attitudes."

"But they're a great support group," Betsy said.

"I'm sure they are," George said. "And when I'm in need of them, I'll know where to look. Right now I'm doing great the way I am."

"They're more than a support group," Karen said. "They have the truth."

"Karen, I already told you I didn't want to talk about it, and I meant what I said," George's voice rose. "You guys walk around like you're so much better than I am because you supposedly have the truth. I'm sick of it."

"Sorry," both Karen and Betsy said together.

"Perfect!" Mikey said, jumping out of the mop closest. "Mom, you and Betsy had such emotion in those words. Very believable. I really felt like you guys were embarrassed by what you've done. Didn't you, Dad?"

"I guess," George said.

"Mikey, I thought I told you—" Karen started to say.

"Have to go. See you for lunch," Mikey called as she raced out of the kitchen door.

Karen set her spoon against her bowl. "She's starting to really worry me. Do you think she's going insane?"

"Naw," George said. "It's normal teenage stuff. Sam has it too. You should see what he's wearing today."

"I don't want to know," Karen said.

"But, I do. Tell," Betsy said.

"First off he has on a white blouse with ruffles, dropping down the front and on the wrists."

"Like they wore in Ben Franklin's time?" Karen asked.

"Exactly. Then he had on black jeans and long black boots with sliver buckles," George said. "My son looks like a fem."

"At least he hasn't dyed his hair turquoise or lime green. I've seen a lot of those teenagers do that."

"That's real encouraging," Karen said. "What are we going to do? This could be bad. That kind of thing leads to drugs, crime—"

"Let's talk to him before we get all hysterical," George said.

Karen sighed. That should be an interesting talk.

✧

Brother Kirby's handout made the perfect fan. Karen wiped at a few bubbles of sweat on her forehead and noticed her classmates didn't seem hot at all. Their hearts probably weren't skipping out of their chests either. The hot flashes and racing heart must be from the herb then. Never, would she trust Betsy again. At least with medical advice.

Karen refocused on the chalkboard, tuning back to the lesson. She couldn't even remember the subject they had been talking about.

Relief Society time came shortly after that. When she walked into the room, she looked at the patrons who waited for a friend with their hands and purses on chairs next to them. Quickly her gaze flashed over the back row—it was mostly filled.

Ladies bumped into her as they passed by. She sighed and stepped forward to take a seat two chairs in when June walked up behind her, resting her hand on Karen's shoulder.

"Come up front and sit by me." June gestured with a slight tilt of her head.

Karen agreed, noticing the floral maternity dress.

"Are you pregnant?" she asked.

June patted her stomach with a smile. "Yep. I find out what it is on Wednesday. I hope it's a girl."

"You already have a lot of girls," Karen said, "and they're so much harder to raise." She thought about Mikey and her excessive dramatics. Give Sam a soccer ball and some weird clothes and he was content.

"Girls take care of you better when you're old. I'm starting to get to the point I need to invest in my future."

"By the way, where's your sister-in-law, Betsy?" June asked as the noise in the room increased.

"She teaches the eleven-year-old boys in Primary."

"Chad's class?" Her face deepened in color.

"Yes, of course, he's in that class," Karen said, wondering why such a reaction.

"How long has she been teaching?"

"Awhile. She really enjoys it."

"They can be rascals," June said.

"Nothing Betsy can't handle."

"You don't say," June said weakly. "Did she start dating Jeff before or after her calling?"

"I think it was right after, but I can't remember for sure. Why?"

"No reason."

"There must be one."

"I'm wondering if Jeff put her in there so Chad and Betsy could become better friends."

"Could be."

"I hope not."

There was anger in June's voice. Why? "What would it matter?"

"Jeff's wife has been dead for less than a year. Don't you think that's a little early for Jeff to be dating?"

Karen snickered. "Some men don't wait until their wives are dead."

"It just bugs me. If he loved his wife enough, her memory should fill his needs."

"Being single can be lonely."

"Doesn't matter. Don't misunderstand me, I don't see anything wrong with Betsy as a person per se, but I don't want her hanging around Jeff."

Karen blinked, gathering her thoughts. "I guess I don't understand."

"I'll clarify," June said. "Chad suffered a major trauma in his life losing his mother. He was really close to her then he lost his legs. He needs his father and shouldn't have to worry about losing him to a stranger and being forced to accept her as a replacement for his mother."

"Betsy wouldn't dream of replacing his mother."

"Good, because it's not going to happen. I'd appreciate it if you'd help me out."

The Relief Society president stood and gave the announcements to the sisters. Karen sighed, having no idea how she should've responded to June. But she did know one thing, she liked Betsy dating Jeff. He seemed more stable and responsible than the others did. He also appeared to possess the virtue of being faithful. That'd be a definite change for Betsy.

◊

After Karen left for church, George found his boy in his room talking on the phone. He sat on the corner of Sam's bed and waited for his son to get off the phone, which Sam did quickly.

"What Dad?"

"I wanted to have a talk with you."

"What about?"

"Why the sudden change in clothes?"

Sam sat nestled against the wall on the floor. He set the porta phone on the carpet. "Because I'm tired of everyone being the same around here. In California no one was alike. Here there's a lot of pressure to become a punch-and-cookie type of person and that's just not who I am."

George leaned back on the bed with his arms behind him. "I can understand that. Your mom and I are just worried that you're getting into some things that might be dangerous."

"Come on, Dad. It's just clothes. It's a way of expression."

"Are you sure you're not getting into—"

"No, Dad. No drugs. I'm not stupid enough to ruin my life."

George patted the mattress. "Well that's good to hear. Your mom and I love you and wanted to make sure everything's okay."

"It's fine."

"What are you going to do today?"

"I got a new camera and Mikey agreed to let me take her picture. I have some real rad ideas I'd like to try."

"Sounds good. Where are you getting all this money for the clothes and camera?"

"Remember, I mowed lawns the entire last summer."

"Be careful not to spend it all." George stood to leave. Things seemed to be under control.

Chapter 5

Betsy changed positions carefully in the small child's chair in the primary room. It was quite a challenge to find a spot on her body not covered with a tender bruise, but despite the pain, it had been worth it. Snowboarding, once she figured out the weight adjustment, was a much freer experience than skiing, with its entanglements of poles and boots, which offered no flexibility. She'd be back up the hill soon. Her goal was to fly down the moguls.

Once she found a position that didn't hurt much, she turned her attention to Chad. It was song practice. His shoulders slouched and his brow furrowed like a scolding teacher. He refused to sing. The lesson that Betsy had so diligently labored over for the sole purpose of breathing life into him seemed not to even scratch the surface of his wall. As Betsy continued watching him, she understood better Jeff's concern. Still, it'd be best for Chad to go to a counselor, but Jeff didn't agree. She knew if she mentioned it again, Jeff wouldn't take it kindly. Perhaps he might even end their relationship. Betsy wasn't sure she wanted that. She definitely didn't want it terminated on a bad note. Karma.

◊

June's heart thundered. She had to excuse herself from Relief Society. Just the thought of Betsy and Jeff together caused an irregular pulse to echo in her throat. It was wrong for Jeff to not hold onto her sister's memory! Nothing could replace her sister, especially not that strange New Age purple finger nailed—red-headed-middle-aged-woman. Later she'd talk to Jeff, right after visiting with the bishop. Earlier that morning, the counselor had called her setting up an appointment with the bishop. What could he possibly want?

◊

Sister Coons stood and presented a positive, funny, and thought provoking lesson on marriage. She discussed how it was an equal partnership between the mates and God.

When the lesson moved into the blessings of a temple marriage, Karen fidgeted in her purse for a hankie, to wipe the tears. She tossed around the idea of leaving, but decided to stay. Fortunately for her, Sister Coons didn't dwell on temple marriage long, instead she asked the ladies, "What should we do if our husband's don't do what we wish they would?"

A lady who was several chairs down from Karen raised her hand. "You know I've found all nagging does is drive people away and builds hostility. I tried something new with my husband. I've always felt that we shouldn't watch television on Sunday. Not that anyone who does is wrong, it's just my own personal choice. I wanted my husband to support me so we could spend Sunday evenings together. But he saw nothing wrong with catching up on Sports Beat Sunday. He'd invite me to come watch with him. At first I gave in and did, but then my conscience bothered me. When he asked me why, instead of giving him a holier-an-thou speech, I'd simply say I choose not to watch television on Sunday.

This went on for years until last month. He flipped off the television and said, 'You know I don't feel right on Monday mornings if I watch TV on the Sabbath. It's as though I didn't have the proper rest I needed.' He hasn't turned on the TV once since then."

Karen twisted the Kleenex in her hand. It'd never work with George. He wouldn't notice the blessings of the church if she wasn't the one pointing them out.

The teacher wrapped up her lesson and the song and prayer were given. As Karen stood to leave, she felt someone tap her on the shoulder. Sister Jenkins from the scrapbook party, asked, "Are you feeling better?" Her expression was that of a caring mom.

Karen smiled. "Yes, thank you. It's hard to get much worse than having those migraines."

"Ahhh, that's awful. I understand. I've suffered from them for years."

"Sorry."

"Have you tried Doctor Bringley?"

Karen shook her head. "Haven't."

"I've been to countless doctors. Believe me, I've tried everything. A friend finally recommended this doctor. I decided one more doctor couldn't hurt. She put me immediately on a yeast-free diet and a mild drug. In my research, I haven't found any side effects. That's much better than the Imtrex I was taking. The second day I was on the medicine the migraines had stopped, and so had the other headaches that used to be a constant."

"How long have you been doing this?"

"Five years and still headache-free. You should try it."

"Thank you for telling me. I'll keep it in mind."

◊

When church ended, Betsy called after Chad. He stopped rotating the wheels on his wheelchair and maneuvered to face her. "Yeah?" he mumbled. He gazed downward.

"I want to talk to you privately."

He shrugged.

Betsy pointed to the corner of the primary room where they stored the folded up chairs. No one was there. "How about in that corner?"

He rolled to where she had suggested with strenuous movements. "What?" he asked, glancing up at her.

"Your father's worried about you."

"What business is that of yours?" There was a sharp edge to his voice.

She put her hand on the corner of his armrest. "I care about your father and I care about you."

"If that were true, then you'd leave us alone."

Betsy wiped at her dress in an effort to keep the hurt from flaring into anger. "That's not true."

"Both of us would be better off if you left us alone."

"How exactly am I intruding?"

"You're stealing my dad." He spun his chair around and left the room. The primary secretary, Sister Edwards, held the door for him and looked at Betsy with a questioning expression.

Betsy sank onto the floor to think. She crossed her legs Indian style, then made sure her dress covered everything. She closed her eyes and prayed. "Dear God, is it my fault?"

She remained there for at least five minutes before Jeff found her. "Betsy, what are you doing?"

She opened her eyes and saw the bronze hue of his eyes penetrate her with inquisitive surprise. "A meditating prayer," she answered as she offered her hand to him.

His strong arms quickly lifted her to her feet and she straightened her skirt once she stood.

Others in the room watched with curious interest. Jeff took her by the arm and guided her into the hallway. He spoke in a low voice. "Come on, let's go for a walk."

Betsy nodded. They strolled to the front of the building, grabbed Betsy's long lavender coat which he helped her put on. She also slipped on her tall furry boots. She had come prepared for the weather.

Like a true gentleman, he escorted her out of the building and onto the sidewalk. They stepped in the melting snow as the sun warmed their backs. Betsy spoke first, "How's your son getting home?"

"They wanted him to stay and help plan a scouting event. Sister Jensen volunteered to drive him back."

"Hmmm," Betsy mumbled.

Jeff's soft chocolate eyes swept over her. "Please tell me what's wrong."

"I tried to help him," Betsy said, feeling a mixture of foolishness and being ashamed. "Honest I did. I worked all week on the lesson and prayed so hard, and then nothing, not one hint suggesting that I reached him. I see why you're so worried about him. He looks awful. He's definitely suffering from clinical depression." The smell of burning wood in a fireplace brushed past them.

"Now, I wouldn't take it that far."

"Jeff," Betsy said. She stopped walking and gazed into his hypnotic eyes. "I know you don't want to admit things are out of your control, but they are. I've seen clinical depression many times and in many different ways. I've suffered from acute bouts myself. My sister-in-law had an awful struggle. My mom—it's in the family. It's nothing to be ashamed of. We all have circumstances that are extremely difficult to handle. And now I'm a Mormon, I know why. God is testing us. But He doesn't expect us to always know what to do. He has given us helpers along the way who guide us to the light."

"I don't want to hear about counselors again," Jeff said.

"Why not? It would help." Betsy bit her lip. Despite her promise to herself, she had brought up counselors again. Instantly, sick nervous waves shook through her body.

"We're fine. Now please tell me why you sat on the floor?"

"I had a talk with your son after church. Will you please forgive me? I was trying to help. Really." Betsy felt like a sinking boat.

Jeff took her hand and squeezed. "Tell me."

"I told him that his father and I were worried about him. He flipped telling me to stay away from you."

"I see," Jeff said. His thick salt and pepper eyebrows pointed downward as he pondered the new information. "That still doesn't explain why you were on the floor." He shoved his free hand into his olive green suit jacket.

"I needed to meditate and pray. I felt awful, and I wondered if Chad was depressed because of me. Maybe I shouldn't see you any more. I'm coming between your son and you—" She choked. Her soul screamed, "disagree with me."

Jeff grabbed Betsy's shoulders. "That's not true. Cindy led you to me because she knew you'd make me happy. I need you to help me go on living. Chad's adjusting to the idea. Yes, it's difficult for him, but he'll learn. It's better this way."

Betsy stepped into a slushy mess. "Are you sure, Jeff? Your relationship with Chad is more important than ours."

Jeff pulled Betsy tight for a hug and then his lips searched for hers. Comfort and desire flowed from his touch.

"Does that answer your question?" he asked.

She grinned, feeling slightly light headed. "You shouldn't have done that."

"Why not?" Jeff asked, his face coming close perhaps for another kiss.

"It's making me sweet on you."

Jeff drew her in tight. "Does, huh? Then I better do it again." As their lips touched, they heard a distant holler.

Betsy looked up, wiping her mouth. The wind blew strands of hair across her cheeks. Her heart sank. Chad.

"You're filthy pond scum!" He pointed at Betsy.

"Chad!" Jeff's voice demanded control.

His son's face darkened. "She is. She's clawing her long fingernails into you."

"Stop this instant. She's the best thing that's happened to us since Mom died."

"She's not Mom."

"I didn't say she was. She could never replace Mom but she can make living more bearable."

"You mean miserable."

"Chad!" Jeff turned to Betsy and with sad eyes asked, "Can I call you later? I'd better go."

"Sure," Betsy whispered. She had positioned herself so she didn't see Chad's angry eyes. He wouldn't want to see her face either, though she doubted he'd even notice the torment. Depression was extremely contagious.

◊

The bishop's door was closed when June arrived, so she flipped open her *Ensign* and read the First Presidency message. She tried to do that monthly, feeling it was important to hear what the Lord's prophet wanted them to know. Time passed slowly as she progressively found it more and more difficult to focus on the words. What could the bishop want?

The solid wooden door finally opened and the bishop smiled at June. "Come in, come in, Sister Thomson. It's good to see you.

June sat and folded her hands neatly in her lap.

The bishop cleared his throat and steepled his fingers. "We'd like to issue you a call."

June's back straightened. She had been Homemaking leader for four years and the job was quite demanding. Perhaps now they'd give her a break. With a new baby coming and her five other kids, an easier assignment would be a welcome relief. Her hands tightened into a fist. The bishop didn't continue. To prod him along she said, "Yes?"

"I'd like to thank you for the wonderful job you've done as the Homemaking Leader. My wife raves about what fun crafts you have arranged, and the education activities have done a lot of good."

She blushed.

"We're in a transition period. I don't know if you heard, but Sister Coons is moving."

Her grip tightened on the chair.

"We've prayed about it and feel impressed the Lord wants to call you to be the Relief Society president."

June swallowed. This had to be a joke. A very bad one. She blinked. The bishop hadn't burst into laughter yet.

"Sister Thomson?" he asked as if trying to edge her out of her daze.

"Yes?" Her voice sounded far away and unfamiliar.

"Will you?"

She took a deep breath, which helped dispel some of the shock. "You're kidding, aren't you?"

"No," he said.

"I have little kids."

"We realize that and have already talked to your husband."

"My husband knows!"

"He's on the high council and—" his voice trailed off.

"What did he say?"

"He said it was wonderful and he'd support you two hundred percent."

"He did, did he?"

"He'll be released and given a job with less demands so he can be the support you'll be needing. We feel strongly we don't want both parents out of the home when they have small children."

"How can I? My family! I can't leave them to go visit the elderly or those needing special attention."

"I realize this," the bishop said. "We wouldn't have called you because of your children, but we're strongly impressed you're the one. No other name came. It happened time and time again with my counselors and myself. For some reason, the Lord wants you to have the calling now. There's something only you can do. He'll give you the strength and the way to make it happen."

"If that's the case," June said. "Yes, but truly, I'm no Superwoman."

✧

When June arrived home, Kendall had a wide grin on his face. "Have a nice chat with the bishop?" He was laughing.

"Oh," was all she said before she chased him around the room with the diaper bag. "Would you stop so I can swat you?"

"I'm no fool. And you can't hit me. What would the ward think of their new Relief Society president? That's not something she should do."

"Kendall, why did you let them do it? You know me. I don't have the skill to be a Relief Society president and I have my hands full with the kids. There's no way. I don't know enough and am not spiritual enough to do that kind of thing. I've always told you how bad that job is and how glad I was I'd never get it."

Kendall smiled broadly and wrapped his arms around her. "I told the bishop you said, 'you'd never get that calling,' then I added, 'never say never.' He agreed with my advice."

She pulled from his embrace. "Kendall! What am I going to do?"

"Be an awesome president. You underestimate yourself. You'll be good at it, and I get to brag to my buddies that I'm married to a Relief Society president."

"Would you stop that?" June lurched forward, trying one more time to hit him. This time she used her hand, which he grabbed hold of and then pulled her close. He kissed her tenderly on the lips.

She looked at him, smiling.

He whispered, "There's more than one way to tame a woman, but I like this way best." He lunged for another kiss but instead got a mouth full of hair. "Hey," he said. "Get back here."

"Why should I? You betrayed me."

"I did no such thing," Kendall said, "I believe in you."

"Do you really?" June asked.

"Yes, of course. Why do you doubt me? I've lived with you for fifteen years, and I know you have all the skills to be successful at this job."

"But—"

"Plus, I know you'll rely on the Lord to help you through the rest. The Lord wants you to be successful. I want you to be, the bishop, and the ward does, too. With that kind of backing there's no way you'll fail bringing Christ's love to people."

"Thank you." June rested her head on her husband's shoulder. "I like your way of looking at it. I can use this new title as an excuse for serving people. I hope—"

Kendall silenced her doubts with another kiss.

✧

When Betsy walked into her apartment, the phone was ringing. She paused to decide if she wanted to answer, and finally concluded to find out who it was. It couldn't possibly be Jeff so soon.

"Hello?" she asked.

"*Mon cherie,* you sound sad. *Mon petite choux,* is having a bad day?"

"Philippe."

"*Oui.*"

"Why are you calling me? I said no to your proposal and led you on."

"*Non,* you were right. If we were meant to be together, we'd have worked it out the first time or the second. It would've caused us more pain. We make better friends than lovers. Do you agree?"

Betsy laughed. She had missed Philippe's romantic, flirtatious talk and his light floaty conversation. "I agree, and I'm happy we're friends once more. You're right, it is better this way. Besides, I've missed your wise counsel."

"You're too much like me, *mon amie.* Too much. I called because I wanted to know what kind of trouble you have gotten yourself in."

"What makes you think I've gotten myself into trouble?" Betsy pulled the phone cord to her bed. Talking to Philippe was always interesting, fun, and long.

"*Mom cherie,* we are talking about Betsy. The wild, wonderfully interesting, Betsy who always has herself in a pickle. Last time it was two men fighting for her hand in marriage."

Betsy laughed. "It wasn't quite like that Philippe. I'm not unfaithful to you."

"I deserved it. I did the same to you."

"No, you did it while we were married. That's not the same thing," Betsy pointed out.

"That is true."

"I made no promise to you, Philippe. I was still thinking about it."

"With my two karat diamond ring on your hand."

"Beautiful ring," Betsy said.

"Can I have it back?" Philippe asked.

"Not in this lifetime," Betsy said. "Last I talked to you, you said I could keep it."

"Yes, I know *mon cherie* and I meant it, but I got myself in a *la petite* mess."

"You need money fast?" Betsy asked, shaking her head. Some things never change; no matter the time or the age of a person.

"*Oui.*"

"*Pourquoi?*" Betsy asked.

"You know my fabulous line I designed after the impressionist age?"

"Brilliant concept. I'd love to own a pair or two."

"Well, my competition broke into my studio when I was away at Utah visiting you, and he copied my styles and worked like a wacko person and got them out before I did. Now I am stuck. If I reveal my line and it is the same as theirs, then I'll be hassled for being a plagiarist. If I don't release it, I can't pay the rent."

Betsy raised her eyebrow. There was something wrong with this picture but she couldn't quite smell where the stench came from. "I'll put the ring the mail tomorrow," Betsy said. "Don't worry, I wouldn't ever let you starv

"No, you can't mail it. It's too expensive and I don't trust the postal system. I must come and pick it up myself."

"That's a real expensive idea," Betsy said. "How 'bout I sell it and wire you the money?"

"No!" Philippe said. "I have to come to California for business. It would not be much more bother to stop in Utah also."

"But that's at least two extra hours."

"I have a layover there anyway. Besides, I wouldn't mind spending an evening with my favorite friend. That is if you aren't already married to your new fellow?"

"Jeff? No. I don't rush into marriages any more. I like to give myself a little time to think about it before I plow in and make a whole bunch of entanglements."

"Sounds like you have gained wisdom in your years, and that I still have a chance."

"Philippe."

"I know. Do not worry. I have learned my lesson. We are friends even though my life is missing sparkle without you."

"You could always come up with good lines," Betsy said with a smile. "You should try that line on the next pretty girl you meet. I'm sure it'll work."

"You never told me what trouble you are in now. I want to know," Philippe said.

"I just had a few sparks fly between Jeff's son and myself."

"What seems to be the problem?"

"His mom died a year ago. The anniversary is coming up. His son is becoming more and more hostile about the whole situation and he sees me as taking his mother's place."

"Ahh, the sticky situations we get in when we become involved in relationships that have had entanglements from before. It is never fun. They say second marriages are much harder than firsts."

"Now you tell me," Betsy said.

"No worries. You have always pulled through and come out on top. I do not see why you wouldn't do it again."

"It's true. I am a survivor. I don't know if it's right for me to even step in. I don't want to take his mother's place. I have no right to do that."

"You could bring the family happiness that has not been there before," Philippe said. "You did the same for me."

"Thank you for saying that," Betsy said.

◊

The bishop had asked June to pick counselors. It had been a day since he asked and she wanted to get that out of the way. The whole idea seemed mind boggling. She knew prayer and fasting were the key. But what if she chose wrong? If she made a mistake, would someone be overlooked that only the right counselor could reach? Would she be responsible for a spiritual death in the ward? The whole thing overwhelmed her.

She had prayed for several hours, agonizing over the choice. Of course she wouldn't instantly pick a friend, because after this job was over there was a high probability that whoever she worked with would no longer be her friend.

Who should she call? The Lord would make it clear. He did, too. Only one name came over and over, no matter how many times she'd tried to think of someone else. She glanced down at the name she wrote on her note pad, Karen Ashforth.

◊

"You look happy," Karen said when she stumbled on to Betsy in the kitchen late Monday morning.

"My positive waves are floating toward the sky," Betsy answered.

"Why?" Karen asked.

"No reason," Betsy answered, washing her hands at the sink. "I'm still sore from snowboarding, but I'm happy."

"I'd hate to bust your bubble but if this positive wave has anything to do with Jeff—"

"Jeff," Betsy cast her blue eyes downward.

Karen noted a visible difference in Betsy's disposition. It was as if someone had turned off the overhead light, leaving only background lighting on for affect. Curiosity peeked her interest. "Why such a change with the name?"

"Why would you say that?" Betsy asked as if nothing had taken place.

"I don't know if I should tell you this..."

"Tell me." Betsy pulled bowls of food out from the refrigerator.

"I'll tell you only because I believe you'll help this person with her problem. If I know anything about you, you do go out of your way to help someone that you think needs it and you won't stop until they try whatever you want them to try."

Betsy smiled. "That's true. I told you Mormondom would do you good, and was I right?"

"I don't know what I would've done without it. Now you do have a problem with Jeff."

"What is it?"

"Do you really like him, or is he a passing fancy?"

Betsy drummed her long fingernails on the counter. "I don't know. Some days I want to call it quits. I grow tired of it. Start feeling all stuffy inside and get like it's time for me to move on. Then he'll call and his deep baritone voice does something to me. It smoothes my irritation over and I find harmonious peace once more. Sometimes I think I could have a wondrous relationship with him, which I have lacked with others, than other times I doubt. But when I think about leaving him, I worry he won't want me back into his life."

"Sounds like a hard call to me."

"I hardly know him."

Karen looked at Betsy and saw an expression or emotion that she hadn't seen before. "But," she said, raising her eyebrows, "I think you do. There's something tugging at you. It's as if being with him is being home."

"How did you do that? You're so good at reading my soul. You could've made a great psychic."

"I don't know about that," Karen said. She looked at Betsy and wondered if it was right for her to meddle in her life like this. She stood up and walked to the sink. Since she was doubting, maybe she could make it out of the room without mentioning June's words to her earlier yesterday.

"Now you must tell what the problem is with Jeff."

"It really doesn't affect you," Karen said. "I don't know why I even said anything."

"Karen Ashforth, there'll be absolutely no wiggling out of this."

"But I'm not sure I won't be betraying a trust. I don't ever want to do that."

"Karen, out with it. Nobody will ever guess and it'll help me to know what to do. My dear, knowledge is power. Now tell."

"I get the feeling June is concerned that you're stepping in on Jeff too fast after his wife's death."

"It's been a year. That's not too fast. A week after she died, yes, I could see that, but a year? That's a long time and he's lonely and confused, trying to make it on his own being both mom and dad. He'll hardly forget her memory."

"You're right, but she does have feelings."

"Why would June even care?" Betsy asked.

"I don't know," Karen said. "But it'd be interesting to find out."

⋄

"Bishop, hi, this is June." She scraped the dishes as she talked. "The reason I called is because I wanted to know if I could have one more counselor than most Relief Societies have. I have a lot of young kids and don't think I can do it all. I'd like to have a counselor who visits the sisters. I know this is an unusual request, but I really can't get out there and see the sisters like I'd like to. I'm willing to do what I can by phone, but I do have many little ones and don't want to leave them with the babysitter often. They need to be with their family and—"

"June—"

"Yeah?"

"That's a perfect idea."

"It is?"

"Yes."

"Good. I have some of the names for the presidency to consider."

"I'm ready. Shoot."

Chapter 6

The simple yet powerful notes of *I Am A Child of God* floated through Betsy's mind until she burst into song as she cleaned her apartment on Monday morning.

I am a child of God.

And He has sent me here.

Has given me and Earthly home with parents' kind and dear.

Lead me, guide me, walk beside me.

Help me find the way.

Teach me all that I must do to live with Him some day.

She stopped tugging on the bed sheet and squeezed herself in a big hug. She was a daughter of her Heavenly Father and He guided her. What a wonderful message. Knowing God loved everyone and didn't play favorites generated marvelous comfort.

She tucked the sheet under the mattress. The truth she'd found hadn't died. It remained bright as sparkling gold. Nothing tarnished it, except, of course, those few passages in the *Bible*. There were reasons for those and she'd find the answer sooner or later. She had prayed about it and felt prompted that it was okay. No need to listen to Lydia. Her friend had good intentions although those well meaning acts often backfired.

The phone rang. "You sound happy," Lydia commented.

"I am," Betsy said. "I had a good time with Jeff yesterday afternoon. He took me on a short walk and I talked to his kid and everything." More like got my leg chewed off, she thought.

"That explains it. I called and called yesterday and you were never home. I wanted to go night skiing or snowboarding. Now I discover you shunned me for a man. It must be serious if you'd treat your best friend that way. Do you think he'll propose soon?"

"No. He still mourns his wife. He needs time to heal."

"I wouldn't wait. If he doesn't get over it and realize what he has in you, then he's not worth the effort."

Not hard to see why Lydia hadn't stayed married.

"Didn't you tell me awhile back that Philippe had been calling and hinting around that he wanted a resolution?" Lydia questioned.

Betsy pushed herself off the bed to hunt for his ring. She'd wear it for fun today. Might as well enjoy it. Parting with the diamond would be dreadful, but if it helped one of her friends she'd do it.

She scurried over to the cabinets to search through the drawers. She wanted to take the ring to an appraiser and have it evaluated. Just for fun and curiosity. "He proposed," she said at last to Lydia's inquiry on Philippe.

"Oh, Betsy that's so wonderful. I'm sure he's learned from his mistakes. He's so much more your speed. What are you going to do for your wedding?"

Lydia rambled on about Philippe then paused to ask, "Why is Jeff still around?"

"Cause I'm dating him."

Lydia gasped. "Does Philippe know about this?"

"Yes."

"Ah, you modern woman! I'm taking lessons."

"Believe me," Betsy said with emphasis, "you know how to have the guys with a cherry on top."

Lydia laughed. "But Jeff doesn't look like the kind of guy who'd be very liberal minded, if you don't mind me saying."

"He's not. He's the white-picket-fence with several smiling kids attached type."

"How are you doing it? Are you being sneaky, Betsy?"

"Let me make it clear to you. I told Philippe no."

"What? Why?"

"I already tried his route before; didn't like it." Betsy dumped the vanity drawer upside down on her bed. The ring had to be somewhere amidst the paper clips, buttons, and magazines.

"But he's so sexy, and the things he says—"

"He's not faithful."

"You two shouldn't give up. You could go to counseling and learn to work out your relationship. You two are a perfect match."

"I'm an old woman, Lydia. I don't have the time it'd take to do all that."

"But think of the clothes you could buy. The places you could go. The adventures."

"Would you like to be set up with him?" Betsy cut in.

"Me?" Lydia asked with mock shock.

"Yes, you seem to like his taste."

"I have other interests. But Philippe's perfect for you and he's not boring. He definitely knows how to live."

Too well, Betsy thought.

"What's he up to these days? It's been forever since I've seen him," Lydia continued.

"Still designing clothes and taking lot of trips to the States for work."

"Really! I'd love to see him. I miss those good old days when we were all together."

"We did have a lot of fun." Betsy yawned. In reality, those days weren't as good as Lydia made them out. They had been full of heartbreak, hurt, and betrayal, not to mention that something always seemed wrong. It reminded Betsy of how she once felt when she was a teenager, and had told her parents she was out with her girlfriends when in reality she was dating Johnny. Wherever they went, she lived in fear her parents would show up and catch her in her lie.

"So, to change the topic," Lydia broke into her thoughts. "Do you want to go shopping tomorrow? I noticed Provo has a new mall, but I bet Salt Lake has a bigger one."

"It does," Betsy said.

Lydia's first marriage was to an ancient old man. When he died he left her a nice pot of gold. Very few people knew about it. Betsy doubted even George was aware of it. It had happened right after they broke up in college. Lydia loved her husband and the suspicious mumblings directed at her were jealous attacks. Lydia was a truth seeker like herself, not a deceiver. The grief from his death consumed her whole being. Ever since then, her friend liked to shop, perhaps her way of coping.

"So shall we go tomorrow?" Lydia asked.

"I haven't spent very much time with Mikey or Sam lately. I'm clueless as to what's going on in their lives. What kind of aunt is that?"

"We could take them. It'd be fun. I'm sure Mikey wouldn't mind a few more outfits."

"I'm sure Karen would mind paying."

"A couple of outfits to make Mikey feel better. What's the harm? We don't have to buy, just see what's available."

"It'd be nice to get out of Provo. That might not be such a bad idea. We could also catch a movie at Trolley Square."

"Great," Lydia said.

"Let's leave about three-thirty. Then you can have your beauty rest and I can clean the house. Mikey will be home from school by then. I'm sure Sam will be doing something with his friends, or practicing soccer. Sometimes the school lets him play indoor soccer, and when he gets desperate, he'll practice in the garage."

They said their good-byes and Betsy opened up the ring box she had finally found buried in the last drawer, lurking under a pile of socks. Inside, the two-karat diamond ring sparkled. Gorgeous. Rich, although it must have impurities. After all, Philippe wasn't a bank. She slipped the slightly chilled metal on her finger. The ring fit.

As she sat at her vanity to put foundation on her partially wrinkled face, her mind wandered to what it'd be like to wear a ring of that magnitude and to have it truly represent a thing of beauty. Would she ever be the owner of such feeling? Was Jeff capable of giving her that? Or were her expectations so high no one could climb a mountain that steep?

Once she'd applied red lipstick and blue indigo eye shadow, she studied her red hair. It had been purple before red. Now the red seemed too much. Perhaps she should tame her style. The memory of Apostle Paul's words about the stiff neck and the excessive dress floated to her mind. She wouldn't want to be guilty of that before the Lord. Maybe she should try a new color—something truly unique to her. Maybe, just maybe, she should try brown.

Yuck! It might give her a younger appeal and she wouldn't stick out so much. But she would miss the attention. Would Jeff like it better? Would Philippe be disappointed by her meandering to the conservative ways? Perhaps she should follow the Prophet's counsel to the hilt and dress very plain with no expense.

Nah. She liked wearing loud clothes. Bright clothes were different than expensive clothes that caused pride. She surely wasn't guilty of pride.

She glanced again in the mirror; perhaps she'd get a virtual makeo\.. see how bad it'd be. She didn't want to lose herself, but developing a c version, a more classic style, might be tolerable.

She slipped off the ring and watched it glitter as she twisted it. She'd wear it today. She could pretend to own a perfect husband. She smiled at her fantasy. As she gathered her things, she slipped the ring's box in her purse. She had been known to bloat and wanted to secure the ring in its home if that happened.

♦

By Monday morning, Jeff was completely at a loss about what to do. He had thought of the many possibilities through the night and still, as he prepared for work, he continued analyzing the problem. His wife had always guided him on the steps that should be taken concerning their son. She would explain their son's motives and why he acted the way he did. Funny, he had never noticed her talent before she died. He never even once said thank you. Did she know he was thankful even though he didn't say so? Or was that why he found her depressed sometimes, because he hadn't fully let her know her value to him or to their son? Oh, if only he could go back and change his ways.

But none of that helped his current problem with Chad. He couldn't have his son telling off the lady he dated. And his son shouldn't feel like Betsy stole his mom's place. No one ever could do that. Betsy had her own spot.

Ah, Betsy. So alive, so different from the other ladies in the ward. She took no thought about how she appeared to others. She'd douse herself with colors and clothes that she enjoyed. It was so refreshing to find someone who didn't care what other people thought. Cindy had that quality, too. Cindy knew he appreciated that trait before she died. That was one area he hadn't slacked. He tightened his tie as he looked in the mirror. His eyes bagged and several razor cuts dotted his chin.

He took a breath, then knocked on Chad's door. He waited for the "yeah." Nothing. Odd response for a school morning. He entered his son's room, finding no one. Bath water ran. He went into the bathroom. The door creaked open. Before he saw his son, he heard groans of pain. Then he saw his boy's face, color drained out of it, leaving a face as white as the freshly fallen snow outside. His big brown eyes flashed in startled sparks as he looked at his dad from the tub.

"What are you doing in here?" Chad said roughly, unable to hide the tension in his voice and the embarrassment of being caught wincing.

"I came to talk to you."

"Well, there's better timing than this."

"Sorry, I didn't know you were still in the bathtub. You're running late, aren't you?"

"So?"

"You're never late."

"A person can change. How do you get a ghost clean?" Chad asked, moving the water around him.

"I didn't come in here to hear jokes. I want to know what's going on with you."

"I'll tell you the answer since I don't know if you'll ever figure it out."

"Thanks," Jeff muttered.

"Give him a boo-ble bath." Chad laughed. "Get it?"

"Yeah, that was pretty clever."

"Here's another one: Why was the ghost sad?"

"Why?"

"Because he missed his ghoul-friend."

"Do you miss yours?"

"What are you talking about?" Chad drew his gaze from his father.

"Mom."

"She wasn't my girlfriend."

"No, she was better than that. She was your best friend."

His hand stopped waving in the water, but he didn't respond to the comment.

"Isn't that true, Chad?"

Another long delay of silence than a choked out yes came. "She was a good Mom."

"Yes, she was and I'll always remember her. You know that, don't you?" Jeff asked.

"Of course."

"Chad, because I've started dating someone else doesn't mean I'm trying to replace Mom."

"I know," he said. "I just want Mom back."

"You figured that out?"

"I'm not dumb," Chad snapped.

"Don't get me wrong, I never thought that. I can't tell you why I do half the things I do. You're a smart boy, did you know that?" Jeff ruffled his son's long wet bangs.

Chad shook his head.

"Love you, son."

"You too."

"Now, let me see that bedsore of yours. You'll have to pat it until it's extremely dry when you get out."

"I know. Stop babying me. Mom was never this bad."

"All right, but I still want to see it."

"Dad!"

He grunted as he pulled himself out of the tub.

Jeff looked away. His son shouldn't be a cripple. He bent down by the hip and the reddened skin had transformed into a more purplish tone and the rawness seemed painful. "It's getting worse."

He shrugged.

"I'm calling the doctor."

"Don't. It's no big deal."

"I don't want it to become more serious."

"It won't. Will you please trust me on this one?"

Jeff stared in his eyes and knew if he didn't start earning the trust of his son their relationship would grow progressively worse.

✦

Early Monday morning Karen woke up in her husband's arms about five minutes before her alarm buzzed. She scooted closer to him, feeling the warmth radiating from his strong body. He breathed lightly in her ear and she caressed her fingers through the brown hairs on his arms. She wanted to remain like this forever. Of course she wouldn't, but the thought was nice. If only George would hear the gospel, he'd have to accept it because it was the truth. Then they could work on being sealed forever. What purer love could there be? How would she get him to listen?

"George?" she spoke lightly. "I love you."

"You too," he said, then rolled over onto his stomach.

So much for the dream. The weight of his arm pressed heavy and lifeless across her side. She scooted herself from the confines and sat up. Once a yawn had stifled out of her mouth, she lowered on her knees for prayers. She needed to call down the very powers of heaven like she had been studying the prophets had done. After she rose from her knees, she sat on the mattress to wake-up a bit more before jumping into the shower.

Suddenly a big strong arm wrapped around her and pulled her in. George. "What do you pray about?" he asked.

"That you'll find the truth of the gospel," she said flatly.

"Gees, can't you think of something else?"

"What's wrong with praying about that?"

"I'm happy as I am. I wish you'd stop thinking I need something in my life."

"George, its 'cause I love you."

"If you love me, you'll stop cramming religion down my throat and pay attention to me and my needs."

Karen lunged to break from his grasp but the hold tightened. "I pay attention to you."

"When was the last time you asked me how I was doing or how my work was?"

"I ask you those things," Karen said through tightened lips.

"Name the last time."

She tugged on his arm lock. He wouldn't budge and give her any space. "See you can't name a time. Well, I have news for you; my work isn't going good. I'm stressed and it'd be nice to have someone I can talk to and depend on once in a while. Other people have noticed that you're not there for me."

"Who?" Her eyes darted over him in angry rapid movements.

"Just other people."

"Tell me!"

"Don't ask," George said.

Karen felt herself go faint. Lydia. "I've been sick with migraines or otherwise I would've been a better support."

George offered no response.

"Does this have to do with Lydia?" Karen finally asked.

"No," he snapped. He spoke the word so quick and short Karen suspected she'd hit a nerve. Was her husband trying to hide something? Her empty stomach cramped with uneasiness. Not Lydia. Not now.

"George, I want you to stay away from her."

"Are you saying you don't trust me?" He let go of his grasp and pushed on her back. "Go. You want to leave anyway."

"Don't push me away." Karen sat, refusing to budge. She flung herself over George's chest. "Love me. I love you. I'm sorry."

He gently put his arm over her like she might break. "I'm sorry, too."

◇

Jeff drummed his fingers against his desk when he found out it was his sister-in-law on the other end of the phone. "Hi, June how are you?"

"I heard you were dating Betsy."

The drumming stopped as the smell from the doughnut on his desk tickled his nose. "You heard right," he said before biting into the chocolate.

"Why?" Her voice had broken into emotion. "Wasn't Cindy good enough for you?"

"Of course she was."

"You have a funny way of showing it. She hasn't even been dead a year and you're already being unfaithful."

"I am not."

"She's watching you. She wouldn't want to share you with anyone. I know my sister. You can't say she would. You should really think about this before you go out on any more dates."

When Jeff hung up the phone, his stomach felt ill. Perhaps it was the sugar so early in the morning, perhaps it was June's attack.

Was she right? Was he being unfaithful to his beloved?

◇

Karen ran into Mikey in the hall.

"Mom, look at the picture Sam took of me. Don't I look wonderful?"

Karen grabbed the photo out of her hand. It was a large black and white picture—head shot. Mikey had her brows raise and a far off dreamy expression. "This is great. Do I get a copy?"

Mikey beamed. "I guess." She pulled a felt pen from her pocket. "Would you like my picture personalized?"

Karen blinked. It was too early in the morning for this. "Whatever you want."

She wrote, pressing the photo against the wall, "Thanks for being such a great fan. Mikey."

"Ah, Mikey, I thought we—"

"I know. I know, Mom. Just kidding. I need to get ready for school." She kissed Karen on the cheek and was gone.

Rubbing her temples, Karen found Betsy in the kitchen cleaning. She grumbled hello.

"About three-thirty today Mikey, Lydia, and I are going shopping up in Salt Lake. Do you want to come?" Betsy said.

Karen wanted to say no, but then she thought about it. It wouldn't hurt her to get a few new outfits. And it also wouldn't be bad to keep Lydia busy. "Yes," she said. "I can go to work early tomorrow to make up the time I'll miss. That'd be fun."

Betsy smiled. "Marvelous. I have to admit I'm kind of surprised but I'm glad you're coming." She dumped the swept up dirt into the trash compactor.

"It'll be fun." She walked over to the medicine cabinet to find an aspirin. What she wouldn't do for a cup of coffee right now. She was going to need it to make it through this day, she thought.

"Have a rough night?" Betsy inquired.

"I didn't get much sleep," Karen admitted, "and I feel like another migraine is lurking in the recesses of my brain."

"You had a headache yesterday."

"I know," Karen said. "I have headaches everyday and those darn migraines seem to attack me at least once a week. I don't think I can stand it if I keep suffering from them."

"They're painful."

"They're interfering with my quality of life." Karen pictured Lydia's hourglass shaped body and shuddered. She could be replaced because of those headaches. They needed to end.

"Have you called that doctor the lady at Relief Society told you about?"

"No."

"You should give her a call."

"I will first thing when I get to work. It's too early now."

"Promise me you'll do it," Betsy said.

"I promise," Karen said as she worried about losing her husband to Lydia.

Chapter 7

The slow repetitious motions of scrubbing scum off the cabinet eased the worry from Betsy's mind. Before she knew it, notes floated from her lips only to be interrupted by the ringing phone. She ignored the phone on the counter, knowing if she answered that one she'd be glued by the cord and not able to finish other household chores. Frantically she searched for the cordless phone and found it under the living room couch. She answered breathlessly.

"Is Betsy Ashforth there?"

"Speaking."

"Bishop Hawthorne would like to meet with you tomorrow night. Would that be good for you?"

"Did he hear about what happened with Chad on Sunday? I can explain that. He didn't mean what he said. He's just a confused child, and with the anniversary of his mother's death coming up... Actually, I think the exact day is this Thursday. The bishop has nothing to worry about. I have it under control, even though it didn't seem like it on Sunday. Tell him everything is okay."

"I-I-I don't know why the bishop is calling you in."

"That's why. I explained it. If you can't remember all that, tell him I have it under control and thank him for his belief in me."

"But—"

"Thanks a lot, you're a doll." Betsy hung up and grabbed the broom.

The phone buzzed again.

"This is Betsy and you are?"

"Brother Erickson, I just called you."

"Oh, yes? I thought we had things worked out."

"I think the bishop still wants to meet with you."

"You haven't had time to tell him everything?"

"I'm confident he wants to see you anyway."

Betsy leaned on the broom. "Well if you really feel that way, then I guess I could come in. But I don't want to waste mine or his time."

"We appreciate that. About eight-thirty?"

"I have a date with Jeff tomorrow night. Don't worry, Chad had already made plans with some friends so I'm not taking him away from his dad. I'm definitely not a Dad-stealer, despite what he yelled."

"Um, so you want to meet earlier?"

"That'd be wonderful. Five?"

"He'll still be at work. Six-thirty is the earliest he can make it."

"Will that give him enough time for dinner? I could bring him some and we could eat as I explain my side of the story. Really, this is a big misunderstanding."

"He'll manage dinner on his own, but thanks for the offer."

"Then I'll make him cookies. I have this great new healthy recipe doesn't use an ounce of sugar. He'll love it and it'll be good for him. I gue I better dash though, because I'll need to run to the store to grab a couple of ingredients. Oh, I can triple the batch and give some to Jeff and my brother's family. I'm sure everyone will love it. Thank you for calling." She hung up and swept the floor in a flurry. She had a lot to do before her shopping trip later that afternoon.

◇

The dark drug of depression crept upon Karen from the moment she realized another phantom migraine headache had hit her. She rubbed the center of her forehead where it throbbed. She would lose her husband if she didn't get control of her health, she thought, swallowing an Imtrex. A small tear of self-pity welled up in her eyes and drifted down her face when her co-worker approached her.

"Here's a list of people you need to call back."

"Thank you," Karen said as she watched her manager leave. She pulled out the telephone book to call the doctor Sister Jenkin's had recommended.

"Doctor Bringley," the receptionist answered in a hurried tone. "How may I help you?"

"I'd like to schedule an appointment."

"The soonest one available is in three weeks."

"Three weeks!" Karen said. "It has to be earlier. You don't understand, it's very important I get in right away."

"Just a minute please."

Karen shuffled the papers on her desk as she waited.

"Looks like we had a cancellation for tomorrow morning."

"Great."

The lady took her name and number and Karen got off the phone shaking her head. Doctors, first they're booked and next thing you know if you throw a stink, you're in. She was going to become a skunk.

◇

"What movie are you working on now?" Betsy asked Mikey at the breakfast table.

Her niece gave her the classic where-did-you-come-from look that teenagers are so famous for. "What?" she asked before digging her spoon in for another bite of Sugar Smacks.

"I know you're always making a film in your head and I want to know what you're shooting now."

"Aunt Betsy, I gave that up ages ago."

"What has replaced it?"

"Nothing."

Betsy walked over to her niece and waved her hands in front of her face. "Earth to Mikey. Come in Mikey. Your aunt is trying to communicate with you and she isn't appreciating this nothing response. When you lie it always comes back. Please talk with your aunt before she shrivels away from disappointment."

Mikey turned her head from the waving hands.

"Your Aunt Betsy is getting lost in the static." She slowly bent her knees. "Please, I'm going to get sucked away by the 'non-communicator blob.'"

Mikey burst into a smile.

Betsy slumped to the floor, moaning. "He's got me. He's got me." Then she fell silent, sprawled out. She squinted her eyes to see if Mikey watched. Some crumbs she had missed sweeping, stuck to her hands. She wiped them on her pants as she stood. "I'm going to Salt Lake this afternoon to do some serious shopping. I planned on taking my favorite niece with me, but now I seem unable to communicate with her so I doubt I can convey the message."

"Okay, stop. I'll talk. I'll talk," Mikey said. "I don't feel like making movies in my head much anymore, but Agatha and I are going to try out for the school play next week. It's going to be so cool. They're doing the *Wizard of Oz* and I want to be Dorothy. Don't you think I would make a good Dorothy?"

"Perfect," Betsy answered. She'd have to tell Karen her daughter was losing her movie dream world. "Don't you have to sing?"

"Yes, and I have a wonderful voice."

Mikey broke out into a scale of notes that brought to mind wailing stray cats and shrieking house mice who were dying a long agonizing death from food poisoning.

"I hear," Betsy said, struggling to pull a pleasant face. "I wish you all the positive waves when you try out."

Mikey beamed. "Thanks, but I won't be needing them. There's no way they won't see my great skill. I'm so excited. This is my first step into making it big. I've put in years of practice. Now it's time for my talent to be recognized."

Betsy nodded. She had done well in teaching Mikey to project positive vibes.

"Now can I go on the shopping trip with you? Please, please, please?" Mikey grabbed hold of Betsy's hand and shook it as she spoke.

Betsy looked into her niece's brown eyes. It was interesting how situations reversed in life. One just never knew.

"Well I don't know—"

"I told you. That was the deal."

"You didn't tell me about your grades."

"Ah come on—"

"The communication's growing fuzzy. I'm starting to lose contact."

"Stop. I'll talk. I'm doing okay in most of my classes."

"Which one gives you trouble?"

"Math."

"That's completely understandable. Don't worry about that unless you want to be a doctor. People at school always tell you that you'll need it in your life when you grow-up. It's not true. I never use it. There have only been a couple of times when I was cooking that I wished I knew how many teaspoons were in a tablespoon. What class is it anyway?"

"Geometry."

"That stuff makes no sense. Just survive, and if you can, get a C going to go shopping after school. It should be fun. It'll be you, your mom, and Lydia."

"Lydia and my mom together?" Mikey questioned, her brow furrowed.

"Yeah, I was a little surprised myself. Your mom didn't even complain about Lydia coming."

"This might be a more eventful shopping trip than I thought. With Lydia there, I bet I can get mom to buy me more outfits than she would otherwise. She'll be so distracted."

"Ah, Mikey, we think a lot alike."

✧

When Karen pulled up to her house, the first thing she spotted was Lydia's black Porsche. The slick, shiny black seemed almost as cold and impersonal as the owner. Too bad the only way she could keep an eye on that woman was to baby-sit her at the mall.

She took a deep breath before marching into the kitchen, straight into her foe. Lydia flipped her hair as a greeting. Immediately Karen noticed the black fish net lace nylons. The gray skirt graced the top of the hose a yard or two short of needed fabric. A silky white blouse hid under a gray suit jacket. Her make-up and hair were stunning with a short tailored stylish flavor. Karen wished she had done something with her moppy hair.

"Hi, Lydia," she said flatly.

Lydia smiled. Karen noted her red lipstick matched the red bold stroke in her bangs.

"Oh, Karen, it's good to see you. How was work?"

"Fine."

"You look exhausted. I don't know if I could ever handle a job like yours. If I don't sleep until at least one in the afternoon, I'm an absolute wreck. You wouldn't even recognize me."

Karen offered a faint smile and headed for the cupboard for aspirin. Betsy bounced into the room and said, "Oh, good, Karen, you're here. Now all we have to do is wait for Mikey and then we'll be riding happy trails."

"We should shop with style. Let's take my car," Lydia said.

"But there's no room in it," Betsy said.

"Oh, Mikey and Karen are short. They could ride in the back."

"Where would the shopping bags go?" Karen asked. She wasn't going to cram herself in the back of the small sports car, especially the way Lydia drove.

"We can go in my Cadillac," Betsy suggested.

"Does it have enough style for you?" Karen mumbled to Lydia.

Lydia ignored the question.

Mikey walked in the door and spread her arms wide. "Ready for shopping?"

Everyone smiled and climbed in Betsy's car. Betsy turned around before starting the vehicle and asked, "Do you want to drive with the roof up or down?"

"Judging that it's snowing, I think we should opt for up," Karen said.

Betsy shrugged. "Okay, but it would be real spontaneous to do it the other way. I bet no one else is doing it."

"Do you think it's wise to even drive this car in winter?" Karen asked. This was her first winter and even though the locals had complained how mild it was, she worried about the storm that would come.

"We'll have a great time," Lydia said.

Karen watched Lydia and her charm. Fake. Karen wondered what the true Lydia was like.

"I vote for a four-wheel drive," Mikey said.

"Is that the vogue thing here?" Lydia asked. "About ten years ago that was in fashion in California."

"Some things never go out of style," Karen replied quickly. "My favorite are the good old classics. I put my vote with my four-wheel drive. I don't want to have to go on this mountain in a wimpy stylish car."

"Seems like we have a slight disagreement," Betsy said. "But I have the perfect solution to make the harmony flow between us again."

"What's that?" the ladies asked.

"Lydia and I will go in her car and Karen and Mikey can follow to handle all our many purchases. Truly the way this group shops I doubt my car could manage it all. Besides, I love Porsches."

This satisfied everyone. Karen and Mikey took the lead.

"I'll laugh so hard if they get caught in a snow storm," Mikey said with a devilish grin.

"I would, too," Karen answered. "Shall we pray for snow?"

⋄

"Why won't it stop snowing?" Lydia asked as she edged her feet through the slush with careful steps.

Karen looked at Lydia's high spiked shoes. It was like Lydia, instead of being practical and wearing leather boots, to complain about the weather, and try to get it to conform to her. Once inside Lydia went straight to the bulletin to find out what stores were there. "Nordstrom's, we must go there!"

Karen and Mikey locked a glance. They both turned to their side laughing. How many times had they made fun of that store and the people who shopped there? The prices were outrageous and only the elite rich could afford to walk-in.

"Sounds fun!" Betsy said. "That has always been one of my favorite stores."

"Do you guys mind if I find a store a little more hip?" Mikey asked.

Lydia put her arm around Mikey. "My dear, this store is all class."

"But," Mikey said, "it's not cool to look good. It's a teenager's personal mission to look their worst."

Lydia smiled. "You may have a point there."

"So I'm going to split and I'll meet you here in three hours. Cool?"

Everyone nodded except Karen. She pulled Mikey toward her, causing

Lydia's arm to fall off her daughter's shoulder. "I better keep an eye on Mikey. With her kind of attitude, you never know what trouble she'll get into."

The group agreed to part and once Lydia and Betsy were out of sight, Karen plopped her arm around Mikey's shoulder. "Thank you. Come on, I have an idea that'll definitely shock them."

✧

Chad rolled into the kitchen, maneuvering his chair sideways to the fridge so he could open it. He had amazed himself by not wanting his bowl of ice cream. Actually, he didn't feel like eating anything.

He closed the refrigerator door remembering that his mom had always had a treat waiting for him after school. He imagined his friends were enjoying homemade cookies and ice cream with their moms' smiling at them and asking about their day. He, on the other hand, had no one to talk to. His dad would give a casual, "How are you doing today?" with his hand on the door ready to head-out. I'm no fool, Chad thought. He doesn't want to hear what I have to say like Mom did. All he cared about was dating that New Age lady, Betsy. Chad shook his head. She was pretty good at giving primary lessons, but she had purple hair and she tried to make him meditate.

Too weird, and definitely off limits for his dad.

Chad rolled his chair into his bedroom, using his frustrated anger against the wheels. What was his father doing with that woman anyway? He was supposed to be thinking of his mother. Lately, it seemed like Chad was the only one doing the remembering. Maybe he should do something to make his dad recall how wonderful his mother had been.

✧

Karen tightened her grip on her purse. "Are you ready?"

"For what?" Mikey asked. "To shop? Aren't I always?"

"I have a little surprise planned for Lydia and Betsy."

"A surprise?" Mikey asked, her eyes lighting. She stopped walking and grabbed her mother's sleeve. "What kind?"

"Lydia and Betsy aren't the only ones who can get all done up. I'm going to show them I can compete with the best."

A small boy yelling ran right into Karen's leg. A mother who was jogging behind him apologized and picked him up.

Mikey raised her eyebrows and spoke in a very long, loud dramatic voice, "You don't mean you're going to—"

"Yes, I do. Are you game?" Karen strolled down the tile floor at a fast pace.

"What exactly do you have in mind?"

"I'm going to let the experts go for it. I have already set up a consultation appointment and then I'm fully booked for the next couple of hours. My hair's going to be dyed, cut and styled, and I'm going to get a new approach to make-up. They also mentioned getting my eyebrows done and legs waxed. If you like, I can get you a hair appointment, too."

"I want." Mikey jumped in the air and clapped her hands. "This is going to be so much fun."

◊

Lydia turned to Betsy and pulled her purse back over her shoulder. "Okay, what is the most expensive store around here? Give me the best that Utah has."

Betsy grabbed Lydia's furry coat. "They have Anne Taylor?"

"You're kidding?" Lydia asked, her mouth slightly lowering. "In Utah?"

"We're not just a bunch of dumb cowboys," Betsy said. "I haven't completely lost my marbles moving here. You'd be surprised what Utah does have to offer." Betsy slipped into a quick trot and headed for the store.

Lydia followed. They headed straight to one of the counters. Lydia banged the bell in short quick pats.

"Yes?" asked a lady dressed in a dark suit, gray hair piled up into a hair clip.

"Where are your most expensive clothes?" Lydia spoke in a high tone.

"That'd be over in the east section of the store," the clerk answered. "If you'd like, I'll show you."

"Please," Lydia said without giving the lady another glance.

"Why the most expensive?" Betsy asked, trotting behind her friend.

"Please," Lydia said as though that was one of the stupidest questions she ever heard.

Betsy stopped walking and drilled her fingernails against her lips. There was no reason for Lydia to be so rude. Why would someone insist on buying the most expensive clothes? Betsy had always bought what was "her" not what the price said on the tag.

A purple dress with white lace caught her attention. The cut of the suit was flattering and figure shaping. She found her size as the passages she read the other night on vanity and pride strode through her head. The phrase "very costly apparel" seemed to play like a two-year-old asking why in her mind. Over and over again the phrase came to her thoughts. Was Lydia guilty of costly apparel? Well, yes. She obviously wore clothes so pricey only the few elite rich could afford them, but that wouldn't necessarily mean she had a stiff neck like Apostle Paul had suggested. It didn't say she was a person who had pride, malice, and persecuted others. But that was the path *The Book of Mormon* described would happen to people who became too caught up in their clothes. Could that theory be true? Was she caught up in the snags as well?

Betsy glimpsed Lydia one more time and spotted the heavy pile of outfits in her arm. Lydia would make the perfect test case of the theory. One, she could afford to wear costly apparel and two, she did wear them.

A pang of guilt rushed through Betsy. Lydia had been one of her best friends for years. What kind of friend was she being, thinking Lydia was prideful and caught up in malice? She felt as if she had gossiped behind her friend's back.

Her friend was full of great qualities. Beautiful. Passionate. Enthusiastic about life. And best of all, she was a truth seeker. But still, Lydia did put a lot of dough into her purchases.

◊

"What kind of make over would you like, ma'am?" the model-like asked after Karen sat on the black leather hair cutting chair.

"I want a complete one. I'm tired of my lifeless brown hair. I want to be vogue. In. Beautiful. I'm game for anything classy. I don't want to look like a freak. After two decades of marriage, I want a style that will turn my husband's head."

"No ideas of what you like?"

"Not really. I have to admit I really haven't been paying much attention to fashion lately."

"All right," the lady said, taking a deep breath. She walked behind Karen, studying the different angles of her features. "I suggest for starters we change your hair color. You mentioned you were tired of drab. Let's do an auburn. That would contrast nicely with your light complexion and would hide the gray."

The lady hurried over to the wall and took down hair samples and pointed at what color she had in mind. "This shade would be perfect for you."

Karen nodded as a lump rose in her throat. What if she made a big mistake and ended up like Bozo the Clown? Dying hair seemed so permanent. "Do whatever you think is best," she said, closing her eyes.

◊

They had been shopping for a little over a half-hour when Lydia lugged a pile of outfits to the counter. "I'd like to purchase these on my Visa."

The gray haired store clerk nodded as she gazed over the mound. Betsy figured the lady was computing the commission at the same time fighting jealous impulses of not being able to throw money down on unnecessary clothes like that.

"Looks like you didn't have too much problem finding clothes even though it is Utah," Betsy said to Lydia as she eyed the jewelry on display.

"It's not as good as New York or California, I must say, but it isn't that bad," Lydia said. "I've found some outfits here that I'm excited about. I can't wait to have a night on the town. What other stores does Utah have that are any good, or is this the only one?"

"No. There's a couple of other pricey ones. But how are you going to carry all this?"

"I thought we could run this out to the car and then come back for more."

Betsy nodded.

"What have you found?" Lydia asked her.

"Nothing."

"What? I'm sure we can find you something. Have you looked over at those business suits? They still have some stunning ones left that I didn't grab."

"I haven't, but—"

"Go look. I saw the most pretty indigo blue one. It would go fabulous with your eyes. You have to get it. You'll see it over there. I have to admit, the second I saw it I thought of you. I went to show it to you, but I couldn't find you. Have you been hiding from me? What are you waiting for? Why don't you check it out?"

"Lydia, I appreciate your help, but I really don't need a new suit right now. I have more than enough to fit my lifestyle."

"Naturally, you have enough, but that isn't the point."

"What's the point?"

Lydia seemed startled. "What?"

"Why should I buy that outfit if I don't need it?"

"To have more, of course." Lydia handed her credit card to the store clerk as a vast amount printed up on the register. "We must always appear like we walked out of *Vogue* magazine. Fashions change and we need to keep up."

"Honest Lydia, I watch kids. I don't need a suit. Wouldn't it be silly to be cleaning house in a thousand dollar wool outfit?"

"Well, if you feel that way, why don't we hunt for more casual clothes so you can clean in style."

Betsy laughed. "Clean in style. Now there's a motto for me."

Lydia rolled her eyes and spoke snappily to the clerk. "Can you get someone to help me carry my stuff to the car?"

"Let me see what I can do for you," the elderly lady said.

Betsy couldn't help but think the lady was taken back and confused.

"Service these days is really down to minimal," Lydia said. "I wish I could say it was different elsewhere, but I'd be lying. What has happened to the good old days where the stores knew how to treat customers?"

"Lydia, you're being rude."

"I'm just stating the facts as I see them."

"The store isn't used to people buying out their whole inventory in half an hour."

"All the more reason they should be waiting on me hand and foot."

Betsy sighed and tapped her fingers on her lips.

Lydia gasped. "Oh, the ring."

"What?" Betsy asked.

"That ring. Iiiitt'ss beautiful. Can I see it?"

Betsy held out her hand so the rock could be examined.

"Let me wear it."

Betsy slipped the ring from her finger and handed it to her friend. By that time, a boy from packing had made it up pushing a cart to help lug Lydia's purchases to the car.

"At last, you've come," she said, waving the boy toward the elevator. "I don't know why I had to wait so long."

"Sorry," the boy said, mouth quivering.

Betsy laughed as she glanced from Lydia to herself. They were a scary enough couple to put fear into any male. This poor boy must wish he was back in the packaging warehouse.

Once they made it outside, and Lydia noticed the snow falling to the ground, she insisted Betsy take the boy out to the car. She explained that Betsy had on more suitable shoes for the occasion. Betsy rolled her eyes, growing weary of her friend's prima donna attitude and trucked to the car. After she opened the side door, she realized that Lydia had kept her ring.

Betsy quickly helped the boy throw the purchases into the car and she jogged back to Lydia.

She held out her hand. "Ring."

"Where should we go now?" Lydia asked, turning toward the mall.

"Ring," Betsy said loudly. "I'd like to have my ring back right now."

Lydia headed for the door.

Betsy grabbed hold of her fur coat and pulled the nap backwards. "I said ring and if you'd like your coat to survive a minute longer, you'll hand it over."

Lydia slipped off the ring and slapped it in Betsy's hand. "Gees, you didn't have to get all hyper about it."

"I think I might have. The way you've been acting today, I wonder why we're friends."

"Why would you say that?" Lydia asked, brushing at where Betsy had grabbed a hold of the coat.

"You haven't been very kind and I got the feeling you would've kept my ring if I hadn't insisted you return it."

"I'm sorry you got that feeling. Of course, I would've given it back. I don't steal from friends. When have I ever stolen anything from you?"

Betsy looked away from her probing eyes. "You steal?"

"No." Lydia looked angry.

"I'm sorry. I guess I'm attached to the ring. I really don't want to give it up."

"You mean you want to marry Philippe?" Lydia asked as they walked into the mall.

"No, just keep the ring."

"I have to say I can't blame you there. Let's go find something you can wear comfortably around the house. What do you say?'

"Sure. Sorry I got grouchy," Betsy said.

"That's all right. It happens to the best of us."

Time slipped away until the hour came to meet Karen and Mikey. Betsy pointed it out and sighed. "I wish we could stay longer. With the roads the way they are, I think it's best we go now. I don't want to be stuck in a snowdrift somewhere."

"Are winters always like this?" Lydia asked.

"How am I supposed to know? Remember, this is my first one here, but the locals say sometimes it really snows and other times it's mild. Just depends. January and February are supposed to be the worst months. But it sure does make great skiing weather."

"That's true. It reminds me I need to try out my new ski outfit. How about we go snowboarding again tomorrow?" Lydia asked.

"I haven't got rid of all the bruises from our last trip."

"Ah, come on. I thought you got over your chicken attitude last time. Where has your spunk gone?"

"I actually had a great time. And for your information I still have my spunk. Why don't we make it for a half-day? I just don't think I can rise out of bed early two days in a row. Remember, I did have to clean house today and I still have a couple more bathrooms to do tomorrow."

"They sure work you like a slave," Lydia commented.

"I like doing it."

"You like being taken advantage of?"

"I'm not. They really appreciate me and I do get to stay in their house for free. Serving other people brings me happiness. You should try it sometime."

"Yeah, maybe. What's taking Karen and Mikey so long?"

"I'm sure they'll be here any second. It's not like Karen to be late."

Chapter 8

The house stood dark and lifeless. No lights flickered to suggest inhabitance. Jeff flinched. His wife had always cast a homey warmth in their abode.

If only he had said thank you, held her more often, spent effort and energy on her so she would've known her value. She'd longed for that, but he always rationalized that next time he'd charm her, romance her. He earned money to support her and that was more important he had told her and himself. All lousy excuses.

When Cindy had given birth to Chad in October, Jeff's birthday had been a week later. Cindy was sick and tired from the experience of bringing a lively baby into the world, and she had still managed to bake him a cake and purchase presents. She had the excuses and she chose not to use them.

Her example shamed him. Cut into him, deep like a surgeon's knife, exposing his character. Now he could change it. He clenched his fists. If he became the person Cindy always wanted, then when they joined in heaven he'd be prepared do all the things he so longed to do. He could make it up. If he worked hard enough, he could get his life in order so he could be with his wife. He'd have to try despite the pain of neglect blocking his progress.

His keys jingled as he unlocked the front door. Where was Chad? Surely he wasn't sitting alone in the dark again? Jeff closed his eyes. His son must be at a friend's house. Of course, he knew that wasn't true. Chad had gone over to several friends' homes only to discover they weren't designed for wheelchairs. Humiliation burned his cheeks when people went out of their way to help him up the stairs and into rooms. Sister Hutch told Jeff several months ago she was so sorry their doorframe was so narrow. It seemed when Chad visited Jason he couldn't get through the front hall. Sister Hutch felt awful and wondered if Chad had handled it all right.

In truth, Jeff didn't know anything about it. His son never mentioned it. Jeff had never spoken of it either, afraid it'd embarrass his son. But was that the true reason? Yes, it was the excuse Jeff had used, but was he too chicken to be supportive of his son as he had been with his wife?

The door creaked a mournful sound as Jeff hesitantly pushed it. "Chad? Are you home?" He reached for the light switch and flipped on the entryway lamp. The quiet blackness changed to emptiness. No shoes tossed on the front rug. No coat hunched in a heap a few feet away. "Chad?" Jeff called again before listening. He heard the faint noise of the television. Slipping his coat off, he progressed into Chad's room. His son sat slouched over to the right side of his wheelchair, chin resting on his palm. The blue light of the television engulfed him.

"Hello." Jeff set his coat on a nearby table.

If he hadn't been watching his son closely, he wouldn't have noticed the barely detectable nod.

"What ya watchin'?"

Chad didn't answer. Jeff approached the television to turn it off when he saw her. She smiled before the camera with one of those brilliant grins that he had fallen in love with. Her gorgeous red hair bounced lightly as she spun in circles wearing a purple dress. Her red, full lips he loved so much blew kisses toward the camera. In her best Marilynn Monroe imitation she sang in a long deep voice, "Happy Birthday, Mr. Chadwick." Then she burst into giggles.

Jeff froze as he watched the so alive figure smile, sing, and tease. "Cindy, oh, Cindy," he whispered. "Cindy," his voice shook as he extended his arms out to her. The urge deep within longed to hold her, caress her, and whisper the love that refused to die even though she had.

A tornado of emotion spun around him in passion as he transformed to a little boy-child who sat within the eye of the storm, his hands extended out pleading to hold such a breathlessly beautiful creature. The peace that the eye of the storm was supposed to have wasn't there. "Ciiiinnnnddddyyyy."

Not until his son's hand pressed on his back did he realize he had sunk to the floor. "Dad?"

Jeff looked at his son and grabbed him close. The metal of the wheelchair banged into his side but he didn't care. "I love you. I love you."

"She was so beautiful, Dad."

"Always was. Always. And fun. Oh boy, did she have personality plus. No party ever started until she arrived. Everyone loved your mother."

"Dad?"

"Yes?" Jeff asked, pulling slightly from the embrace.

"Don't ever forget Mom."

"How could I?" Jeff asked, tears rising. He had ignored her when she was alive and now he couldn't do anything but remember. He stood and jogged from the room. It wasn't appropriate for a boy to see his father breakdown. Besides, he wanted to hold one of Cindy's dresses. He needed to feel close to her. The purple dress she wore at his birthday party, pretending to be Marilyn, would be the perfect choice.

◇

Elevator music drifted from the store into the entry where Lydia and Betsy waited on the benches. Karen watched Lydia glance at her watch and sigh in dramatic form. It could have been one of Mikey's acting routines. Karen stepped up to the tired waiting ladies in a fast paced sway. The music on the mall speakers was wrong for her entrance, but she could ignore that. Nothing would take away the satisfaction she'd receive from seeing Lydia's face and having the spotlight glow on herself.

She swayed up in her new pumps to her sister-in-law and friend with confident strides. "Hi," she said in a low voice and looked down on them.

Lydia glanced up, her red lips separated as her eyes widened. "Who—"

"Karen!" Betsy yelled, jumping to her feet, shopping bags tumbling to the floor. "Karen!" Her two arms encircled her neck. "I can't believe it's you. I can't believe it! Spin around and let me see." Betsy's hand guided her in a circle. "You look good. Look at your figure. Wow."

"Isn't Mom a babe?" Mikey asked.

Karen chose to not circle in a quick fashion like a child would in happy euphoria. No, this was her moment and she would shine. She'd play off the steady attention by taking her time to move as naturally and confidant as a model. When the circle was finished, she stared straight into Lydia's eyes.

The satisfaction was complete. Lydia didn't try to hide her feelings. Her lips curled and her face contorted. Karen didn't let the pressure of the eye contact get to her. She could tangle with the pros. She continued to watch Lydia until the woman at last felt compelled to speak. "Karen," she said, in a barely audible whisper.

"I can't believe it!" Betsy said. "You look marvelous." Her gaze went to Mikey. "You look good, too. What did you two do with your hair?"

"Got it cut," Karen said.

"A very sleek style," Betsy said as she nodded.

Karen smiled as her fingers brushed at the long tangled bangs that followed her jaw-line. The bangs framed the length of her face hiding part of her left eye, giving a secretive, seductive flare.

The rest of the style consisted of fullness at the crown, a tapered nape below her earlobes and a sleek, classy tuck on both sides behind her ears.

Her make-up was natural browns and corals, a degree softer than the auburn of her hair. Her lips were full, inviting, like a golden autumn leaf recently exploded into color.

Her eyebrows were highlighted a lighter brown and a delicate trace of eyeliner brought out rich mahogany eyes. Her high cheekbones were shaded just enough to enhance the beauty of her features.

"Your hair color is so sultry. I love that shade of auburn. I'll have to try it next time," Betsy said.

"Absolutely not," Karen said. "I will not look like a twin."

Betsy shrugged. "I like your outfit, too. I had no idea leopard could be so powerful on you."

Karen had found a black velvet jacket with a silver zipper running down the front. The collar and cuffs had leopard fur on it. The store clerk said the outfit would send a powerful message. Karen had agreed and bought it along with matching black stirrup pants. From Lydia's response, she had been right.

Karen smiled. Tonight, she was reclaiming George.

"I don't think the leopard trimming looks powerful," Lydia said. She swayed a couple of paces, examining the outfit closer. "It seems gaudy like the rich ladies wear in the comics. Everyone laughs at them."

"Lydia!" Betsy said.

Karen didn't glance at her. So natural for her to try to shoot a hole right through her. Would it kill Lydia to be nice even once? Obviously it would.

"What? I wanted to tell her now so she could take the outfit back. I'd hate her to waste her money," she said with a plastic smile.

"I'll be keeping it. Thanks anyway." Karen motioned to her daughter who had kept her hair color brown, but had more detail added to it. It edged around her face in curls and she too had some hair tucked behind her ear. She was delightful with the new cut. It made her eyes so prominent. "Shall we go?"

Mikey nodded and darted Lydia a dirty glare. "Yes."

"See you at home, Betsy," Karen said over her shoulder.

"Yeah, wait, we need to stay with you in case we get stuck in the snow."

"Then," Karen said, stopping, "I suggest you keep up." She pulled her bag strap over her shoulder and headed straight out of the mall.

Once the door shut and Betsy and Lydia were in the far distant background juggling boxes and bags, Mikey burst into laughter. "That was awesome! Mom, you really got Lydia. She was so jealous I thought she'd rip your jacket off. Did you see how she stared when you first walked up?"

Karen smiled. "I did," she said in a reserved voice. "Now you know it's best to settle our differences civilly."

"Yes, Mom."

"Let's hurry. Another snow storm is coming."

"And you don't want to be stuck in the car with Lydia if it does arrive."

Karen put her arm around her daughter with the bag of clothes dangling on Mikey's back. "Who made you so smart?"

Mikey shrugged and mother and daughter burst into laughter as they hustled to the car. Great big flakes tumbled from the sky.

Mikey sang at the top of her lungs, "Let it snow. Let it snow. Let it snow."

Both she and Karen laughed hard; Karen had to wipe the tears from the corner of her eyes. "We have to stop," she said still chuckling. "I don't want to ruin my make-up before your father sees it."

"He's going to love it, Mom."

"I hope you're right." Karen flipped on the windshield wipers. The snowflakes had turned icy.

Mikey peered in the back mirror then turned around, staring out the rear window. "I see Aunt Betsy and Lydia still shoving stuff in their car. Do you think we should wait for them?"

"No. Lydia's probably taking some of her own advice and returning one of the outfits she just bought. You know, to save money."

Karen switched the car into four-wheel drive and pressed on the gas.

⋄

"Lydia, we need to hurry. Karen and Mikey have forgotten us."

"We don't need to worry." Lydia lifted her foot. "My nylons are wet," she said with a pout. "My car can handle a little snow. People really underestimate Porsches. They do have one of the best engines in the world. We're going to plow through any drift that gets in our way."

"I hope you're right," Betsy said, holding her hand extended to catch flakes. In seconds her palm retained a pile of snow.

Betsy tossed Lydia another bag to throw into the backseat.

"You know you really should have bought that purple outfit we're looking at. The dress was so flattering on you and the gold sparkles along the bottom are exactly your style."

Betsy sighed. "I did like it, but I can't think of any place to wear it. I'm trying to be more practical."

"Why?" Lydia asked, standing up.

"I shouldn't buy something if I'm not even going to wear it once."

"The outfit is perfect for your Valentine's date," Lydia said as she hurried around the car to the driver's side.

"That's true." She thought for a moment. "You're absolutely right. Would you mind if we go back?"

"Not at all. Hop in and I'll give you front door service."

Lydia started the car as cold air blew on them. "Philippe will love it. That dress has enough taste to impress even him."

"I wasn't planning on being with him on Valentine's," Betsy said as she fastened her seatbelt.

"You don't need to act like your life is in jeopardy with me." She eyed the seatbelt. "I'm a safe driver."

Betsy nodded. "Sorry it's a habit I don't want to break. You never know—it might save my life some day."

"So you're still planning on being with Jeff even though he's hung up on his former wife and it's doubtful you'll get the marriage question out of him?"

"Yes, I'm still planning on it. Sorry but Philippe is—"

"Cute," Lydia cut in.

"Yes."

"Fun."

"Yes."

"French." The car came to a stop by the curve.

"Yes."

"Creative."

"Yes, but we mustn't forget his flaws," Betsy added quickly. "Unfaithful. Unfaithful. Unfaithful."

"Betsy, I promise you he's not like that any more."

The car pulled along the sidewalk and slowed to a stop. "Ah, how can you say that? You haven't been around him in a long time. You wouldn't know."

"I do know how devastated he was when you left him."

"That's right, isn't it?" Betsy said, waving her finger. "You were around when that happened. You rushed right to his rescue."

"I did. The poor man was really devastated. He needed someone to help him feel better. Someone he could talk to."

"Someone to help him forget about me and the consequences of his actions."

Lydia peered out the window. Betsy continued her angry glare for several uncomfortable seconds, unfastened her seatbelt and climbed out. "I'll be back shortly," she said before slamming the door.

Once inside the mall, the cheerful notes of a song filled her ears. It was a nice contrast from the mood in the car. Betsy shook her head wondering how she and Lydia had ever become friends. Lydia didn't seem to be like the person she once knew. Something had changed. Their conversations used to be lively and fun—not so self-indulgent.

Betsy glided over to the rack where the purple dress she had tried earlier had been. It wasn't there. Walking into the changing room, she found it hanging in the stall where she had left it. She scrutinized the purple silk that tapered into a flattering style. The glittering gold. The price tag. Five hundred dollars. Pricey, but didn't come close to Lydia's purchases.

Would Apostle Paul consider a five hundred-dollar dress costly or would he think it wasn't as bad as the more expensive one? Why did she care what Paul thought anyway? He said some pretty eyebrow raising statements. He wasn't actually considered a prophet, was he? It wasn't like President Hinckley had come out and said she shouldn't have spent five hundred dollars on the dress.

She held it up to her and looked at the purple against her hair. Perfect. She wasn't going to change the way she dressed until she knew for sure about Paul and where the church stood.

This would definitely be worth the price. Jeff would agree. It might even help him forget about his wife for one evening.

◇

It took Jeff a lot of searching to find the purple dress Cindy had worn. It was hid in a box labeled summer clothes. Jeff didn't even know his wife packed up clothes depending on the season. Cindy had suggested they get one of those closet organizer people to come over and put in more shelves. He had thought that was silly. Now he realized the gesture would've been so easy and meant so much.

He slumped down in the closet and buried his face in the fabric. The smell was a mixture of dust and old stale clothes. The perfume he'd hoped would still be on the clothes had vanished.

◇

The hands on the clock flipping in a steady rhythm were a welcome sound for George. Work, as always, was tiring. The weekend hadn't gone as well as planned. Of course, whenever he and Karen fought, he felt battle fatigued the next day. Why did she have to go to church? For heaven sakes, she still fought her migraines and she needed to get over them. She'd never get well if she didn't take it easy and rest.

He reached across his desk for a tissue. His nose seemed to be runny, but he wasn't coming down with a cold. He didn't want to give his wife another chance to say, "I told you so."

◇

Plows filled the snow-covered highway. Cars with their headlights on, and snow streaming from the sky made the scene. Betsy had hoped since they traveled south the storm would slow, but it hadn't.

The plows, thankfully, were doing their job in keeping the roads drivable. If they hadn't been, Betsy and Lydia would have definately been stuck.

After Betsy had bought the dress, she slipped into the car and smiled. Lydia had put on George Winston's *Winter* tape. One of her favorite groups. "Perfect choice," she said to her friend.

Lydia smiled. "I'm glad you like it. I remember this was one of your favorites. I wanted you to hear it on my car stereo. It's quite an exhilarating experience."

With the surround sound, and the perfect tone, Betsy had to agree. No other car that she'd been in possessed this kind of crystal clear quality. She fastened her seatbelt, tipped her head against the chair, and closed her eyes. "Oh, such luxury."

"Don't you forget it," Lydia said, picking up speed only to slow because of the car in front of her.

Betsy hummed to the music as she watched out the window. The snowflakes did a spiraling dance from the sky and the headlights reflected off them, making them sparkle. The whole event seemed almost magic.

Lydia cruised down the off ramp, speeding up. No cars were in front of her. The light changed red and Lydia slammed on the brakes, the car spun to the right. She flipped the wheel to the left causing the car to fishtail.

"Foot off the brakes," Betsy yelled.

The car thumped to a stop, slightly off the road. Betsy's hands had wrapped tightly around the seatbelt. Both she and Lydia remained silent except for the hard gasps of their breaths.

"That was close," Lydia whispered.

"You forgot how to drive in the snow."

Lydia laughed, wiping her hands on her hair. "I guess I did." She looked out her window for oncoming cars and rotated her steering wheel to the right and pressed hard on the gas. The tires spun, but the car didn't move. She pressed again. Still nothing but the spinning of wheels.

"Why don't you back up and then go forward?" Betsy suggested. "Rock the car out of the snow pile."

Lydia tried it, but the car refused to move more than an inch either way.

"Looks like we're going to be digging your car out," Betsy said, unfastening her seatbelt.

"Will you?" Lydia asked.

"You're not going to help?"

Lydia pointed down at her feet. "I would, but my feet are already frozen. You're more dressed for the occasion." She leaned forward and switched on the heat.

Betsy buttoned the last button on her coat as she decided to be generous this once with Lydia. She hiked several feet away and squatted to see how much snow the car had high-centered on. She stood, laughed and then peered under it again.

Somehow Lydia had managed to drive up a two-foot snowdrift. Betsy opened up the car door and leaned in. "Out. We're going for a hike."

"What?" Lydia asked, eyes wide. "But I can't walk in these."

"There's a gas station about a mile away and I'm not coming back."

"Let me use my cellular and see what I can do," Lydia snapped.

Betsy slipped back into the car and waited for Lydia to locate it. Lydia found her phone and started rapidly dialing numbers. She muttered then tried again.

The phone flew past Betsy's head. "Darn thing. Battery is dead."

Betsy pushed the door open. "It's walking then."

"Can't you just come back for me?"

"Ha! You're the one who drove up this mound and got us in this mess in the first place. You're lucky I decided to join you in the hike."

"But—"

"I already told you, you're coming."

Lydia shoved her keys into her coat pocket. "At least let me grab my clothes. I don't want anyone to steal them."

"Good idea," Betsy said. She picked up her plastic bag as Lydia loaded up.

Betsy rolled her eyes as she marched ahead of Lydia. Her friend had been full of complaints as they hiked through the thickening snow. Granted, the adventure had become uncomfortable. The wind whipped against their faces and brushed their noses until they ran. Their ears burned and snow seeped into Lydia's shoes. Betsy was positive about that, because Lydia kept mentioning it. At least she was wise enough to wear boots although they were leather and would probably be ruined by the time their adventure ended. The positive was her toes weren't ready to fall off.

"I can't believe one car hasn't stopped to offer us a ride," Lydia yelled to Betsy.

"Count yourself lucky," she called back. Didn't Lydia ever watch the news?

The wind and snow lessened the complaints, and even if Lydia offered them the sound was drowned out. Betsy hummed as the words came to her mind.

Do your duty with a heart full of song.

We all have work.

Let no one shirk.

Put your shoulder to the wheel.

Lydia trotted to Betsy's side. "I haven't heard that song before."

"I learned it at church."

"Oh."

The night pressed on them with a black silence. The only sounds were the distant roar of motors and the squeak in the snow as they stepped in it.

Betsy looked at Lydia's high-heeled shoes and the red that glowed through the nylons.

She stopped walking, opened her purse, and pulled out small sewing scissors, then grabbed a hold of Lydia's fur coat. "What are you doing?" Lydia asked through chattering teeth.

Betsy unbuttoned her coat and tugged on the scarf around her neck. "Here," she said as the fabric blew in the breeze. The sun was long gone but the snow brightened the evening, making the twists and turns of the scarf easy to watch.

"What?"

"For your feet. Wrap your feet in the fabric. It'll keep them warmer."

"But it'll ruin your scarf. You bought that in Europe and paid a lot for it."

Betsy waved her hand as though to brush the comment aside. "That's all right. Your toes mean more to me than an expensive scarf." She took the scissors and cut through the fabric. To hurry the process she ripped it the rest of the way.

"Thank you," Lydia said, pressing her hand on Betsy's shoulder to maintain balance as she wrapped.

"Now, I want no more complaining. It's upsetting my positive thinking."

"You're right. Sometimes, like when you're freezing to death, it's hard to remember those principles."

Betsy nodded as they pushed forward toward the gas station. It wasn't too far away now. Lydia followed behind her, hopping in her footprints, gasping every step.

When Betsy and Lydia finally made it to the station, Lydia had begun to shake. "So cold," she said to the male store clerk who gave her hot coffee on the house. Lydia took the cup and sipped with shaking hands. Coffee spilled on the floor.

Betsy grabbed a cup of hot chocolate and gulped its burning liquid into her body. She asked for the phone. The clerk was kind enough to let her borrow the store's. "You look like you've had enough freezing weather for one night," he said.

She mentally added, "For a lifetime," as she pressed the numbers.

The first place she tried to call was home, but no one answered. Then she called info and got George's number. She offered God a silent prayer that he had worked late and would be there.

"Hello," came a rough-tired voice.

"George, I'm so glad I caught you."

"Betsy, what's wrong? Are Karen and Mikey—"

"I'm sure they're fine. They left the mall way before us, so they probably missed the snowstorm. I bet Mikey's just on the phone and didn't flip over to call waiting. She's been making a habit of that."

"The mall?"

"Didn't Karen tell you we went shopping in Salt Lake today?" Betsy took another hot sip of the rich taste not caring that it burnt her tongue and throat.

"No. Who's we?"

"Lydia, Mikey, Karen and I. Anyway Karen left and we were supposed to follow her home in case one of us got stuck in the snow and—"

"Wait a minute. Why didn't you guys all go in the same car?"

Betsy took another sip of chocolate. She blew into the brown mixture first this time, her tongue throbbing from the earlier sips. "Lydia insisted on driving her Porsche—"

"You drove a Porsche through a snowstorm!"

"It's not as dumb as you make it sound, little brother. Porsches are cars built with some of the best engines. They can plow through just about anything."

"Yeah, they have a lot of power until they get high-centered."

Betsy coughed. "Funny you should mention that."

"You're stuck."

Lydia had joined Betsy by the phone. Betsy nodded to her, indicating it would be a moment. "Yeah, and we need a ride."

He groaned. "All right. I'll come help you. Where are you?"

⬧

George blew his nose into the tissue paper one more time and coughed before he flipped open his cellular phone. The cold Karen had predicted had come. This phone call would be the worst thing about saving Betsy and Lydia.

"Hi Mikey, how was your day?...I'm glad to hear that. Is your mom there?"

George slowed for the red light. It was a frightful night to be out. The fresh snowfall covered the melting snow from earlier that day. Black sheets of ice hid under the illusion of white fluffy stuff. George had passed at least three cars off the road and plenty of others buried.

"Hello," came his wife's voice on the other end of the line.

"Karen, how are you doing?"

"Great."

"That's good to hear. I have a little problem."

"What?"

"Betsy called. She said Lydia's car got stuck. They need me to come and pick them up."

"Why can't someone else do it?"

"Somehow Lydia drove her Porsche up an embankment and high-centered it. They had to walk to the gas station because her cell phone wasn't working. I guess both Betsy and Lydia are pretty cold."

"Lydia was wearing high heels."

"I'm going to go pick them up and then I'll be right home."

"Hurry."

Chapter 9

Karen slammed down the phone. Leaving Lydia in the dust had backfired.

"Mom, is everything okay?" Sam asked, spinning a soccer ball on his index finger. He wore soccer clothes for a nice change, although his hair was moussed and parted in the middle like a hippie.

"Yeah." She headed for the cupboard where she stored the cookbooks. She might as well get going on dinner.

"Are you sure?"

Karen stopped walking and sighed, shoulders slouched. "Yes, dear," she patted Sam on the back as he looked at her with a worried expression. "Sometimes Lydia gets to me."

"Hmm," Sam said. "I wouldn't worry about her. Anyone with eyes can see she's a phony."

"I hope your dad feels that way."

"He does."

Karen gave a tight-lipped smile.

"Yeah, Mom you look good. I'm going to get the camera. We need to capture you like this forever."

Karen laughed. "Sam, I have to cook dinner."

"Not until I get a picture. This is going to be my birthday present to Dad."

Sam ran up the stairs to his room and Karen glanced through the cookbook. Lydia had been wrong. Even her son noticed how great she looked. Not that he could tell she had a different hair color or that her eyebrows were a lighter brown, but he approved of her new overall appearance.

Sam rushed back and asked her to stand in front of the tan curtains. "I want the picture to include nothing but you," he said as he setup his equipment. "I'm going for a strong powerful pose. No, smiling. Just give it to me. A deep serious stare."

Karen gazed into the camera as though she was upset at what Sam had said.

"Tip your head down. I want your eyes glancing up at me."

Karen lowered her chin.

"Not so much."

Karen lifted it a tad.

"Good. Now move to the right."

She did and her bangs fell slightly over the corner of her eye.

"Perfect. Now I want your left hand to rest on the opposite shoulder and the other hand to wrap around the center of your body."

It took Karen several tries to figure out the position.

"Fingers apart. Rest them against you as though you're barely touching your forearm. Curve them like the hand position the piano player uses."

"You're a slave driver," Karen whispered. "Who'd thought you would've been so picky?"

"I know what I want," Sam said, peering into the camera. "This is going to be perfect. Now, give me a strong powerful expression, slightly alluring."

Karen laughed. "I can't believe my son's talking this way."

"Mom. Stop that. I'm going to be a professional photographer and I want to get this shot perfect, please work with me."

"I thought it was soccer and the World Cup."

"I can do both. Off season I need to do something besides training."

"I'm impressed," Karen said. "Most teenagers have no idea about their future."

"I do, so let's get this picture right."

◊

When George drove into the gas station, he spotted Lydia first. She sat on the windowsill of the convenience store. Her black fur-coat was still on. She held a tissue in one hand, and in the other, a mug with steam floating out. She alternated bringing the mug and the tissue to her face.

The store clerk seemed transfixed in their conversation. George searched for Betsy. It would be best to approach her. That'd make Karen happy. His day had been long and he didn't want any more complications.

He spotted his sister. She strolled down the aisles. To keep warm? Exercise? To capture positive waves from different foods? One never knew with her.

He turned off the engine and waited until Betsy rounded the aisle nearest the front door. He climbed from the car. It would be a challenge to pass Lydia to reach Betsy. He'd pretend he hadn't seen her and headed straight for his sister.

Once he started walking, he could feel Lydia's head turn and her conversation die. His sister rounded the corner as he approached. He jogged over to the aisle and called, "Betsy."

Footsteps sounded behind him. Had to be Lydia.

"George."

He could avoid her no longer. He glanced over his shoulder. "Lydia."

"I'm so glad you're here!" She threw her arms around him.

George smelled perfume. The smell was odd and he didn't particularly like it, almost a rusty odor.

He pushed Lydia from him. "Where's Betsy?"

"I'm here," Betsy said from behind him.

George took a step away from Lydia and smiled at his sister. "Is everything okay?"

"We're cold but we're fine."

"Don't minimize our experience," Lydia spoke loudly. "It was one of the most horrific events I've ever been through. I'm still not sure I'll keep my toes."

George glanced at her feet. A roughly cut up scarf covered with black gunk wound around both of them.

"Interesting shoes," George said with a rise of his eyebrow.

"It's Betsy's scarf. My feet were freezing. She made me walk through huge snowdrifts. The snow plows haven't been on the roads yet."

"Lucky for you they just came by. I can almost guarantee you a safe journey to your hotel room."

"Oh, thank you. I'd just love a hot bath right now."

George pushed open the convenience store door and Lydia hustled to him with several bags in her hand. She grabbed his elbow. "Can I hold onto to you so I won't fall?" she asked. "I fell about three times on the way here. It's lucky I didn't break a bone."

"I hope it taught you a lesson on wearing practical shoes," Betsy piped in, grabbing George's other arm. "People are going to think we're polygamists."

"What?" Lydia asked.

"You know they're a few of those around here," George said. The wind rushed around them.

"Let them think what they want," Betsy said.

"I would never. They would never..." Lydia pursed her lips together. "Betsy, we have to get you out of Utah."

"Why?" Betsy asked, grabbing tighter as she slid her feet through the drifts.

"The snow, the polygamists, the malls, everything is awful. Not to mention it's so cold!"

"I kinda like it. It feels more and more like home."

They reached George's car, he swung his arm forward as a hint for Lydia to stand on her own. He unlocked the back door and gestured for her to get in. She climbed into the backseat without protest.

Relieved, George opened the passenger side and let Betsy sit next to him. Karen would be impressed with his cleverness on distancing himself from Lydia.

"My clothes!" Lydia screamed once George settled into his seat. "We must go back to get them."

George hit the steering wheel lightly. "Where?"

They drove to it and Lydia sucked in her breath. "My feet. My feet," she wailed.

"What's the matter?" Betsy asked.

"They're so cold." George heard Lydia say before he slammed the door. He climbed through the snow toward the car. Icy flakes decorated his pant legs. He hoped the moisture wouldn't ruin his suit. Once at the Porsche, he groaned. Of course, Lydia would buy the whole store. He should've known. Determined not to walk through the snow again, he piled bag after bag under his arm. He couldn't handle the last bag. "Too bad," he muttered as he slammed the door. "She'll never know."

He plowed through the drifts and the front door opened when he neared his car. To his dismay, he noticed Lydia sat in the front passenger side. She must have thrown a stink about her frozen feet and Betsy gave in and changed spots with her. Dang. He went to give Lydia several packages when a couple of bags slipped from his arms.

"My clothes!" Lydia shouted. "You're going to ruin them."

George handed Lydia the rest of his pile before picking up the outfits spread over the snow.

"Hurry up!" Lydia said.

"Why don't you get them while I finish putting these bags in the back?" George asked.

Lydia took another package from his hand and handed it to Betsy in the backseat.

"Oh, Georgey, you know I can't do that. My feet are killing me and I need to get them warm."

"Of course," he huffed, dropping the rest of the items on her lap. He slipped on the icy snow. After doing a balancing act, waving with his hands this way and that, he gained control and started for the silk red blouse on the snow. He tossed it at Lydia.

"Hey," she said, examining them.

George slammed the door shut. This was going to be a long ride home.

When he climbed back into the car and brushed off the big chunks of snow attached to his pant leg, Lydia lit into him.

"My new blouse has a water stain on it."

George drove the car on to the road.

"That means it's ruined."

"You're welcome."

"Oh, I'm sorry." Lydia placed her hand on his forearm. "I didn't say thank you, did I?"

"No, you didn't." George narrowed his eyes to decipher where the plowed road was.

"That was rude. I really do appreciate you coming to save us."

"Yeah, my brother is a real bona-fide hero," Betsy yelled from the backseat.

"You're right. He is a hero," Lydia said.

George rolled his eyes. This was growing old. He flipped on the radio.

◊

"The picture is going to be perfect," Sam said. "I can't wait to have it developed."

Karen smiled as she cut fat off the chicken breast.

"Mom?" Sam asked, sitting on the chair at the counter.

Karen looked at her son who bordered on being a man. His chest had filled out like his father's. Actually, his face resembled George's, the younger version—square, defined, pleasing. George had always had an appeal that Sam mirrored and the same kind of down home charm.

"What?"

"Can I borrow your car on Saturday night?"

"Saturday? Why Saturday?"

"I, um, kinda wanted to go out."

Karen flopped the chicken into the frying pan. "Go where?" Sam was being so evasive about the whole thing it must be a girl.

"Mom, out. So can I?"

"I need to know where and with whom?"

Sam's shoulders lowered. "Mom." He used a whiny tone he'd developed at two when he hadn't gotten his way.

"Those are the rules."

"I wanted to go see a movie with a friend and maybe grab some fries."

"What friend?" Karen dashed allspice and garlic on the chicken and noticed Sam's face transform to a hint of crimson.

"A friend from school."

"Does this mystery friend happen to be a girl?" Karen smiled, amused as Sam's blush deepened.

"So."

"What's her name?"

"Mom!"

She leaned across the counter and stared into his face.

"Valerie," Sam muttered.

"What? Couldn't hear you?" Karen cupped her hands around her ears.

Sam said it slightly louder.

"Oh, Valerie, that's a pretty name. Is she a cute girl?"

"Mom!"

"Mothers need to know these things. Tell."

A wide smile spread across his face. "She's cute. She has long blondish-brown hair, which she pulls back, and big baby blue eyes. And she's always talking and happy and—"

"Sounds perfect," Karen said.

"She is." He slapped his hand on his cheek as his face gave way to a dreamy expression.

Karen burst into laughter and Sam joined her. "So can I have the keys?"

"I don't want to be blamed for the rest of my life for ruining your chance with Miss Perfect."

"Thanks Mom."

"When do I get to meet her?"

"I want to take this one step at a time."

"Make 'meeting Mom' one of your next steps. I'd like to see who my son is falling for. I promise I'll put on my best behavior. I won't embarrass you by folding your underwear in front of her."

"Thanks," Sam said hesitantly.

Karen returned to the stove to turn over the chicken. "Where's your father?" She darted a glance at the clock on the oven.

"I'm sure he's coming."

Karen pursed her lips. "I'm sure your right. By the way, what does Valerie think of your clothes change?"

"She likes it. She likes artists and can tell I don't conform to the blah dress of the rest of the high school. She thinks I have important concepts to give to the world."

Karen folded her arms.

Sam sighed. "Mom, don't worry. Like I told Dad, it's nothing. It's just clothes. I'm not getting into drugs or satanic worship or anything like that."

"I hope not," Karen whispered.

◊

When George entered the house, he smelled a whole array of cooked dinner. He took his time hanging up his coat. Betsy tripped over him and bound straight into the kitchen. "Something smells great," she said.

"What took you guys so long?" George heard Karen ask in the kitchen.

He straightened his coat on the hanger.

"You know Lydia," Betsy answered. "She about drove me nuts today. We had to go back to the car and get the clothes she bought. Poor George dropped some of her outfits in the snow and she blew-up."

"Really?" Karen said with a chuckle.

George rushed in for a hug and kiss then stopped in his tracks. Karen's blue eyes darted up at him. He gasped. She looked totally different. Striking, breathtaking... Her make-up took years off her and the hair the prettiest auburn outlining her face. Creamy white skin and lips full and tempting. A tight, black leopard outfit emphasized her attractive figure. "Karen!"

"Hi." She gazed from under thick eyelashes.

He seized her in his arms. Her heartbeat against his. "You—you—"

She batted her eyes, waiting for him to find the words.

"I can't believe the change," he finally said.

"Good or bad?" Karen giggled.

"You look great! I want to eat you up." He lowered his head for a kiss. Karen turned to the side, giggling, but he didn't let her sway his pursuit. Their lips met and he pressed long and hard as though they hadn't kissed for years.

"He's going to go for her blood!" Sam said in the distance.

George grabbed Karen tighter as the kiss continued.

Betsy laughed. "That's quite a response."

At last Karen pulled away, gasping for air. She smiled.

◊

June woke up in a sweat. What if she had been wrong in believing earlier that day that she was inspired to call Betsy to be the Relief Society president? She'd have to work with the lady for years maybe. The thought made her stomach sick.

Of course, on the other hand, it got Betsy away from Chad. That alone would make it worth it.

Guilt hit June in the face. "Dear Father in Heaven," she whispered, "please forgive my hard feelings toward Betsy and please let me do what Thou wilt when it comes to her."

June pushed herself into a sitting position. She needed to get going on dinner.

✧

She was falling further and further away as she heard distant cries. It took awhile for her to realize those desperate yells came from her. Once more she saw the black, motionless baby.

June woke in the late night with a start, sweat covering her. Another flashback of one of the babies she lost. At fourteen weeks, she'd miscarried, a lot later than most women do. It had been years ago, but the pain still remained fresh and new, especially when she went in for an ultrasound. Fear that she might find another one dead pressed against her heart.

"Please, tomorrow don't let me see black," she prayed as she drifted back into a restless sleep.

✧

Karen was tired Tuesday morning. She had to go to work early to make up the time she'd be missing at her doctor's appointment and for leaving early yesterday for the mall. She longed for a cup of coffee to jump-start her. How long would the terrible cravings haunt her?

Today in prayer, she begged God that she'd find the answer to her health problems so she could work toward feeling better. It'd help her marriage. She knew George grew tired of her not feeling well. It was a strained point between them.

Of course George and she were doing better. He loved her new look, and he had given her a ton of attention last night. This should knock Lydia completely out of the picture.

She smiled, finishing the flip in her hair. George had complained loudly about how annoying Lydia was. Karen's fears about her should be over.

Glancing at the clock, she realized she had to put a move on it if she was going to make it to work before going to the doctor. She grabbed a green apple out of the refrigerator, kissed Sam on the cheek as he admired himself in the mirror. His clothes were all black with an assortment of chains and belts today. She yelled goodbye to Mikey who thankfully wasn't shooting a pretend movie.

When she arrived at work, she listened to half her phone messages, then checked out. Today would be a long day. She wanted to stay late to free up the rest of the week. Her house demanded attention. Ever since Lydia landed in town, Betsy hadn't been helping much. She also wanted to work on her plans for Valentine's. She wasn't quite sure what she wanted to do, but had a couple of ideas.

Amber tapped on her cubicle to talk about a change of procedure.

Karen listened for the first five minutes. "I'm sorry. I have to go. I have a doctor's appointment."

"For your accident? Is everything okay?"

"Everything's fine. I have a referral to this doctor who may help me with my migraines. I've been getting a whole slew of them lately and I'll try anything to make them go away."

"Good luck. Come talk to me as soon as you get back and I'll go over the rest of the plans."

"Sure thing. I should be gone about an hour."

Amber nodded and Karen hustled to the car. The office was across town by the Peppercorn. Karen knew the location because every time she drove by she thought she should try out the restaurant. Maybe that's where she'd take George on Valentines. She'd have to call ahead and see if she could make reservations. The place was bound to be packed.

Turning the car into the business section of buildings, she spotted the Peppercorn. She found Dr. Bringley's office around the corner. Karen grabbed the long list of papers to fill out.

♦

Betsy waited until ten in the morning to call Lydia. She knew she would still be sleeping, but it was time for her to get up. "Lydia, let's go snow-boarding! I want to ski down the hill at least once on the board without falling."

Coughing sounded on the other end of the line. "I don't feel good." Sniff.

"What's the matter?"

"I think hiking in the snow gave me a cold. My feet still tingle."

"Oh, I'm sorry," Betsy said. "If you're sick, I better let you get some sleep."

♦

An hour and fifteen minutes had passed and Karen still sat in Doctor Bringley's office. When she had arrived, they gave her a couple more papers to fill out. One was a symptom checklist. She was assigned to rate her problems from zero, which meant no trouble, to three severely troublesome. The items covered everything from neurological, gastoinestial, cardiovascular to musculoskeletal, respiratory, urinary system, and skin. Karen busied herself checking.

After handing the chart back to the receptionist, she scanned through a stack of magazines. When she grew bored with that, she glanced at a rack of pamphlets that had titles like: Multiple Vitamins, Menopause and Osteoporosis, Prostrate Health, Arthritis, Nutrition and Exercise...

Then she studied the atmosphere. The clock on the wall behind the receptionist desk was a plastic round with black numbers. The patients consisted of people with walkers, a couple of ladies in their mid-thirties with short-cropped hair, no make-up. Only one boy sat with his mother, looking around with an expression that said, "I feel stupid." Were they all migraine sufferers?

Karen tapped her hand against her knee. "Come on, come on," she whispered as she stared at the clock that threatened to standstill. She stared out the window at the trees and cars in the parking lot. If she didn't find a cure for her migraines, she'd lose George. She knew she would. He was happy with her new look last night and she had felt good. She wanted more of those kinds of evenings.

But today she had a headache and felt lightheaded. Not to mention her tongue suddenly felt big. She tried to shut her mouth and couldn't. What was happening to her? Was she losing her mind?

⬦

June's hands twisted against the steering wheel. She joked openly to others about how she wished this baby was a girl. Kendall thought she was crazy. "You already have four of them."

"And I have one boy. I've done the boy thing."

"Admit it," Kendall would hug her as he searched her eyes, "You want another one."

She wouldn't admit it. God liked to give her girls and she should appreciate it. She shouldn't get her hopes up. Actually, she was very blessed to have any children at all. Many women desperately wanted babies and for one reason or another couldn't have any.

June had often joked, "The ladies who can't have kids and I have the same problem just opposite extremes." It was true, but not to be able to have children seemed so lonely—so hard.

Whenever she thought about it too long the old familiar feeling of guilt cropped up. Why should she feel guilty over something she had no control of?

Earlier that morning, when Kendall again asked her if she wanted a boy, she said, "Why don't you come to the ultrasound with me and find out?"

"We've been over this before, I have to work."

"Can't you take an earlier lunch? I'd like to have you there."

"It's not like you have any problems. The baby's fine."

"If you don't come, I'm not going to tell you what sex it is." June had pulled from his embrace and folded her arms across her chest, resting it on her swollen stomach.

"You wouldn't do that."

"You don't care enough to come and see."

"I have to work. I was there all the other times. I'm sorry, but I can't go to this appointment."

"I need your support."

"I support you, dear. Tell you what, I'll make sure to wear my pager and if there's any problem, give me a beep and I'll drop everything and come. Okay?"

June had lowered her head as a big lump rose in her throat. She didn't care what was going on at work. It wasn't as important as his own child and wife. She needed his support and he had chosen not to grant it. Tears surfaced.

"I have to leave now. You're going to be all right, aren't you?"

"Fine," she snapped. "Have a nice day at work."

"What?" he asked.

"You were excited with Agatha."

"She was the first. I'd never fathered a baby before. June, we've been over this a thousand times. I know what a baby looks like. Take a tape if you want. I'm going to be late for my meeting and I have to go. I wish I could be there. Could you reschedule for tomorrow? The visiting representatives will be gone by then."

"This has been scheduled for months. You can't just reschedule. Besides, I don't want to wait any longer. Even though you don't care if the baby's healthy, I do."

"That's not fair. I care. I care so much that I'm going to provide for it. Now, take a tape and I'll watch it when I get home. When you get done, page me, okay?"

June had shrugged and Kendall gave her another kiss. And that was how their conversation ended. She shook her head.

She stopped at the red light, wondering which way would take her to the Utah Regional Medical Center. That was silly. She had been to this hospital seven times before for the ultrasound—when she had lost her baby. She knew the way. She used to live in the trailer court a couple of blocks from the hospital when she and Kendall were newlyweds and very poor. She had even walked Agatha to her doctor's appointment because her husband was away on business with their only car. The fact was—she knew the way to the hospital.

She pulled up to a stop sign by BYU. How had she ended up clear over here? Was the hospital east? Or was it more left or more right? How could she not know? Her stomach swished inside her. What if it was another girl? It had to be a boy. She had always felt another boy should come to their home. She couldn't go through another pregnancy. She was getting old.

She needed to find the hospital soon. Her appointment was in five minutes.

Seven minutes later she pulled up to the only available parking space in the hospital car lot and raced to the door. As she ran, the baby pressed down, causing a few Braxton Hicks. She had to stop running when the sharp jabbing pain grew stronger. It wasn't worth losing the baby to be on time for the ultrasound.

Twenty minutes later, she lay on the metal bed, with her swollen red-lined belly exposed to the male nurse who cracked jokes that made June blush. Where was her husband? He should be here at a time like this.

They snapped the monitor on her belly as June's eyes became transfixed on the black and white screen revealing the bone structure of a child. A small veiny fist waved. June laughed. The baby was alive.

The monitor moved over the heart. She could see the four different chambers and the strong beat. A sweet warmth spread over her. She had always loved to see the baby alive and moving.

She'd lost her child because he formed only three chambers instead of four. Thankfully the black images from the night weren't here in the daytime. "Thank you Lord," she screamed in her mind. "Thank you for another glorious blessing." Another miracle.

"Do you want to know what it is?" the nurse asked.

"Yes," June whispered, her eyes not lifting from the monitor.

"Definitely a boy."

June gasped. It couldn't be. "Are you sure?"

"Look lady—" the nurse continued to go into graphic detail, describing the where's and how's it had to be a boy, nothing but a boy, and completely one hundred percent a boy.

"A boy," June muttered. "Won't my husband be surprised." That was if she told him. She couldn't believe it. Now she knew she was done having babies. A satisfied feeling came with that thought mixed with gladness, relief, and a hollow longing. How could she be longing?

Because she didn't yet have her son in her arms, she decided.

Chapter 10

Betsy pulled up to the University Mall midmorning on Tuesday. She twisted the wedding ring on her finger. Time for an appraisal.

She passed several stores before being greeted by an elegant array of jewels. She paused at the window display to gaze over the alluring gems. Bracelets, rings, and earrings pulled on her desire. She had to admit when it came to jewelry she was normal. Diamonds were the best. Something about the sparkle, the shine... She glanced at her ring. The brilliant reflection teased her eye.

She slipped the ring off her finger and walked up to the dark haired, mid-twenties salesman, browsing through pages in a book. "May I help you?"

"Yes," Betsy said. "I'd like to know how much it costs to have a ring appraised."

"That depends on what kind you want. If you want me to look at it, I can give you a rough estimate. I won't sign a paper to my figures, but it should be pretty close. If you want a more exact amount, I'd have to get my manager involved and he'd charge fifteen dollars. We can also take the diamond out of its setting and send it for a more thorough investigation. That'd run about sixty dollars."

"The free estimate would suit my needs." Betsy handed him her ring.

The man held it up to his eyes. "Wow," he said, before walking behind the counter. He pulled out a Proportion Scope and peered into it. "This is definitely a Hearts On Fire, round, brilliant."

He scooted the scope toward Betsy. "Go ahead and look. You can tell a Hearts On Fire from any other diamond because they have eight hearts cut into them. Do you see that?"

Betsy glanced into the scope. Tiny little heart shapes circled around the diamond. The points of each heart shot toward the center. "Were those hearts carved into the stone?"

"Yeah, by laser."

"You can't even see the shapes with a naked eye."

"That's why this is one of the most expensive diamonds on the market."

"You're kidding?" Betsy questioned. She blinked several times, but the store clerk continued to nod.

"I'm not. Let me show you what else is completely unique to the Hearts On Fire series." He pulled another gem from the case. "Since your diamond is set, I'll show you on one of our own gems." He lifted the diamond around and turned it so it faced up. "When you look at it from the top view, you see eight arrows."

Betsy sneaked another glimpse into the magnifying glass. "I don't see what you're talking about."

The clerk straightened the diamond to balance more upright on the black velvet surface. He double-checked the magnifying glass. "Now look."

This time Betsy saw white arrows shooting out from the center of diamond in a fancy design with intricate cuts. "My heavens. That's inc ible."

"The stone cutters have mastered the way they cut the stones to have perfect cut. No other diamond in the world has that."

"So is it valuable?"

"The one carat diamond we have in our store on an average rating scale runs about ten thousand dollars. Your diamond's definitely bigger."

The clerk set to work examining the rock as Betsy wandered around the displays. Philippe sure didn't spare any expense when he picked a diamond. Why hadn't he mentioned it?

"This stone is 2.85 carats and as far as I can tell on quality, it's borderline from an IF to a VVSI. I detected a slight flaw on the upper right hand corner."

"What magnification are you using?"

"The tenth power. That's what they use for all diamond tests. It appears like you may have a near flawless diamond."

"Is that good?" Betsy peered into the magnifying glass again.

"It's very rare, especially with the Hearts On Fire. That'd make this rock worth a lot."

"How much are we talking about?"

"I don't know. It's also colorless. Let's just say if you wanted to go and pick out the perfect diamond in the categories of the color, quality, clarity, and cut, you have it. I've never seen one before. I don't think this store ever has." He signaled to a co-worker across the room. "Hey, Ron, come here."

A man in a blue suit with kind blue eyes and soft wrinkles walked over. "What can I help you with?"

"What do you say a colorless Hearts On Fire with a clarity quality of IF and grade level D would run?"

"I don't think that exists."

"Look."

The manager examined Betsy's ring. "I can't believe I'm seeing this. Where did this come from?"

The sales clerk pointed to Betsy.

She swallowed. "I got engaged."

"That's quite a rock you landed."

"So it seems." Betsy leaned toward the men and talked in a softer voice. "Can you tell me what it's worth?"

"I'll have to make a few phone calls." The manager left.

The store clerk pulled out a booklet and slid it over to Betsy.

"Some reading on the subject," he said.

"I always like to get enlightened."

"Why don't you check it over while I pull out our diamond book?"

Betsy lifted her ring and admired the sparkles. "So I don't have just a normal diamond." She examined it from the side. The sparkles weren't there. By then the store clerk had joined her. "Why doesn't it glitter from the side?"

"The cutters only worry about the top, allowing all the light to reflect to you. My boss is on the phone with the corporate office right now."

"Do you have any guesses?" Betsy batted her eyes.

"If I have to make an estimate right off of what I know, a one carat of that qualification, it'd be at least $50,000.00."

"This is almost three carats, that'd make it at least $100,000.00. Wait, the price increases with the ratio—Wow," Betsy said.

"But I don't know exactly how rare it is. I've never even heard of it. That'd increase the price too. The only true way to figure it out is through a bidding war."

Betsy gasped. "It can't be worth that much."

The manger returned. "It is. Even the corporate office is up in arms about how you came across the stone. They knew nothing of it. Where did you get it?"

"I told you from my fiancé." Betsy was tempted to say former but figured that wouldn't help her situation.

"Perhaps it's a phony," the clerk suggested.

"There's an easy way to find out. Let me see the ring."

Betsy slipped it on her finger and pulled it away. "Why?"

"I'd like to check the serial number."

"What?"

"Every Hearts On Fire has a serial number that'll match the number on the certificate you received with the purchase. The main store would like to trace the numbers."

She didn't know if it was from the shock of finding her ring was priceless or if it was the Holy Spirit guiding her, but she had the distinct impression she should get out.

"I appreciate all the help you've given me. I don't think that will be necessary."

"No, it really won't be a problem," the manager said, stepping out from behind the counter.

As he rounded the corner, Betsy waved to him and blended into a slow paced group of teenagers who strolled by. She headed straight for the food court, then shot into the bathroom. Once there, she dashed into a stall and dug into her purse, hoping to find a disguise. Her heart raced to the point she had to focus on not breathing hard.

She pulled out her tissues and noticed the scarf she kept tucked in the bottom of her bag in case a harsh windstorm decided to blow through and destroy her hairdo.

She sighed when she noticed the color of the scarf was lime green with deep purple background. Why did she always wear loud colors? She heard a group of teenagers giggling as they fixed their hair.

"I can't believe your mom almost saw us!" one said.

"I'd be so dead. Grounded forever if my parents found out I ditched school."

"My mom isn't supposed to be here. She and my dad were up all night arguing about her not spending money."

"Use that against her if she catches us."

"What?"

"If she catches us, tell her you'll tell your father about her buying another outfit if she punishes you."

Betsy peered through the frame in the bathroom stall. The girls brushed at their hair and applied lipstick.

"That's a great idea."

The girl with long straight blonde hair smiled. "Let's go. I'm sure she's gone by now." She tossed her hair to her back.

Betsy opened the door to the stall and joined the girls. The teenagers continued talking, never noticing her. She blended in with the group until she came to the first door exit, then made a hasty get-away. Once outside, she realized she was on the other side of the mall from where she parked. It'd be safer for her to be out of the building, so she took the sidewalk toward her car, head bent and feet shuffling.

The pounding in her heart continued. She was being silly, thinking the store clerks searched for her but their reaction to her leaving was a bit on the dramatic side. She must be exaggerating to create excitement in her life. She had been a happy homemaker too long and was inventing adventures for herself to keep entertained.

Still, that didn't explain the value of her ring. Why would Philippe give her such a costly jewel and never tell her about it? How could he afford it? The jeweler in France must've made a mistake and put the wrong diamond in the prongs.

✧

Karen focused on the deep maroon carpet that went up to the desk. The color nauseated her. It was a shade Betsy especially enjoyed, particularly when she'd dyed her hair a deep pink. Thinking of her sister-in-law, she realized Betsy had tamed a bit. Perhaps it was because she became a Mormon or maybe it was Jeff. Of course he wasn't bound to last much longer. Betsy had a way of chasing men away whenever the relationship appeared like it may transform into a trip down the aisle. Philippe must've really hurt her.

She stared at the maroon carpet so long it began to be blurry white dots when the receptionist walked into the waiting room.

"Karen Ashforth," called a girl with long brown hair swaying over the chart as she looked into it. She proceeded to weigh Karen and then showed her into a small examining room. There Karen spent another fifteen minute scouring through more magazines. Finally, the door opened and a thin older woman walked in.

Humming and hahhing, she glanced over Karen's chart. "Do you have a history of taking antibiotics?"

"I get strep throat at least once a year. Does that count?"

"It does." The doctor buried herself back in to the chart, jotting notes.

"I used to have a lot of ear infections when I was younger. Funny, since I moved from California I've never had that problem."

"Probably the altitude change. Do you have a congested nose?"

Karen nodded. She had not paid much attention, but yes, in fact she did.

The doctor kept asking her about different symptoms and she confessed to each one. She felt red crawl up her face. This doctor would think she was a hypochondriac.

"It looks to me like you have a condition called Candidiasis. That's where excessive yeast attacks your immune system." The doctor talked in a fast paced monotone. "When this happens, it's like mixing warm water with yeast. It rises and bubbles. That's what's happening to your insides. I can't say for sure you have it, but from all the symptoms it leads me to believe this is the case. You probably thought I'd wonder if you're crazy from all the side effects you've listed."

Karen laughed. "Yeah."

"Actually, it's common. You'd be amazed to learn that after we put you on a yeast free diet and medicine that'll eat the existing yeast, you'll feel a lot better. The overgrown yeast contribute to symptoms as varied as diarrhea, heartburn, headaches, depression, tiredness, and it keeps weight on that would normally fall off." The doctor continued. She told about several other severe cases and how as soon as the next day after being on the strict diet and using the medicine, patients headaches had vanished. After a month they didn't complain of any side effects. "Would this be something you'd be interested in trying?" she asked.

"Yes." Karen sat up straighter.

"The diet is a strict one. I used to apologize for it when I first started out, but I no longer do that. This will give you improved health and make you feel better. I'll give you a book and a paper outlining the schedule. The book will explain the treatment, symptoms, and cure. It also has some good approved recipes at the back."

Karen nodded. The doctor had spoken so fast she was sure she'd missed half of what she said. It'd be nice to go back and read the information again at a leisurely pace.

"Let's start off with all the do's," the doctor continued.

Karen sat back, wondering what her new eating life would be like. Naturally she'd start with the pluses.

"You can eat all meats, vegetables, legumes, and whole grains."

Short list.

"The foods you need to eliminate are all sugars, that includes fructose, honey, and molasses."

Karen stared at her. "No sugar?"

"No. Remember when I talked about yeast mixing with sugar and water?"

"Yeeeaah?"

"Yeast thrives on sugar. It's one of the culprits for yeast overgrowth and for the poor immune system."

"You mean no sugar at all? I can't have just a bite here and there?"

"This needs to be a full commitment. Are the migraines worth it?"

"No. But life without sugar?"

The doctor frowned.

"Okay, I think I can live for a month without sugar."

"Do you understand your health problems are most likely caused by suξ It makes it so your body isn't receiving it's proper nutritional needs and that why you have many more colds, flu's, and other infections than you should."

"Okay, okay. I'll give it a try, if you promise me my migraines will go away."

"It's an almost one hundred percent bet."

"The next thing you need to avoid is all white flour such as white-flour pasta, bread, and processed foods."

"Ahh, that's all the food I eat!"

"That'd explain your health problems."

"I guess it would. This is hitting straight home. I can't believe the way I eat is causing all the pain." Karen tugged at her wedding ring.

"It's fascinating how it works. Others on the list include avoiding all yeast breads and pastries. Anything with yeast is out. Avoid all cheese, except cottage cheese."

"No cheese? You're taking away my fun."

"But you'll feel good enough to make up for it."

"I'll have to take your word for it. One month chance," Karen said, biting back her words of protest.

"You'll be surprised. Also avoid alcoholic beverages. No fruit juices or fruit. No coffees, teas, including herbal, and no leftovers. That has the fungus on it that you're susceptible to. No mushrooms or processed meats. That's the end of the list."

"Oh my," Karen whispered.

"I'll set you up with my nutritionist and she'll go over some ideas on what you can fix. And with the allergist. From the swelling in your tongue, it looks like you're having a reaction from something you've eaten today. It's common for the swelling to be the result of an apple."

Karen groaned. The diet sounded awful. This appointment was going to take longer, and she had grown lightheaded from not eating. And now she was told no more apples unless she wanted to have a tongue bigger than a gallon of milk.

⋄

The door to Betsy's apartment stood wide open when she drove up to the house. "How odd," she thought, climbing the outside stairs. Dull pain throbbed in her chest from the exhausting workout it had received today.

Halfway up, she stopped. Did the jewelers find out where she lived? She shook her head. That was impossible. She had just come from there and if they had followed her, they'd barely be finding her address.

She turned around and searched the street below. No cars drove by. No unusual cars parked in the distance. Nothing out of the ordinary.

Her heartbeat much harder than climbing a few stairs should cause. She shot a glimpse at her ring, then slipped her hand into her purse and grabbed her mace. Just in case.

With her pulse racing and throat constricting, she climbed the stairs. "Hello?" she called out when there were three stairs left. "Hello?"

Nothing.

She swallowed a dry lump as her grip tightened. When she walked into her room, papers, books, and clothes lay scattered everywhere.

⟡

"No, nothing is missing. I can't think of a thing," she said to the short Pillsbury doughboy policeman.

"Do you know of any other reason someone would break in and paw through your stuff?"

"No." Betsy tapped her fingers against her cheek. "I believe in having good karma. I never burn a bridge. Never! I'm even good friends with my ex-husband. The other one was killed in a car wreck, but before that I was friends with him too."

"You can't think of anyone who has anything against you?"

"I just told you, I ride positive waves with everyone. If I sense turbulence, I immediately remake the situation and achieve peace with them and myself."

The officer blinked. "Does that mean you can't think of anyone you have offended?"

Betsy dropped her hands to her side. "Of course that's what it means. Weren't you listening?"

"Has anything unusual happened in your life that might lead to this?"

"The only out of normal thing is an eleven-year-old boy told me off on Sunday."

"Do you think he could have—"

"Of course not. He's in a wheelchair. Besides, he's not like that. He has one of the greatest hearts." Betsy walked to her scattered books and picked up the first one she came to and unfolded its bent pages. "Can't you take fingerprints or something?"

"We could try madam, but I don't see what good it would do. They didn't steal anything and no lives were in danger. It appears to me like pranksters. I'd suggest next time you keep your door locked."

"I always do that!" Betsy planted her hands firmly on her hips.

"No evidence of forced entry. You must've forgotten this once." With that, he nodded and left.

She took in the sight of her scattered things and her heart dropped. Who would do this?

Her finger twisted her ring. Did the price of the diamond have anything to do with the destruction of her apartment?

⟡

The work on the computer program was long, hard, and exciting. Jeff was always on the cutting edge of technology. He had grown tired of people cracking jokes about how boring work was. Jealousy.

Today the excitement he normally felt over writing the codes wasn't there. Seeing his boy scream after he had kissed Betsy replayed in his mind.

The phone rang. He jumped. "Hello," he said.

"Jeff, this is the bishop. I wanted to know if you could go visit more new families in the ward tonight? I'd like to get as many as I can off the list."

"That's fine." Jeff glanced into his day planner.

"Have you gone skiing recently?"

Jeff leaned forward on his desk. "Huh?"

"I heard the snow is perfect this year."

"No, I can't say I have."

"You should take some time off."

"I wish I could. I've been so busy with work and Chad—"

"Jeff, you need a break. You can't take it all on at once. You need time to unwind."

"You don't understand, I have to—"

"This is the bishop you're speaking to. The bishop. Don't talk to me about not having time and not understanding. The Lord said we need to have balance in all things. That includes recharging yourself.

"Even Jesus took a break. What do you think He did for forty days and forty nights by himself? Now, I'm going to stop preaching to you for a second to give you a chance to agree to go with me to Alta on next——."

"I'm sorry, Bishop, but I've got this really important deadline due that—"

"I didn't ask to hear excuses. I want to hear a yes."

"Are you speaking to me as a friend or the bishop?"

"Does it matter?"

"I guess not. Fine, you win. I'll go skiing with you under one condition."

"What's that?"

"You don't tell anyone we're going and also we need to come home long before school gets out. I don't want my boy to know. It's hard enough for him to be in a wheelchair, I don't want to be a painful reminder of the things he can't do."

"He can ski. I've seen people skiing on wheelchairs—"

"I know, but frankly we're not ready to climb that mountain. We're still trying to deal with our grieving." His voice choked.

"How's he doing?"

"Maybe we can talk about that on the slopes."

⋄

By the time Karen finally made it out of the doctor's office, with a list of items she was allergic to, which included green apples, she had passed the point of starvation. Her head was floaty and she had a headache, her stomach growled as a sharp pain jabbed at her side. She glanced at her watch. The appointment had taken two hours! Doctors. She'd needed to have lunch before she went to work.

Maybe she'd stop by Hogi Yogi and have a sandwich and a smoothie. Wait, she couldn't eat sugar. Darn. Just a sandwich then.—No yeast. This diet was going to be hard. Where could she go and grab a fast bite? She thought and thought as she drove past one restaurant and then another. There wasn't time to stop and go in, and a salad wasn't going to cut it. She was starved.

After about five minutes of racking her brain for a place she could drive through and pick up something, she gave up. She'd have to start her diet on the next meal. She simply didn't have time to mess with it now.

◇

Betsy locked the door behind her after the police left. It looked like nothing would be done legally about the situation. The only thing to do was straighten the mess and pretend the whole thing hadn't happened. She mustn't let her harmonious peace escape. She had worked too hard to achieve it.

She bent and picked up the first few books by her feet. This task had an ill sense to it. Someone had been in the room and invaded her things, tossing around the items that meant so much to her as though they were nothing. They had learned a lot about her by seeing how she surrounded herself, the colors she chose to spray the wall, and with the book she read and marked. Who was the creep that dared invade her property?

She picked up clothes first. Each dress, blouse, and skirt she examined closely. No damage except to the ironing job. It'd be at least a whole day of re-ironing. Besides that she couldn't find so much as a stain.

Next she worked on organizing her books. Slowly she unfolded the bent pages. That damage was more severe than the clothes. Her books, her precious books. It was then that she noticed a new book she had just bought to help in her search with Apostle Paul. McConkie called it *Doctrinal New Testament Commentary Volume 3*. Since she had it in her hand, she might as well read what he had to say about women and dress.

She flipped the pages to where it referenced 1 Timothy 2. Betsy smiled, what luck there was a section entitled: Paul Speaks about Dress of Women. This would hold the answer. She scanned on page 79 and read the first few sentences of commentary which read, "Worldly styles and fashions in women's dress, whatever they may happen to be at any moment, being of the world, which those who join the Church are commanded to forsake, are improper and to be avoided."

Betsy's heart sank like a paper ship. Her clothes, her identity, were they wrong? Would she have to give them up for this church she had joined. For this church that had given her such peace? Such happiness.

She read on. "Almost always the apparel so involved is excessively costly, with those who wear it being lifted up in the pride of their hearts. The Nephite prophets repeatedly identified the wearing of costly clothing with apostasy and failure to live by gospel standards." The commentary listed scripture and verses.

Betsy's hand shook. She read on. A line or two later, "In this dispensation, the Lord had commanded: "Thou shalt not be proud in thy heart; let all thy garments be plain, and their beauty the beauty of the work of thine own hands.""

Tears rose to Betsy's eyes as she shut the book. Everything was becoming too much.

◇

A celebration was in order, June decided as she pulled up to the Mom and Me store. Kendall had been doing well at work and she'd spend some of his earnings on new maternity clothes.

She slipped into the store and grabbed outfits that seemed comfortab young girl with short blonde hair approached her. "Can I help you?"

"I'm looking right now, thank you." June continued to wander between the racks filling her arms high.

"Would you like me to put that in the dressing room for you?"

"Yes, that'd be nice," June said. She put her hands on the lower part of her back and stretched after the lady took the clothes.

She proceeded to gather another pile and then went to the dressing room to weed it out. When she was done with all her selecting, she had gathered three new pants, four tops, and two Sunday dresses.

She put the stack on the counter and the store clerk smiled. "Looks like you found some nice things."

"I did. I hope my husband doesn't get mad. It's kinda of a celebration. I'm finally having another boy."

"Congratulations."

"Thank you. I already have four girls and one boy."

"Wow!"

"This might sound crazy but this boy means I can finally quit having kids. I can't tell you how relieved I feel."

The lady nodded as she bent the price tags.

June tapped her credit card on the table. "I shouldn't be buying all new pregnancy clothes now that I'm done, but I kinda wanted to go out in style."

"So you had your ultrasound?"

"Yes."

"I love seeing the baby inside wiggling. Mine was sucking her thumb."

"How cute," June said. "I never had one do that."

"I hear it happens a lot." The clerk pressed in the numbers. "I also hear those children are normally the thumb suckers after birth."

"That means they'll probably have the blanket, too. I know about thumb suckers. I've read from the experts that from sucking their thumbs they learn to emotionally comfort themselves."

The clerk smiled. "Really? That's cool. I hadn't heard of that."

"Is this your first?"

"Yes. A girl."

"How fun. Enjoy the time while it lasts. It'd be nice to have only one to dote on. Right now I have to worry about so many I'm getting scatter brained."

"I tell you, I don't know if I could do it." The clerk folded the outfits. "I had to baby-sit my nephews the other day. One kid was making a mess in the kitchen the other spilled water in the bathroom at the same time. It drove me nuts."

"Thank heavens this is the last time I'll have to go through this. I can't wait until I can act like the grandma and say, 'I'm so glad I'm past those days.'"

The girl laughed. "I had an older lady in here that used that exact phrase when I told her my daughter had wet all over her dress during her baby blessing."

"Why do babies do that? I haven't had one baby yet that didn't mess all over. My last one not only got the dress, but the blanket, and me, and the floor. I was so embarrassed. She did it in Relief Society while this poor lady tried to teach the lesson. If the teacher looked my way, she would've seen me stripping my daughter. Then I asked my mother to hold the baby so I could run to the bathroom to get toilet paper to wipe up this straight line of green stuff."

The store clerk laughed. "That'd be embarrassing. Please sign right here."

She slipped the credit card receipt out.

"Believe me it was." June put her hand on a sharp contraction that shot across the upper part of her abdomen.

Chapter 11

With her arms full of a burrito, a drink, and a purse, Karen pushed open the office door with her shoulder.

Amber laughed. "Finally made it back, I see, and loaded up with food."

"It takes more time to go to the doctor than it does to manually defrost my freezer. I thought I'd never get out. But that's not the worst. She put me on a diet where I can't eat yeast, sugar, or white flour for a month!"

"Let's put you in a coffin now. That'd be less painful. What are you doing with that burrito? Doesn't that have white flour?"

Karen shoved another bite of burrito into her mouth. "I was so hungry. I couldn't think of anything I could eat and had to get back to work."

"That reminds me." Amber tapped Karen on the back, "so do I."

They strolled toward their cubicles while Karen chatted. "Sometimes I miss staying home. If I did, the house would be clean and I'd bake homemade treats for the kids."

Amber laughed. "Nice dream. It wasn't like that when I was there. It was a lot of stress and crying babies every other second. Trust me, it's much better to work."

"I forgot." Karen waved good-bye with a yawn. Tonight she'd have twenty minutes to change and grab a bite before the meeting with the bishop at seven. Had she done something wrong? After the bishop, she'd stop by the pharmacy to pick up the prescriptions, then she'd drop into bed from exhaustion.

The time dragged by until six thirty. As predicted, she dashed into the house, kissed Sam on the forehead as he talked on the phone, red-faced. It must be that new girl. She opened the refrigerator, scanned the carrots, half-rotten lettuce, and the two cups of milk.

Betsy walked into the kitchen.

"What's there to eat?" she asked Betsy.

"Carrots."

"I'm starving. I have to meet with the bishop in a couple of minutes."

"You, too?" Betsy looked at her with wide blue eyes. "I have one with him at seven fifteen," Betsy said. "We can go together."

"Did we do something wrong?"

"I doubt it. There's some Frosted Flakes in the cupboard."

"Oh good," Karen said, reaching for the box. Her hand slumped to her side. "I forgot, the doctor put me on a diet that she thinks will help with my migraines."

"You went to Dr. Bringley?"

Karen nodded.

"That's great news. What kind of diet?"

"No white flour, sugar, or processed meats."

"Sounds perfect." Betsy washed a carrot.

"What are you talking about? It's absolutely dreadful." Karen glanced at the clock. Out of desperation, she grabbed the oatmeal box and dumped the oats in a bowl, slipped water on it and put it in the microwave.

"I've heard of similar diets. White flour's supposed to be one of the biggest culprits for ill health. Whenever I want to clear my body of impurities, I eliminate yeast and eat whole wheat. It tastes a lot better."

"I don't think so," Karen said, grabbing the milk.

"It'll take some getting used to. But I need to know something, do you have any enemies who'd want to scare you?"

"What are you talking about?" Karen asked, feeling her voice crack. "Is this another one of your—?"

"Somebody broke into my apartment. The police think it might be a person who doesn't like me. I can't think of anyone, so I thought maybe you had someone."

"I don't know of anyone," Karen choked. "It must be some acquaintance or a bored teenager. What did they steal?"

"Nothing."

"Nothing?"

"That's what's so odd about this whole thing."

"Scary."

"It's a little nerve racking." Betsy pointed her carrot at Karen. "We gotta go. We don't want to keep the bishop waiting."

Karen glanced at the clock and gasped. She shoved in two mouthfuls of oatmeal. So much for dinner.

⟡

When they arrived at the church, Betsy noticed Karen's hands twist. "Don't worry about the apartment," Betsy said, "I'm sure it was a prank."

Karen nodded. "It makes you feel exposed to know someone raided your home, and pawed through your personal belongings."

"I agree, but it's very important we don't dwell on it. Think positive thoughts. There's nothing we can do."

"Bull. An alarm system goes in tomorrow."

"That's a good idea," Betsy said as Karen parked. The two ladies climbed from the car and headed into the church.

Betsy stopped halfway and ran back to her car, grabbing the extra-healthy cookies she had baked for the bishop. He'd love them.

"With a house your size that's almost a must," Betsy puffed when she returned. "If you do get an alarm, can you have it hooked up to avoid my apartment?"

"Yeah. Why?"

"I have my reasons," Betsy said.

The bishop peeked out of his office to greet them. "Looks like we have both Ashforths here."

Betsy shook his hand. "I'd like to go first." She turned toward Karen, "Is okay with you?"

Karen nodded. "I can do my scripture studying while I wait. Maybe even take a brief nap. When Betsy meets with anyone, it always takes a while."

"We won't be very long," both the bishop and Betsy promised.

Soon after that she set the plate of cookies on top of his papers and plopped into a chair in front of his desk. "Bishop, you must've been inspired to call me. I really needed to talk to someone and I didn't know who. I think I'm in trouble."

The smile on his face faded. "Care to tell me about it?" He selected a cookie from the plate.

Betsy proceeded to inform him about her marriage to Philippe. The divorce, their courtship again, the engagement, and the beautiful two point eight-five carat ring he had said she could keep.

"That was really nice of him," the bishop commented, putting the crescent bitten cookie onto the plate.

"I thought so too until I visited the jeweler today."

"What would the jeweler have to do with this?"

"Philippe called a couple of days ago asking if he could have the ring. He said someone broke into his apartment and stole all his designs for the spring line up. He needed the ring for the money. He'd pay me when he gets on his feet."

"I see," the bishop said, forming his hand into a steeple. "He lives in Paris?"

"Yes. He'll have to fly out here to get it. I suggested I'd mail it. His vibes grew hostile. Definite no go. Neither was selling the ring myself and sending him the money. He grew real insistent that he'd be in the states and would stop by to pick it up. He acted like it was a nearby town. That made me suspicious. You don't fly across the world if you're low on cash."

"It does seem strange," Bishop Hawthorne agreed. "What does this have to do with the jewelry store?"

"I felt uncomfortable about the whole thing so I had the ring appraised." Betsy filled him in on the experience she had at the mall, leaving out the part that she hid in the bathroom stall. The bishop didn't have to know everything. Then she proceeded to tell him about the break-in at her apartment.

"Are you sure they didn't steal some other jewelry or money?"

"Positive."

The bishop shook his head. "I've never—I've never—Wow, invaluable."

"That's what they said. What am I supposed to do?"

"This is a sticky situation. Let's think about it. Your ex-husband Pil—"

"Philippe."

"That's right. He gave you the ring and then asked for it back. When you went to have it appraised, you found out it was invaluable and the clerks grew suspicious after they called their company's headquarters. They told you that they never produced this diamond and they're the only company who cuts Heart On Fire. Am I correct?"

"Yes." Betsy leaned toward the oak desk.

"Right after that your apartment was searched and totally messed up."

"That's what I said."

"Don't mind me, I'm problem-solving out loud. If they didn't want you to know that they were in the apartment, they wouldn't have made a mess and you'd have never known."

"Probably true," Betsy said. "So they're trying to suck me up into an unhappy vortex."

"Ahhhh, yeah." The bishop raised his brow. "There's a strong possibility you're involved in something illegal."

"What?" Betsy stared hard into his wrinkled face. "I've been involved in a lot of strange things, but never anything illegal!"

"Let's calm down," the bishop said.

"Why? You're saying I'm into something really deep."

"Betsy, I don't want to alarm you, I'm only suggesting a possibility. If the ring was stolen and you're caught with it in your possession, you could become an accomplice. Your ex-husband might be setting you up."

"That's not possible. I know Philippe. He's a good guy. I bet he's as clue-less about this situation as I am."

"I hope so. In the meantime, I think it'd be best if you turn the ring over to the police."

Betsy pulled backwards as if struck with the suggestion. "Why?"

"I don't want to see you in jail."

"Jail!"

"Yes, jail. If that's a stolen ring, you could very well take the fall for the real crooks."

"I don't know about going to the police. The ones I've dealt with didn't project warm fuzzy auras."

The bishop agreed. "I'm not going to force you to do anything, but I do have a friend that's an officer. He'd be on our side. Guarantee it."

"Do you really think I should?"

"I do."

"Okay. But what am I supposed to do with the ring until then? I feel like a huge cash magnet walking around waiting for the first metal attraction."

"I can understand that. I'll call my friend right now and see if you can meet with him tonight."

"But I have a date."

"Have him go with you. A bodyguard would be nice."

"Bbbbuttt..." Betsy struggled as the words mixed around in a sea of jumbled meaning.

"The idea perplexes you?" the bishop asked with a slight twinkle in his eye.

"Well it's just that..."

"What?"

"I can handle it on my own."

"It's your decision, but I'd advise you to have someone go with you for your protection."

Betsy burst into resistant laughter. The bishop raised one eyebrow si
as he made the call. His friend agreed to meet with Betsy in an hour.

She gathered her purse straps and stood, extending her hand to the
bishop. "Thank you for your—"

"Just a minute, Sister Ashforth, we're not done."

"We aren't?" Betsy asked, sitting.

"No. Now, for the reason I called you in."

"I thought it was because you knew I needed to talk—"

"Maybe I have been guided to call you in at this time, but I had another
reason."

"What?" Betsy said.

"We'd like to issue you a new calling—"

"Is this because of what happened last week with Chad? I promise you, it
won't happen again. I've really been trying to reach him and I'm going to do
it. I know June Thomson is upset about me teaching Chad but that's because
she doesn't like me dating Jeff. I don't know what business it's of hers—"

"Betsy, calm down. June is Cindy's sister."

"She is?" Betsy hands flew to her lips. "That explains a lot."

The bishop leaned forward, his hazel eyes looked straight at Betsy. "I don't
want you to get the wrong impression. We're not releasing you from teaching
the eleven-year-old class because you didn't do a good job. On the contrary,
you did—"

"Why are you releasing me?"

"Because we've been inspired to put you into a different program."

"Where?"

The bishop held up his hand. "Let's slow down. I want you to know I've
been very grateful for what you've been able to accomplish with the eleven-
year-olds. You were the answer to many, many prayers. You were the only
person who could've done that job. You did marvels with those kids. Now
their new teacher will be able to step in. Before you got in there and straightened them out, they'd learned nothing.

"Your next calling is going to stretch you and help you with your own testimony. I prayed long and hard about this because I was selfish, and I didn't
want to take you out of the eleven-year-olds' class when you were doing so
well. But the Lord has different plans."

"Would you please tell me?" Betsy asked.

"The title is the Compassionate Service leader for the Relief Society. Since
Sister Coons is moving, we're calling a new Relief Society president—Sister
June Thomson. She'll have three counselors. You'll be working closely with
the third counselor in the presidency."

"And who is that?" Betsy asked.

"We haven't called her yet. We'll be letting you know as soon as she
accepts."

"Karen."

"Are you willing to accept the call?"

"You're calling Karen. Boy, won't she be overwhelmed when she hears this—"

"Please don't say anything—"

"Like I have time. That's why you called her in and wanted to talk to her first. But I messed it up."

"It wasn't a problem, really." The bishop waved his hand. "But will you—"

"Of course. I plan on following the gospel to the letter." She looked at her bright purple and pink dress. "I know I'm dressed a little wild right now, but I just barely read about the dress code and haven't had time yet to go to the store. But from now on, all I'm going to wear are plain black dresses. Promise. It'll be up to the collar and down to the ankles. I'll follow the rules to the letter of the law."

"What are you talking about?"

"The dress code. You know the one that Apostle Paul said in Timothy where women should be modest and have shame-facedness and sobriety."

"I think I know what you're talking about."

"Well I read in McConkie's commentary, he's a reliable source for comments on the church, right?"

"He was one of the twelve apostles, so, yes."

"He said women shouldn't be caught up in the fashions of today. That when we join the church we're commanded to get rid of improper attire. He went on to say clothes caused pride in people's hearts."

"You take that to mean you have to dress like a Puritan and wear drab clothes?"

"Yes."

"You're misinterpreting the verse. God wants us to be happy people. *Men are that they might have joy.* He doesn't want us to put on drab faces. I don't believe that's true humility. Instead it is a big show of your righteousness as much as wearing expensive costly clothes. That was one of the great errors of the Pharisees."

Betsy drummed her nails against her lips. "You really think that's true?"

"I do."

"But what about what McConkie says?"

"His warning is true also. If you wear clothes that no one else can afford, how does that make others feel in your presence?"

"Uncomfortable, maybe jealous."

"Exactly. Is that charity? Does that show love to your neighbor?"

"No."

"If someone wears plain black clothes from their head to their toe in the United States, where that isn't their culture or religion, how does that make others feel?"

"Depressed."

"Exactly."

"So you're advising that I wear clothes that make others around me feel comfortable."

"I'm advising you to use charity as your guide in what you wear."

Betsy's hand flew to her mouth. "Oh, thank you, Bishop. Thank you. Thank you. Thank you. You don't know how much finding this out means." Her hand wiped a couple of tears away. "I thought I'd die if I wore boring, ugly clothes. I don't think I could stand it."

"Just make sure you don't spend too much time thinking about yourself or how you look."

"All right. I'll pay attention. Would you like me to send Karen in?"

"Please. Thank you for the cookies."

"They have no sugar in them. They're extra healthy. I'm glad you like them."

The bishop offered a half grin.

✧

Karen had read perhaps a chapter in *The Book of Mormon* before drifting to sleep. She didn't dream, except for hearing Betsy's voice raise to a yell occasionally. The words she said made no sense and she quickly forgot them, although she had told her subconscious mind to remember them to tell Betsy. Her sister-in-law always got a big kick out of those things. Before she joined the Mormon Church, she'd consult her many different dream books to see what the dreams meant. She wondered if that had changed since joining the church.

"Karen. Karen."

She rolled onto her back. "Hum?"

"It's time to wake-up and meet your fate."

"What are you talking about?" Karen asked.

"Nothing, just go in and meet the bishop. I need to find a phone."

Karen stood, rubbing her eyes. The nap was too short. She felt a smothering, heavy weight pressed on her and her body screamed for more rest. This was one of those times it would've been better if she wouldn't have slept at all; and to add to her horror, she had spread herself across the couch like she was at home.

Blinking and stretching, she walked into the bishop's office. He smiled at her gently, his kind face, soothing her. "Have a little nap, Sister Ashforth?"

She nodded.

"Well, I have just the thing to wake you up."

"What's that?" she mumbled.

"Betsy's cookies and a church calling."

Karen smiled. "I'll pass on the cookies."

"Okay then, on to the calling. The Lord would like to call you to be the third counselor in the Relief Society presidency."

"The what?"

"You'd be helping out the new Relief Society president, June Thomson."

"June's the new president?"

"Yes, she is and she has asked you to be one of her counselors."

"What exactly would I do?"

"June has the added pressure of numerous children and she has asked for an extra counselor to help her. Basically, your job is to be my eyes and ears of the ward and to visit people who she believes needs help. She'll still handle the more critical situations, but what she'd like you to do is help with the other sisters. Be a support for them. She'll be contacting you and telling you more about what she has in mind. Will you accept the call?"

She bit her lower lip.

◊

Betsy called Jeff and cancelled their date. He said, "Okay." He didn't even ask her what was up or why! If she didn't know better, she'd have thought he sounded relieved. Was this relationship doomed to fail? She tugged on her purse and headed for the couch. By then Karen walked out of the office. "How'd it go?" Betsy asked.

"Okay," Karen said.

They went to the car and Karen asked, "Going out tonight?"

"Yeah," Betsy said. "I planned on wearing the new purple dress I just bought, but now I have doubts." She recounted what she'd learned from talking to the bishop. "I'm going to take the dress back and use the money to buy sleeping bags for the homeless."

"Sounds good," Karen whispered.

"Hey, what's the matter?"

"This new calling. I don't know if I can do it."

"Of course you can. You beat your depression, your fear of the Mormons, and you're taking positive steps for your health. You can handle this one."

Karen smiled. "You're right." Later, as they pulled up the driveway, she asked, "What's your new calling?"

"Close to yours. Hopefully this time I'll be more successful."

After dropping Karen off, she drove aimlessly around before making her way to the police office. Dread built in her heart. She didn't want to worry about the ring or Philippe and what he might be up to any longer. Her body, mind, and every sense screamed for a hot bubble bath and a good book. She had heard there were some good young writers coming up in the Mormon world and she wanted to try them. The idea excited her to actually read about characters that were Mormon and faced with some of the same challenges as she. Or at least confront life with a similar value system. She'd have to give it a try.

She stopped the car for the red light and flipped on the defrost. Her windows fogged. As she waited, she watched a homeless looking man stumble down the street. A bar was close by. Unbelievable. A bar in Provo.

Shaking her head, she realized if she was in that bubble bath she had dreamed of, she wouldn't be secure. Her home had been invaded. She didn't know why. She wouldn't be safe until she knew the reason and that they wouldn't come again.

The light changed to green, reflecting off her windshield. She switched on her left blinker and turned. A few minutes later, she walked into the Provo Police station with a steady confident stroll. The receptionist looked up at her. "Mr. Rex, please."

"One moment." The young boy, thin, with brown, indistinctive eyes stood and headed out into an office.

Betsy tapped her fingernails against the counter and waited until a white haired man meandered out and shook her hand. He was short, plump with a greasy glazed doughnut in his palm.

"You're the lady Mr. Hawthorne called me about."

"I am."

He extended his hand. Betsy noticed oil still dotted the top of his fingers, she paused, then shook. She waited until he had turned around to guide her into a private office before she wiped her hand on the inside of her coat.

Once he shut the door, he spoke. "From what Mr. Hawthorne was saying you are in a pickle."

Betsy nodded. "But I didn't mean to get into it and I don't know exactly what it is I'm in to. Let's just say, I'm growing suspicious that I'm involved in something illegal, without my knowledge, and I wanted to talk to someone before anything happens. I don't want to go to jail."

"A lot of people have a fear of that place."

"Is it justified?"

"Absolutely."

Betsy then proceeded to tell the policeman the same story she told the bishop. She did leave out some of her reactions and the fact she hurried away from the jewelry store when they asked about the serial number. She worried any detail might make her appear guilty.

"Sounds to me," the detective said, going over his notes, "like the diamond is hot. I can't be sure, but if you'll let my team have it for a day, we'll write down the serial number and do an investigation ourselves."

"But what if it is stolen? Then I'll be held accountable."

"Your participation will waive any guilt."

"Will you sign a legal document saying that?"

The police officer glanced at her. "I rarely get asked that."

"I like to have all my bases covered. I've never been in trouble with the law and don't plan on starting, especially if my ex-husband is behind this. He's not going to get the best of me."

"I can understand that, but nothing is going to happen."

"I'm sorry I can't part from my ring without a signed paper."

The police officer stared, testing her bluff, then gave in. "A hard head. Fine, you win. It'd be interesting to see what kind of mess you've gotten yourself into."

"Me?" Betsy practically yelled.

"I meant your ex-husband. Where is he right now?"

"I'm not sure. He lives in France and said he'd stop by my house to pick up the ring."

"Did he tell you when?"

"No, he just said he'd do it soon."

Chapter 12

"I thought you had a date with Betsy tonight," Chad said. He glanced from the Jazz game on TV to his father.

"I did." Jeff planted himself on the couch. He leaned over and grabbed the remote control.

Chad stared at the remote as though he was going to say something. Instead he eyed the frog commercial. "It's getting late."

"She cancelled."

"Why?"

"Tired."

A Jazz player dribbled the ball, tossing it to another team member. "That's strange," Chad muttered. "I didn't think *she* could ever run out of energy."

"Betsy has been doing a lot of things lately. Actually I'm relieved."

"Why?"

"Cause I decided to stop dating her."

John Stockton passed the ball. Chad leaned to his left. "Come on," he mumbled. Louder, he said, "Good."

Jeff stayed for the remainder of the game with his son and never mentioned Betsy again. When the Jazz won, he stood and patted his son on the arm. "Love you."

"You too, Dad," Chad said.

"I'm going to turn in. You probably should too."

"After the post-game show, I will. I love hearing what they have to say after they win. We sure whipped them tonight."

"Yes, we did."

A slight smile crept onto Jeff's face. Dumping Betsy and spending the time with his son seemed like a good choice. He only had a few precious years left with him. He could chase women forever. There would always be women.

✧

Karen decided not to tell George about her calling. If he knew the church was going to require more time and sacrifice from her, it'd make the distance between them as low as the Dead Sea. She promised herself she'd no longer be a nagging wife. It seemed liked the more she pushed, the greater the distance. She'd have to let it rest even though she longed for the day when they'd walk to the temple hand-in-hand with smiles, to be sealed for eternity.

When she entered the house, George was scouring the shelves in the kitchen along with Mikey and Sam. "Where's the food?"

"There is none. Would you like to go out?" Karen asked.

George closed the cupboard. "Looks like we don't have much choice. What have you been doing today?"

"I went to the doctor's. She took forever. It really put me behind."

"A woman?"

"Yes. I find them more sensitive than men. She said the migraines will stop if I try her diet for a couple of months."

"What kind of diet?" George's brow wrinkled.

"Why don't I tell you about it on the way to the restaurant? I'm sure the whole family's starved."

George nodded and Mikey and Sam smiled as they yelled out different places they'd like to go.

"I'm under a stressful deadline and I don't have a lot of time to spare," George commented. "Let's go to Chuck-A-Rama."

✧

When the bishop called to inform June that her counselors had accepted, she was in the middle of putting frozen bread in pans. One of the many short-cuts she'd taken lately. Her husband had been thoughtful enough to suggest that since he was doing so well at work they could afford some help once a week.

At first she said, "Absolutely not. I can keep my own house running."

"I didn't say you couldn't," Kendall said as he folded the laundry with her. "I just thought since you have the sixth kid on the way and a very heavy church calling, you'd welcome the relief.

"The bishop had a long talk with me about being a support to you and how my calling was to make sure you didn't burnout. I thought about this maid thing hard and I feel good about it. Does it matter who cleans the toilet?"

"But I can do it," June protested.

"This isn't a matter of what you can do and what you can't. Pretty soon you'll have the full burden of being a Relief Society president. What's going to be more important—rendering service to a sister who needs your support or cleaning our toilet?"

"Having a clean toilet is important."

"I'm not minimizing that, but almost anyone can get it to sparkle, but you have a calling to do that's unique and only you can do."

"I disagree. Very few people can clean a toilet right. But I guess having someone come in once a week wouldn't be a bad thing."

Kendall bent over the laundry pile and kissed her. "You're going to be real pleased to have help. I know lots of ladies who'd kill for it."

June forced a grin. For some reason agreeing made her feel like a failure.

✧

It was black outside when Betsy left the police station. She had agreed to come back early tomorrow morning to pick up her diamond and find out what the police had discovered. She glanced down the deserted street and felt safer to be rid of the ring. If the diamond was that rare, she'd put it in a safe deposit box in the bank until Philippe came.

What to do with Philippe when he arrived? She wasn't sure. The police would probably have suggestions. At least she didn't have to cross that bridge until tomorrow or the next day. She nestled her chin deep into the collar of her coat as the chilled air lapped at her ears and top of her nose.

It'd be nice to soak in a hot bubble bath. With George home, she'd feel more secure. Perhaps she'd open the door between her apartment and their house so they could hear if anyone tried anything. Or maybe she'd spend the evening on their living room couch.

When she pulled up to the house, she saw an unfamiliar vehicle parked in front. The muscles in her shoulders tightened. Perhaps George had a client over. Or Karen had a friend drop by. Or Sam or Mikey had friends visiting. The car could be explained a million different ways.

She did a couple of arm stretches before getting out of her car. She looked at the circling stairs to her apartment and opted to go straight in the house. Silly, but last time she climbed those stairs she'd had a bad experience. She shook her head at her superstitious impulse.

She slipped into the garage to go into the kitchen. Once there, she noted that Karen's car was gone as she looked at the dark space it normally filled; a cold chill of dread blew against her senses.

"Betsy!" a voice said.

She screamed, her heart pounded, and her eyes searched the blackness. She flipped around and fumbled on the wall for the light switched. At last her fingers tumbled over the rough surface of the metal plate and the light snapped on. The low hum of the florescent destroyed the silence. There stood Philippe, leaning against the garage wall dressed in an expensive suit with a long cashmere topcoat. He finished taking off his leather gloves, snapping them in his hand as a broad smile crossed his handsome face. Curls outlined his thick neck in a rugged, sexy manner. *"Bon soir."*

"It's not good for one's soul to be crept up on in the dark," Betsy said, scrutinizing him. There was an air of confidence about him she found almost choking. Perhaps she could chalk that up to her nerves. "How did you get in here?"

He smiled, a brilliant grin that must've stopped a hundred women's hearts over the years, and approached her, arms outstretched for a hug. *"Mon amie,* the door was unlocked."

Betsy instinctively took a step backwards.

A slight lowering of his brow was the only suggestion of his disapproval. "I've missed you so."

"Philippe, you look nice. You're all dressed up."

"One must look one's best," he said, shoving his gloves into his coat pocket. He checked her outfit. "The stores haven't been friendly to you here."

Betsy glanced at her purple triangle dress. "What's wrong with this?" Her hands ran over the smooth fabric.

"Nothing, really, but it's so bourgeois. You have a lot more style than that."

The florescent light burned strong, but still cast shadows. She tightened her hands into fists and scooted to the door, feeling like a trapped mouse with a huge cat preparing to attack. "Would you like to come in from the cold?"

"I don't have much time." He talked as she brushed passed him, unlocking the kitchen door. "As I told you, I'm in-between flights. I've come for the ring. I can't tell you how much I appreciate you helping me."

Once the door cracked open, she felt for the lights. The more lights the better. She flipped on the kitchen ones and headed into the hall to turn them on.

Philippe followed behind her and she almost ran into his tall form when she tried to return into the kitchen. She side stepped him and took several steps back before saying, "It's nippy tonight. I'm going to put on some hot chocolate."

She trotted to the cupboard and pulled out a pot.

"Betsy, I really don't have time. I have a plane to catch. I need the ring."

"Where did you buy the ring anyway?" Betsy asked, turning her back on him as she walked to the sink to fill the pot. She mustn't let him sense her panic. She had a sweeping feeling that if he found out she suspected its value, she'd be in trouble.

"In Paris, why do you ask?"

"I don't know. I just love how it sparkles. I was thinking about buying one myself. I've grown fond of it."

"I paid you too much alimony."

Betsy laughed. "No, you didn't. I just invested well. You need to learn to play the stock market better."

"So that's your secret. Do you read the auras on money?'

Betsy laughed. "I don't, but I hear others do." She set the pot of water on the stove and turned the gas on when she felt powerful arms wrap around her. Expensive perfume filled the air, reminding her of times of old. He had often worn the thick rustic scent on their dates when he took her to dance clubs. Those were the days he had swung her in circles until she fell into his arms in hysterics. Other times he wore the scent as he strolled with her in the moonlight, peering into the closed gift shops, quoting Shakespeare ballads or prose. He'd also recited his own talented poetry. Philippe always had a way of making her feel like a woman with his strong arms and powerful chest, the way he commanded the room when he entered. Others had sensed his presence, giving him revered glances, or expressions full of envy. The delight of wrapping her arm around his, claiming her man, smiling at the gaping women had often been her pleasure.

The smell had a soothing effect on her, reminding her of happy times. It also aroused the passion she thought died long ago. The urge came over her to embrace him, feeling herself drown in his arms. All these emotions mixed with the fear that hadn't lessened since the moment he spoke her name.

"Mon choux, je t'aime boucoup."

His fingers pressed down on her shoulder, requesting her to turn toward him. Urgently he beckoned her to hold him.

Betsy battled within herself as she stood perfectly still, her thoughts racing. Rarely had she ever found herself speechless, but this moment was an exception.

Philippe continued to whisper in her ear. "I know we are no longer together, but I long for you. My dreams are filled with your memory. I don't know how I can go on without you. You are always on my mind, *mon cheire*. I can't get you out of my blood. You are such an important part of my living. I was wrong to let you go. If I had not made that mistake the first time, you'd still be mine. Do you know how many splinters this thrusts into my heart?"

Goosebumps raced over Betsy's skin as his hot breath continued to spill on her flesh. Her head spun as she closed her eyes. "Dear God, HELP!" she prayed silently.

Philippe pulled her to him. She still hadn't turned around so her back nestled against him. His lips touched her neck. Desire shot through her as her body became aware of him.

How was she going to get away? His temper had the tendency to grow hostile when he didn't get his way.

She let him kiss her neck gently as she fought for an answer. None came. A huge scream erupted from her body. A silent inner scream, "NOOO. Please help me God. Please. I need Thee. I need Thee. Please! Please! Please!"

The prayer seemed to give her the power, the strength she needed, and she ripped from his grasp. "Philippe. It's over."

He grabbed her tight, his fingers pressing hard into her shoulders. "Betsy, no. Come to Paris with me. I will buy you diamonds much prettier than the one you have. Like I told you earlier, I am a little short now, but I will be coming into my own real soon. I will have more money than I ever had before. I am not a loser, Betsy. I would take care of you in the finest fashion. We will see the world. You will be my queen. That's much more than any other man can offer you."

Betsy shook her head. "NO!" she yelled. "No."

Philippe tipped her chin up so she had to stare at him. His eyes burned with passion, longing, and something mysterious that Betsy didn't understand. "Look in my eyes, dear, tell me you don't want me. You forget I was once your husband. I know how to awaken your senses. You used to whisper that to me. Do you not remember? You used to say how much you loved my strength, my passion, and my drive. Now those very characteristics have come to claim you. No man can compete with me. That fellow you were dating lives a run-of-the-mill life. He's not strong and powerful like me."

"If you're so powerful, then why are you taking my ring? If you have all this power and money, then why are you begging from your ex-wife?" Betsy met his eyes as she spat out the words. She saw how the phrases cut into him. She was doing the unforgivable. She had voiced doubt in him.

He looked away from her with a spark of anger. Betsy bit her lip, wondering if she had pushed too far. Would he hit her? He never had before, but she'd never been so openly defiant.

"There are things you do not understand," he said in a low, chilling tone.

"Then explain."

"Pack your bags. You're coming to Paris with me."

"I am not!" His complexion transformed into a dark storm.

"Yes, you are." He spoke in a commanding tone, oozing each word.

"You can't choose my life. Like it or not, I don't care about your money, your fast life, your power. That type of life strikes me as empty."

"Empty!" Philippe repeated as if struck. His grasp on her shoulder lessened a bit. "How can you say that when it is the very thing everyone wants?"

Betsy moved her shoulder up slightly, and then met his questioning and confused glance. "I don't want it."

"What is it then that you do want?"

"Peace."

Philippe laughed in her face. "You're a fool."

"Perhaps I am, but I've made my decision."

Philippe let go of her, but he didn't back away. "May I please have my ring back?"

This was the moment she'd dreaded. The blood drained from her face. How was she going to explain she'd given it to the cops?

✧

"You do look great," George said to Karen as she sat.

She smiled.

"Betsy said you had a meeting with the bishop this afternoon," George said once everyone had piled their plates with fresh greens.

Karen nodded. Leave it to her sister-in-law to blab.

"What did he want?"

"I thought you didn't care."

George spoke with his mouth full of broccoli. "I don't, but I care about you and what's going on in your life."

Karen used the fork to cut the lettuce in half. "He called me to work with the women of the church. Betsy was assigned to help me."

"What kind of work?"

"I'm not sure. Service, I think. June is the Relief Society president and she'll be contacting me soon about the details."

"Don't you think you should consult me before you decide to add more to your life?"

Karen laughed. "Controlling. You've never been like this before."

George smiled. "You're right, I was out of line, but still, I'm a little worried. You work really hard and I notice you're having a difficult time keeping up with the house. How are you going to find more time to help other people?"

She shrugged. "The Lord will provide."

Mikey looked up from her plate and watched. "Do you really believe that, Mom?" She leaned in close to the table and furrowed her brow. The way she said it gave an air of over-dramatics.

"Yes, why?"

"You've changed. You got so angry with me when Agatha told me about families being together forever. You said there was no such thing as a god and when you die, you died. That's it."

Karen jabbed at a carrot. "I did, didn't I? Mikey, I'm sorry. I was wrong. Will you forgive me?"

"You didn't do anything wrong. You have just changed." She waved her noodle-filled fork around.

"For the better, I hope," Karen said.

"It is," Sam said.

"Maybe you should start going to church too?" George said.

Karen watched her son for a hint of how he'd respond to that challenge. She held her breath. It'd be more awesome than she could ever believe to have him there with her. This would be the first step in having the forever family, and maybe it'd squash his Gothic dress.

Sam avoided his father's eye contact.

"I'd love to have you come," Karen said, not able to wait any longer. "You wouldn't have to be baptized. Just see what it's like."

"I'll think about it."

"What?" George asked, his mouth falling open. "Since when did you care about religion?"

Sam shrugged.

"Since he fell in loooove with a Mormon," Mikey said in a child's voice. "Oh Valerie, oh Valerie." She puckered her lips up into a big fish kiss.

"Shut up," Sam said, pushing his sister on the shoulder.

She laughed.

Karen looked at the brilliant red crawling up her son's neck and face. "Valerie's a Mormon?"

Sam gave a slight hint of a nod.

George set his fork on his plate and stood to get another serving of food. "Well, that definitely explains everything. When I was your age, I got into a lot of strange things for girls."

The muscles in Sam's neck throbbed as he stared at his half-eaten plate of food. George went back for seconds and Karen played with her lettuce, wondering what to say. The whole religion issue now had gone from a disturbance between her and George to the relationships with the children. It seemed like an endless ripple in the water spreading bigger and bigger. Surely God didn't want her family destroyed. How was she going to stitch together the wounds? She popped a carrot in her mouth. She was wrong with that thought. How was God going to bring them all together? He was the only one who could.

❖

Even though it was only eight in the evening, June felt exhausted. The day had been a long one and her energy had been sucked up by the growing *boy* in her womb. After assigning the older children to do the dishes, she slipped quietly off into her bedroom. Kendall would be busy doing the finances for the next couple of hours. Relief Society work waited for her, but she decided to let it sit. She had this strong impression there would always be work to do there. Nothing too pressing, except to call her counselors and get them going on their assignments. That could wait. She had learned long ago not to run faster than she had strength. She'd have to keep that scripture in mind as she took on this new challenge.

She'd have to see how it went, but it seemed reasonable to limit herself to two hours of church work a day—most of that by cutting out nap time. Of course when emergencies arose, she'd put more time in. Her family wasn't going to hurt from her calling. She'd make sure of that.

The idea that kept coming to her was to dump more and more of her household responsibilities on her husband. It'd be good for him and for the children.

The door to her bedroom creaked as she pushed it open. Sleep was what she needed if she would maintain her strength. Quickly she changed into her sweats then buried herself under a thin layer of blankets. Even though there was snow outside, and the rest of the family complained about the freezing house, she was incredibly hot. A sharp pain shot through her belly. She put her hand on the source, allowing the warmth of her palm to deaden the pain. Her eyes grew heavy and she had almost slipped off to sleep when she heard her two-year-old daughter say, "Mommy?"

She closed her eyes tighter.

"Mommy?"

Playing dead didn't trick Michelle. They came to earth with a radar sense of where their parents hid out.

"Mom?" her two-year-old said again, pulling herself onto the mattresses.

"Snuggle," June whispered, longing to hold and caress her daughter. Michelle might need the assurance of her mother's love.

The little girl giggled and pulled from June's arms, jumping over her mother like she was at the track. The child didn't achieve enough height and tripped over June's stomach landing right on top of her swollen belly. "Ooooo," was all June choked out.

The child laughed again and stood to jump back from where she came from. June extended her hand and blocked the motion. "That's enough," she mumbled as she pushed herself off the mattress to tuck this overactive child in.

"No bed," her daughter wailed as June headed down the hallway toward the bedroom.

Odd, how much children hated rest and how much she longed for it. Kissing Michelle on the forehead, her daughter smiled so big it filled up the whole world along with June's soul. Loving and taking care of these little ones was what it was all about. She knelt at Michelle's bedside, said prayers with her, received several tight squeezes, and three wet kisses before she told the story of when John leapt in the womb when Mary was carrying Jesus in hers.

"Jesus, Jesus," the child muttered as the heavy eyelids closed despite the strong will and protest of the two-year-old to remain awake.

Watching her daughter sleep filled June with warmth. She was so lucky to have such beautiful children. All the other mothers must be jealous of her because she ended up with the pretty ones. "Thank you, Heavenly Father," she whispered as she closed the door.

Chapter 13

"Betsy, the ring." His voice cut into her thoughts like a sharp jagged ax.

"I've changed my mind," Betsy mumbled.

"What do you mean?"

"I want to keep it. I've earned it."

"Earned it?" Philippe's eyes flashed with a spark of anger. Betsy knew a storm brewed behind them.

"Yes, from all the pain and suffering your affair has caused me."

"...Lady, I paid you an exorbitant amount of money to cover that. It's not like an affair is a big deal. People have them all the time. It's accepted in a lot of my friend's marriages. You could have had one yourself. I wouldn't have minded."

Betsy bit her lip. This was the man she thought she loved seconds ago? How could she even be tempted by a person who obviously had no character? "Philippe, you don't actually believe that!"

He still stood uncomfortably close. His pale blue eyes gazed into her face, showing puzzlement. "Why wouldn't I? Betsy, my dear, no matter how many classes you take or books you read, you are still tense. You need to learn to relax and not take things so seriously."

She straightened her shoulders. "What makes you think I'm too uptight and who decided your free living style is so much better?"

Philippe laughed. "You have so much to learn. I wish I could stay here and teach you how to capture happiness in life, but I'm afraid I will miss my plane. I love you, *ma belle.*" He put his hands tenderly around her shoulders again.

Betsy tried to shrug it off only to have him crush her in a fierce hug. "*Mon choux,* the ring please."

She shook her head, avoiding his gaze. "I can't," her voice stumbled, betraying her nerves.

The grip around her tightened. Pain quivered through her body. "I don't have time for games, my love."

"Then go."

Philippe snatched her purse off the counter and dumped the contents.

Rubbing the shoulders where he had squeezed her, Betsy scanned around the room. The phone. That was her only line of defense. She'd never make it to her keys and out to the car before he caught her. She'd have to call the police and hope they'd arrive to scare him away. Even after his hostile manner toward her, she still didn't want to see him in jail and she definitely didn't want to be the one to put him there.

Philippe had almost finished rifling through her things. She needed to act fast. She darted over to the counter where the phone sat. Philippe looked up and saw her aim. He lunged, but Betsy was faster. She held the black porta phone in her hand. "I must ask you to leave."

"Betsy, there's no reason to overreact." Philippe hurried toward her with his hand extended. "Give me the phone."

She stepped backwards. "I'm not kidding around, Philippe, go or..."

"Or what?"

"Or I'm calling the police."

His laugh turned dark and menacing. *"Mon cheire,* I hoped it wouldn't turn to this." He dashed forward, seizing her arm. Then he squeezed her hand until it lost all feeling and she dropped the phone. He caught it and threw it on the floor. It shattered.

"I must now demand you tell me where the ring is."

Betsy glanced where the pieces of the phone lay and then at her ex-husband's contorted face. This was a side of Philippe she hadn't seen before. How could someone be married to a person, then be friends with him for years, and know so little about him? What a horrible mistake it would've been to marry him again. How could she have trusted him?

"Philippe, what has happened to you? Anger comes out of bad karma and solves no problems. Remember what we learned—"

"Formidable. I don't care about karma or peace or any of that other nonsense. I need the ring and I need it now!" His yells had grown loud. Betsy hoped the neighbors would call the police. Of course, people tended to mind their own business.

"You can't have it," Betsy challenged.

Before she could blink, a powerful force hit her on the side of the head, knocking her to the ground. Philippe swore at her in French and English as she pulled her arms over her head, crying. Not again, she thought, remembering husband number two. The scares, the pain, the betrayal of his physical abuse was too much.

Philippe grabbed her arm, yanking her to her feet. "The ring. I want the ring."

Betsy's head swam. "I need to think."

Philippe shook her. "Now."

"My room," Betsy whispered.

He let her go, biting his tongue. "Was that so hard?"

"No," she whispered.

He pushed her in front of him and said, "Show me." His hand remained on her shoulder.

Betsy jerked from his touch. "Let go of me and I will."

He complied, stepping close.

"Please give me some breathing room. You're frightening me."

Philippe's face instinctively took on a hardened expression but he retreated a couple of inches.

Betsy led him through the house to the stairs up to her apartment. She didn't say a word. All of her outrage and feministic philosophies raced into her mind. How dare this man try to control her and bulldoze over her just because his physical strength was greater than hers! He had no right to dominate her! The anger rose like yeast when mixed with water.

When she reached the top stair, she was fully prepared both mentally and physically, to do what she had to. She whirled around and kicked the unsuspecting Philippe as hard as she could. She chose his most vulnerable spot, rationalizing that if this attack wasn't successful, she'd be dead.

Philippe fell, with a primal scream. Betsy maximized this gift of time by running into her apartment. She slammed and locked the door behind her. It wouldn't be very long before he was after her again. She pushed the couch against the door. She threw off her shoes, bent to pick them up, and raced out the back. She tore down the outside stairs in her nylons, snow soaking into them.

When she reached the bottom stair, a loud booming noise came from her bedroom. She cursed. She hadn't snatched her keys. She needed to disappear fast. Philippe would easily outrun her. Where could she go?

A loud yell came from within the house, "Betsy!"

She ripped down the paved road as fast as nylon covered feet in slippery snow would allow. She had seconds to disappear.

✧

When the Ashforths arrived home from dinner, George went to take the trash can out and Karen gathered papers, napkins, and old homework assignments from the car. She had filled her arms about halfway before Sam screamed, "Mom. Dad. Come quick. Something's wrong."

Karen flew into the kitchen with her arms still full. She discovered Betsy's keys on the counter and the range still on, burning a pot.

"What makes you think there's anything wrong, Sam? It looks to me like Betsy got caught up with something else and forgot she was making hot chocolate," George said.

"But she left her keys on the counter. She never does that."

"Maybe she's extra tired."

"But look." Sam pointed at the counter where her belongings were dumped out of her purse.

Karen glanced at the pile. That was odd. Betsy never left messes. She felt it was like drinking poison to leave clutter to haunt you.

Mikey scurried into the kitchen. "I found Betsy's coat in the living room on the floor. The pockets were inside out."

Karen looked at George. "Something has happened to your sister."

✧

Jeff kissed Chad and tucked him into bed at about nine o'clock. It was one of the first times he could remember his son allowing him to do that. Chad didn't seem happy at this parental gesture; he just didn't care to protest. All the fight had been zapped out of him.

Jeff stood outside his son's room, praying the right words would come and he'd know what to say to snap his son out of this depressed trance-like mood. No inspiration came.

His mind was a clean slate. Jeff offered a silent prayer on behalf of his son then wandered upstairs to his own room. He sat on the chair by his bed and thought what to do.

He desperately wanted to talk to Betsy. She had been right. Infuriating. His son needed counseling. He wasn't going to be too proud to admit that. He'd do anything to see a smile on his boy's face. "Oh, Cindy, Cindy, how do I help our son?"

Jeff walked to the calendar. Two more days until the accident's anniversary. Two, he had left last year to be with his precious wife and how did he spend his time? Working.

Jeff suddenly remembered the day he asked Cindy to marry him. He had felt bad and was apologetic because he didn't have enough money to buy her a diamond ring. She'd hushed his apologies with a finger to his lips. "Shhh," she whispered softly as the words penetrated him deeply. "Remember, always remember, love is more precious than diamonds and all I ever want is your love."

He slumped to the ground. He hadn't even told her that he loved her on the day that she died. He had failed with the diamond ring and more importantly with the love she so much wanted. "Oh, Cindy, oh, Cindy. Oh, Cindy."

♦

Mikey had been the one who searched for Betsy in her apartment. When her daughter's screams pierced the eerie silence of the house, Karen cursed herself for not going herself. Fear flooded her as she raced to the stairs, hoping no one had grabbed Mikey.

Her daughter's screams continued and tears stained her face.

"What is it?" Karen gasped.

"Someone broke Betsy's door down," Mikey yelled, pointing at the splintered wooden door laid on the couch.

Karen turned to George who just arrived on the scene. "Why would her couch be in front of the door?"

He shrugged and Karen wrapped her arms around her strong husband. "George, I'm scared."

His hands stroked her hair. "There now. It'll be okay."

Karen moved from him and gazed into his eyes. "I hope your sister is all right."

"Don't you worry," he said, pulling her close.

Karen decided to turn her faith to God. He was the only one who could help Betsy. She prayed, with a deep yearning in her heart, that her sister-in-law would have the wisdom to get out of the situation she had found herself in. Please, Karen begged silently. I promise I'll serve you with all the energy I have. Karen took a big deep breath then said, "We need to call the cops. The sooner we get them involved, the better chance we have of finding Betsy."

About thirty minutes later, the police arrived taking notes and asking questions. They said they couldn't officially file a missing person's report until Betsy was missing for twenty-four hours. They admitted there was strong evidence of foul play.

When Karen heard this, her head swam. She was going to be strong even though the thought of living life without her sister-in-law's craziness to spice it up, seemed unbearable. She offered another silent prayer to her Maker asking for strength.

The officer explained, "The tracks out back aren't fresh and there's too many to discover any clues. Has anything unusual happened around here?"

Karen sat at the kitchen counter. "My sister-in-law's apartment was broken into this morning."

"The other police officer who investigated blamed restless teenagers who had skipped school."

"What did they steal?"

"Nothing."

"Are you sure?"

"Betsy would know. She's the type that notices if you move the pencil on her desk half an inch."

The tall officer nodded as he jotted in his book. "What did Betsy say about the break-in?"

"She said not to worry about it." Karen's mind went to their conversation. "She did have an unusual request when I talked about getting an alarm system hooked up to the house. She asked me not to wire her room."

"Do you have any idea why?" The police officer had brought his pen to his mouth, tapping it against his thin lips.

"None. I thought it odd, but I was too caught up with my problems to ask," Karen's voice faltered. "Now I wish I had."

The questions continued in a similar fashion. Karen had a hard time focusing. She kept starring at the door, hoping, praying, almost wishing she had the mental power to force Betsy through it.

When the police left, Karen collapsed in George's arms. "I feel so helpless. I want to do something. I want to solve this mystery, but I can't."

George rubbed his chin. "I'm going to drive around town and see if anything comes up."

"I'll come with you," Karen said, walking over to the kitchen counter where she had left her coat.

"No. I think it's best you stay with the kids. I don't feel comfortable leaving them alone tonight."

"But you do feel comfortable leaving me alone with them?"

"Karen, you'll be fine. You know where my gun is and don't hesitate to shoot. Just make sure it's not one of the kids before you fire."

"George!"

"Karen, I have to find her."

"I know," she said, looking down. "Go. I'll be praying for you."

George smiled at her. "Karen, there's one good thing about your religion, it makes you strong."

She smiled, too. "Funny how an emergency comes and then you realize that."

"Nothing else would have showed me. I love you."

He kissed her long and tender. She wrapped her arms around him and pulled him in close. "Be safe. I still need you."

"I'll try," George said, heading for the door.

♦

June awoke in the early evening to her husband's complaining. "Darn tr. child." The light in their bathroom was on.

"What?" June asked.

"Your daughter got into my shaving cream. It's all over the place. She has completely ruined the carpet."

June closed her eyes, wishing she were still asleep. "It's all right, dear."

"No, it isn't. She also got into your fingernail polish and that's all over the walls, too."

June sat up in her bed, a lump in her throat. She had barely finished painting the bathroom a few months ago. "How bad is it?"

"Come look for yourself."

She walked into the bathroom, hoping Kendall was overreacting. He had a tendency to do that when it came to the house.

She stared at the swirly bright circles. The fingernail polish covered the entire side by the toilet and most of the wall near the vanity. The only other wall in the bathroom was filled with cabinets; and, fortunately, their terrorist hadn't felt inspired to paint that surface yet. Kendall hadn't overreacted.

She snapped off the bathroom light as she turned on the bedroom lamp. "I can't handle this right now."

"June, it's going to dry."

"It already has. And no amount of scrubbing will get it off."

"Where's Michelle?" Kendall asked

June shrugged. "I put her to bed before I went to sleep." She then walked back to the bed and lay down. Contractions had flared again.

Kendall paced out of the room, calling Michelle. June heard her child's grunt and then her husband's firm voice, "No. No."

Michelle burst into tears.

"Go back to bed," Kendall said.

June hated it when he punished the kids. Her heart longed to hug her daughter. Kids weren't trying to be bad, just exploring. Having the whole house covered in shocking pink stripes wouldn't be a pretty sight, either. At least Kendall hadn't spanked her. He used to. It took June a long time to convince him it didn't help. He still swatted the kids occasionally when he didn't know what else to do. He claimed he wasn't being mean, just getting their attention.

June had always thought there were other ways. When her dad had hit her, all she learned was that Dad was mean.

Sleep quickly reclaimed her, only to be disturbed by pounding on her door. She waited to hear Kendall's footsteps, but they didn't come. Why would someone be here this late?

She pulled herself up and wandered to the back door as the pounding persisted. She unlocked the door and peeped out to see Betsy, blood trickling down her face, hair awry, and no coat. "Betsy, what—"

She charged into the house. "Thank heavens you're here." She rubbed her hands up and down her arms. Her eyes darted around the room. "Your drapes are open!"

"So?" June started to say when Betsy dashed into the hall. "What?"

"I'm sorry to intrude on you like this, but he's after me. If he comes, please, don't let him in. Please, June, I beg you."

She stared into a frightened middle-aged face. Betsy looked very different with her make-up worn off, older—less vibrant. "Who is after—" The doorbell interrupted her question.

"Oh," Betsy said, her fingernails flying to her mouth. She bit down on them.

"Should I call the police?"

"No," Betsy said. "Please don't. I'll explain later."

June turned to answer the bell. Betsy grabbed hold of her dress. June glanced back at her.

"I know you don't like me much," Betsy said, "because I'm dating your brother-in-law and you want him to be true to your sister's memory, but please don't tell him I'm here. Please."

The doorbell rang again. June looked at the door then back to Betsy. "Who is he?"

"My first husband."

June felt her eyes enlarge in shock as she went to the door. There stood a man, his bulk filling most of the opening. He had long curly brown hair and a sexy strong jaw.

"Sorry to bother you ma'am," he spoke in a heavy accent. "But I wondered if you'd help me out?"

He stepped into the house and June felt her pulse race. Where was Kendall?

"I was supposed to go on a date with Betsy Ashforth and I just spoke with Karen and she said that Betsy was visiting you."

"I-I-I don't know what you're talking about," June said, feeling relieved that she hadn't lied. Relief Society presidents don't lie, not even in a pinch.

Philippe walked around, peeping around the furniture. Finally, Kendall came into the room. His arms folded across his chest as he glanced over at the visitor. "What's going on?"

He looked to June for answers. She shrugged and focused on this strange man who continued to snoop. She walked in front of him to stop him. "He was just leaving. We can't help you."

Philippe turned to Kendall. "I'm sorry to bother you. I'm looking for Betsy Ashforth and I thought that maybe she was visiting you."

"Betsy? Here? No. Why would she be?"

The man shrugged and started to go. He glanced at the Thomson's and said, "One more thing, when you see her, will you tell her I will get the ring."

"I will get the ring?" Kendall asked, confused.

The man nodded. "Yes, that's the message." After that he opened the door, allowing the February wind to escape into the house.

Kendall turned to June, "What in the—"

June scooted into the hall. "Betsy, you come out now and tell us what's going on."

Chapter 14

She studied June's cold blue eyes and felt no compassion. "I sense negative waves from you," Betsy said, patting her hand. "Believe me I didn't mean to offend you, and I wouldn't have got you and your husband involved if it weren't such a dire emergency."

"What's going on?" June snapped.

"I'm not all that sure."

June puffed.

Betsy waved her hand as if to settle the situation. "Don't you worry. I'll tell you everything I know."

"That angry fellow is your husband?"

"Ex," Betsy said taken back. "I'd never date your brother-in-law unless I was free of entanglements. You must at least believe that." She waited for June's reassurance, but none came.

"We believe you," Kendall spoke, eyeing his wife. "Before we get into this long story, why don't we sit down where it's more comfortable?" He gestured toward the living room.

"If you don't mind," Betsy said, surveying the area, "could we go downstairs?"

He seemed confused until his wife snapped. "Betsy doesn't like windows."

"Ooooh," Kendall said, his thin eyebrows raising.

She smiled weakly. "I'm sorry. Everything will become clearer after I explain."

"I hope so," June said. "Before that, let me get my first aid kit to take care of your bleeding."

Once they sat on the old dusty couches in the basement and bandaged Betsy, she began her tale with as few details as possible. June switched back and forth in her seat with a skeptical glare.

Ironically, June didn't know things had turned sour between herself and Jeff. Betsy rambled on about the story.

When she told the Thomsons that Philippe said she could keep the ring, they gasped. "The ring sounds expensive and he gave it to you?" June asked.

They continued with more questions and Betsy patiently answered them. When she came to the part about the jeweler, Kendall asked, "What day did you have it appraised?"

"Today."

"Today?" husband and wife said in unison.

Betsy nodded, as the events of the last twenty-four hours seemed to overwhelm her. Her soul sagged. She continued with her tale, explaining how she escaped Philippe.

Kendall seemed surprised. "You escaped him?" He sized her up.

A mixture of irritation and pride bubbled inside Betsy. She explained, "The Lord must've been with me. Heaven knows how much I prayed. Well, anyway, I knew I couldn't get far from Philippe. He was hot on my trail and I was on foot. So I decided—"

"To come here," June said.

"Exactly. I'm so sorry to barge in on your hospitality."

"Put that silly thought aside," Kendall said smiling. "Any friend of Jeff's is a friend of ours."

June sat up straighter, her gaze narrowing.

"This worries me," Kendall said. "It sounds like you're in this situation real deep."

Betsy nodded. "I won't know how bad it is until the police trace the rock."

"If that gem is worth as much as the jewelers think, I bet your ex-husband is dealing with a bad group. A crowd that doesn't stop at anything to get what they want," Kendall said.

"Kendall, is our family in danger?"

Betsy glanced at June. Her whole disposition had completely changed to withdrawn and pale.

"I doubt it. We gave no clue we knew anything about Betsy. I bet he's giving the same performance at every house on the block. We need to take extra precautions for the next couple of days."

"Like what?" June asked.

"We must face the fact that our phones might be tapped. So, no, Betsy, you may not borrow the phone. We also need to realize our house might be watched and people might follow us. No one must see Betsy until we have a better understanding about what's going on."

Betsy noticed June's face draining color. "I'm so sorry. It didn't dawn on me that by coming here I'd be putting your family at risk. I wasn't thinking. I was just so scared and—"

"You were right in coming," Kendall said. "The ward is a big family. We help people when they need us. Isn't that right, June?"

She crossed her legs. "Yeah."

"I think the best thing is for Betsy to hide in our home."

"What?" June asked.

"It'd have to be a secret. Not even the kids should know. If Philippe is watching, which I'm sure he is, then it's very important he has no hint Betsy's here. That means you can't ever be caught by a window, absolutely no going anywhere.—None."

June bit her fingernails as her husband spoke. "I don't see how that's possible—"

"She can hide in our storage room. The kids never go there. It'd be the perfect place."

"She'd freeze." A crease appeared between her soon-to-be hostess' eyebrows.

"I'll get a heater. Are you up for it, Betsy?"

She nodded. "I'd be most appreciative of your support. You don't know what it means. Would you mind if I give my sister-in-law a call and ask her to bring over a few things?"

"NO!" Kendall said. "You mustn't use the phone."

"Oh, yeah," Betsy said. "I forgot. I'm going to be living like a prisoner."

"Looks that way," Kendall said.

"But I need to let the family know. They'll be so worried."

"I know this might sound cruel, but for their safety and ours, they must not know. I'm sure their phone is tapped too and they're being watched. Do you understand that, June?"

June nodded. "Poor Karen. That's so mean and scary."

"It might save her life," Kendall said. "Tomorrow I'll go to the police and see how things stand."

"They won't tell you a thing. I have to go with you," Betsy said.

Kendall mulled that over. "I guess we're going to have to risk it and smuggle you in."

Betsy nodded.

"Until then, June will be happy to set you up in the storage room and I'll work on getting you a heater."

Betsy stood up and crossed the room, first grabbing June's hand, then Kendall's. "Thank you so much."

Kendall smiled. "Not a problem."

June didn't respond. Betsy knew she'd have to smooth over the raw edges. As she headed up the stairs, Betsy called out, "June?"

The young tired mother turned around. "Yes?"

"Did the bishop tell you I accepted the call?"

"He did. You're going to have a hard time doing that though, locked up in my basement."

"I'm not planning on staying forever. I know Philippe lied to me, but I doubt he'll stay in town long. He doesn't like Utah."

"People do worse things for money than stay in a town they don't like."

The muscles in Betsy's shoulders tensed. She had grown weary of June's negative outlook. So draining. "They're many good people out there who do a whole lot of wonderful things."

With that, June climbed upstairs to find the cot. Kendall gave the grand tour of the overcrowded storage room.

"When that big earthquake hits, I know where I'm coming," Betsy said, reading the labels on the five gallon canisters.

Kendall moved the bins away from the wall. "You and everyone else in this ward."

"A lot of people have said that to you, huh?"

"Yeah. I don't mind helping them. It's just that when everybody thinks they're safe and going to be dependent on us, I worry we aren't going to have enough. There's only so much to go around."

"That's a good point. What exactly have the brethren said?"

"To get your food storage and get it soon. They think it's only a matter of time."

"That's pretty scary."

"I think so."

"That's what I'll get working on the second I'm released from my jail sentence. Do you think I'll get out early for good behavior?"

Kendall laughed. "I doubt it. But if you're serious about your food storage, I have a couple of books down here you can read to keep you company. We have a lot of books upstairs and if you're into reading, we can bring a few down for you."

"That'd be great. I love books."

"So does June. She always tells me when she buys a new book, that she's working on her year's supply of book storage. When the power is knocked out, there won't be TV and computers, so books will be the in thing."

"Great point."

Betsy helped move the buckets to make room for the cot, which June brought down. Betsy smiled at her hostess. "Your husband informs me you're a reader."

"Yes."

"What kind of books do you like?"

"I like Mormon and Christian fiction."

"Really? Which authors in particular?"

The conversation continued until Betsy had a pile to read so big it'd take three years.

After Kendall found the heater, he hooked it up. Then they wished her good night before shutting the door. Betsy lay on the creaky cot and her thoughts wandered. She and June had found something in common. That was good.

Her mind drifted to Philippe. Just at the thought of his name her stomach lurched. How could she have been such a fool for the second time?

Her head throbbed. She had to stop these negative thoughts. She took a deep breath as she closed her eyes and visualized her peaceful spot. The tension eased from her as tired exhaustion took its place. Her eyelids grew heavy as her body's aches decreased.

✧

Jeff awoke to a pounding headache. Would the pain of his wife's death ever lessen? He closed his eyes, willing himself back to sleep, but when it became apparent it wasn't going to happen, he dragged himself out of bed to grab an Advil.

He kept the drugs in the kitchen. He staggered through the darkness, feeling like a bomb had exploded and had blown away the most important parts of him, leaving him with a few bleeding organs he needed to live.

He popped the pill and sat at the kitchen counter with a drink of cold milk. Life was supposed to be hard. After all it was called a test. But did God really have to kidnap the most important person from him? He shook his head and said out loud, "God, what do you want me to learn from this?"

He didn't worry about waking Chad. The boy was a heavy sleeper. You could put a blaring alarm clock next to his ear and he wouldn't flinch. He and Cindy used to joke about that.

"Heavenly Father, do you want me to understand pain? Do you want to test me and see if I'll still be loyal to you and still believe in you even though I've lost what's most valuable? I've proven that. I'm still here. I still love you. I don't always understand why things happen, but I believe in you."

He set the cup on the counter. "Please take care of Cindy for me until I can be with her."

When would he have the peace Christ promised? He finished his milk and wandered downstairs into the family room. This was where Cindy had spent her free time. The place where her energy came. He wanted to feel part of Cindy, closer, somehow, by being near the objects that made up her life.

He laid on the couch and grabbed the pillow she had labored hours sewing. She had developed carpal tunnel from the hours she spent on her craft. She'd sold several wall hangings for a good price. With the money she earned, she always brought him a present.

He clutched the pillow to his chest. His fingers reached out and stroked the checkered fabric as he waited for morning.

◊

George glanced at his wife. Her nervous habit of tugging on and off her ring was enough to drive a sane person crazy. "Would you stop?"

"I'm sorry," Karen whispered.

"My sister is a big girl. I'm sure she's fine."

Karen tugged her nightgown over her head. "I didn't say she wasn't."

"Well, the way you're taking to your ring, it's like you think she was killed by an chainsaw murderer."

Karen rolled her eyes. "No I don't. I know she's okay. I'm just tired of the waiting."

"Whatever you say." George reached for Karen in the bed. "Come snuggle."

"Why?"

"Don't you want to?"

Karen scooted into his arms. He whispered against her ear, "Let's not fight. It won't make the situation any better."

The couple fell into silence as Karen watched the clock strike two. "George, I do believe she is all right."

He squeezed her tight. "I know."

She prayed. As the words rushed from her soul, she had a change come over her. Warmth, worry, and care flowed together, filling her heart and oozing from it. After she offered her last plea, she opened her eyes. She had never prayed like that before. Never really opened herself up and begged. It was a shame she had to wait until an emergency. She promised herself that her prayers would remain as strong and full of belief as they were tonight. Just please, protect Betsy. Please.

◊

Betsy awoke to the door opening. It was hard to call her senses into action.

Her body still ached and sleep wanted her to pay more of its debt. spilled across her bed. She groaned, blinked her eyes and looked at intruder.

"Good morning," June sang, her hands full of dishes. "I brought you pan cakes and orange juice. I'm sorry it's so early but I needed to bring it before my kids' wake. We don't want them to find out. They can't keep a secret. Not ever."

Betsy yawned as she sat up. The smell of Bisquick pancakes brushed against her nose. "Thank you, my dear. You're so kind."

June acted like the comment meant nothing to her as she pushed with her foot a five gallon bucket closer to the bed and set down the plate and drink. "I'll be back to check on you."

"Actually, a bathroom would be wonderful."

"To be on the safe side, let's wait until my older kids leave for school. I'll send the other ones outside to play then they won't hear the shower."

Betsy nodded, lying back down. It'd be best for her not to get out of bed until the bathroom visit became a closer reality. As she went to leave, Betsy called, "I meant what I said about you being a dear." The door stopped closing and June stood there. "I know this isn't easy for you," Betsy continued, "Karen told me about your feelings concerning me dating your brother-in-law. Trust me, June, I didn't know he was married to your sister."

"Yeah, well there's a lot of things you don't know."

"You're right and I'm willing to learn."

"If that's the case, then I hope you're not offended with what I'm about to say."

Betsy tightened her sensitivity muscle, preparing for the attack. "Try me."

"You can never replace my sister."

Betsy let the words seep in as she surfed through to understand the hidden meaning. "Of course not, my dear, I'd never thought of doing that."

"Don't call me dear," June snapped, "and don't lie. You thought of doing that ever since you accepted the first date with him."

"There's a difference between replacing and having a relationship."

"Where exactly do you want this relationship to go?"

"I haven't thought that far."

June gave a sarcastic laugh. "Don't give me that. A single woman at your age has only one thing on her mind."

"Chocolate," Betsy blurted out.

"No. Marriage."

"Good grief, that's quite a judgment. I don't like being pigeon holed like that. I've had my experience with marriage and I'm not sure that's the type of thing I want to get involved in again. I mean a person can have a whole lot more fun single. You don't have to report to anyone. No worries about toilet seats being up, or cooking breakfast for anyone, or even who's playing in the basketball or football games. No concerns over what anyone thinks about the way I've chosen to do my hair, my wallpaper, or the way I live my life. Being single is a very free lifestyle."

"Also very lonely, I imagine."

"Then you can understand why Jeff is dating me."

June's eyes drew narrow. "No, I can't understand that. I can understand it for someone like you. You have no good memories to reflect on. Jeff has my sister to keep him company. They had the perfect marriage. Their love still beats strong through the veil of death. There is nothing that could break them apart, especially some lady who doesn't know what she wants."

Betsy stood, taking deep breaths. "Just a minute, little missy, you're still very young and naive. You have no idea what it's like to be old and you definitely don't know what it's like to be old and single."

"I don't have to."

"Why? Did Jeff tell you these things?"

"I know his heart. He has a good one. He might be messed up right now but that's because he's grieving for his wife. He's confused, but when time passes he'll become stronger and he'll realize I'm right."

"You're entitled to your opinion," Betsy said, looking at June's angry flashing eyes. "I'm sorry that my dating your brother-in-law causes you so much pain."

"Are you sorry enough to quit dating him? You'd not only be doing me a favor, but you'll also be doing one for his son and Jeff."

"Why do you say that?" Betsy asked in a weak voice.

"Because he needs time to grieve. He doesn't need you butting in confusing him."

Betsy wanted to protest, to point out that Jeff was the one who pursued their relationship, but didn't. Anything she might say would only upset her hostess. "I'll give your point some thought."

June looked at her doubtfully. "I guess that's the best I can ask for. Sorry I got so heated."

"I can tell your sister was close to your heart."

"Is. Is," June said, clutching her arms to her chest. In the distance, a child called for her mom. June gasped. "I better go." She closed the door and left Betsy in silence.

After five minutes of thinking of points that proved her argument, Betsy closed her eyes. She needed positive energy flowing through her. She took a deep breath and thought about her dad. He had always loved her. She remembered being five, and running into his extended arms. His face held delight as he swung her around in a circle, his thin hair bouncing "My cherub," he used to call her. This phrase always filled her with warm satisfaction.

She froze that memory in her mind, letting the flow of his acceptance, caring, and love nourish her depleted soul. Once the experience replenished her with happy thoughts, she opened her eyes. She wouldn't allow herself to think about her father's accident and how her mom was left on her own to raise George and herself. She wouldn't go there. Too painful. Too non-productive. The point of this exercise was that someone loved her as she was.

Time passed slowly while she waited for the kids to leave. She read a chapter in one of her books, set it down and fell into a foggy sleep until June came. "The bathroom is straight down the hall the first door on your left."

Betsy pushed herself off the mattress and nodded. "Thank you."

"I put a clean towel and washcloth in there. There should already be shampoo and soap."

Betsy headed for the bathroom in welcome relief. An hour later Kendall appeared in the doorframe of her dungeon. His straight narrow eyebrows rose and Betsy flushed with embarrassment. No one had seen her without make-up, not even her ex-husbands and now she was stuck for perhaps days with this fate. She kept her head tilted downward.

"Are you ready to go to the police station?" he asked.

She straightened her wrinkled shirt. "Yeah. Do you think we could stop by ZCMI on the way?"

"Why?"

"I don't feel like myself without my make-up."

"Good," Kendall said, throwing the bags he had in his hands at her.

She tugged on her bangs above her brow, blinking at him.

"Remember you're suppose to be in disguise?"

"Maybe we're overreacting here."

"We'll find out that answer at the police station when we hear the value of the diamond."

Betsy sighed.

"You need to get rid of those nails and put on the wig I got you."

"I'm not ruining my nail job. Do you know how much time and money it cost me?"

"Would you like me to do it for you?" Kendall offered.

"No."

"I'll give you fifteen minutes to get rid of the nails and to slip into disguise. I purchased some clothes, too. Sorry about the choice but I don't want you to draw any undue attention."

Betsy examined him. His face threatened to smile and his blue eyes twinkled as though it was a starry night. "You're enjoying this."

He grinned.

"You probably always wanted to be a spy."

"Actually Superman, but this will do. I also wanted to be the biggest, meanest cop around who out-smarted everyone."

"I see. And what's your job?"

"FBI agent." Betsy waited until he said, "Okay a dentist, but I'm a FBI agent on the side. You'd better get busy. Those nails are going to take awhile to come off."

She looked at her hands as Kendall left, her long perfectly polished nails. Actually a couple of places had been nicked in the tangle with Philippe yesterday, but still it wouldn't take much to undo the damage.

Her situation had gradually gotten worse. First, she had to eat breakfast made with white flour. It'd filled her body with pollutants. She was already getting a headache from it. Then she had to take a shower and change back into the same clothes in which she'd slept in and wore yesterday. She felt like babies must feel when someone sprinkled powder on them in an effort to cover the odor of the dirty diaper.

Next she was forced to be witnessed without her make-up and her nails would be destroyed. She felt nothing like her old normal, happy self. Nothing. She closed her eyes, imagining a beautiful scenic waterfall with lush green vegetation thriving around the borders. Banana yellow, baby blue, and tea rose flowers decorated the grasslands. She inserted an owl soaring in the sky, releasing a distant screech. When she opened her eyes, she realized she was the screeching owl.

She sucked on her throbbing finger as she listened carefully to the noise upstairs. Had any one heard her? She'd have to rip the other nails in dead silence. Perhaps she'd lay her face straight into the pillow to muffle her cry.

Chapter 15

Karen woke with a gasp. Had Betsy come home? She slipped off the bed, ran up the stairs into her sister-in-law's apartment. The broken door and couch had been moved out of the hallway. The bedspread had wrinkles, but it was obvious no one had slept under it last night. Karen rubbed her arms.

George found her a couple of minutes later. "What's going on?"

Karen peered deep into worried eyes. "Nothing. I hoped maybe she had made it back."

He examined the room. "Doesn't look like it."

"I know." Karen twisted her fingers.

"It'll be okay." He tipped her chin and pecked her on the lips.

"Will you do me a favor?" Karen asked.

"What?"

"Will you pray for your sister with me?" She watched her husband listening to his gentle breathing. She wanted to hurry him along, but felt it wouldn't be a good idea.

He reached out and touched her shoulder. "Karen, I know nothing about prayers. Never really needed a God or maybe I haven't thought about Him. But if you want to offer one, go ahead. I'll listen." He sniffed.

Karen held back a protest about how anyone, even he, could pray. She shouldn't push, especially with something as important as this. "All right." Her husband said yes to be nice. His action had a sweetness to it.

"Thank you, dear." She kissed him briefly before saying, "I'd appreciate it if we knelt. It's more reverent that way."

They sank to the floor. George squirmed like a kindergartner on the first day of school. He mumbled, "I'm not sure what to do."

"Fold your arms and bow your head."

"That's all?"

"Say amen at the end if you approve of my prayer. It's like you're agreeing to my words."

"If you want that, then you need to be careful what you say. I don't second things every day and I'm going to pay extra attention if I'm doing this in front of God."

"Good point." Karen folded her arms and bowed her head, offering a silent prayer that she would have the Spirit they talked about at church.

"Dear Heavenly Father," she started and then proceeded to thank her Lord for the many blessings that had been poured from heaven upon her. She thanked Him for improving health—she hadn't had one migraine since visiting the doctor a few days ago. She also expressed her gratitude for their two beautiful, healthy children. She thanked God for their employment. And then she poured her feelings out, telling her Father in Heaven of her hurt, worry, and concern for Betsy. "Please, if it be Thy will, let her be safe. Guide us to her. Let her know of our love." She continued, some phrases she repeated, but they rang true with her desires and wishes. Tears mixed within the plea. Then the prayer ended.

She kept her eyes shut, grasping for control of her emotions and dreading her husband's response.

"Karen?"

She saw the wrinkles across his forehead. "Are you all right?"

She nodded.

He squeezed her forearm. "I said amen."

Tears escaped. Something had touched him. Maybe now he'd listen to the missionaries, get baptized, then a year from now they could go to the temple to be sealed for—

"Do you think there really is a God listening to you?" he asked.

The question popped Karen's hope like a needle puncturing a balloon. "Yes, I really believe it and you can find out for yourself, too, if you pray and ask. That's the beautiful thing about our religion."

"Karen, let's not get carried away here. I prayed with you because you asked me to, not because I believed, or was suddenly interested in religion. I don't have time to add more things to my life."

"You're too busy for God?"

"For religion. I highly doubt there's a God. That doesn't seem probable. The scientific theory of evolution seems more realistic. Now, I have to get to work. Will you call the cops and see if there's an update about Betsy?"

"All right," Karen mumbled.

George hugged her. "You be careful today. Why don't you call the alarm company and get going on the estimate?"

She agreed, a bit surprised. Before, when she'd suggested an alarm, George had laughed and said, "You're being paranoid."

After she watched his car pull away, she rushed to leave for work. The house felt spooky with everyone gone.

✧

The nails were bruised reminders of what they once were. Kendall had come back and given her clippers and watched her until every last nail was cut. All the beauty destroyed. The hair was a drab brown wig that hung shapelessly. The skin was a canvas of wrinkles. Betsy shuddered when she glanced into the mirror. She was the perfect person to stand in a spook alley to cast fear in paying patrons.

She shook her head and vowed she'd never appear this way in public, or private for that matter. Her appearance would shoot out ugly, negative, self-defeating waves into the universe and then they'd re-splash on top of her.

Kendall knocked on her door. Soon after they had pulled an old brown blanket over her head and smuggled her onto the floor of the backseat of their car, which was in the closed garage, Betsy listened to the soft rock music spilling from the radio and tried to let the notes carry away her negative fear. She closed her eyes ignoring the muggy smell suffocating her from the blanket. Sweat bubbled onto her face and head.

She lifted the blanket, allowing the cool life giving air to reach her. The breathing hole was small and wouldn't be seen from someone looking in from the car window.

Kendall began to sing a popular song and Betsy's ears groaned. The man couldn't carry a tune. She forced herself to listen to the radio and ignore Kendall's voice. She banged into the front seat.

"That light turned red quickly," Kendall said as if to himself.

Betsy wanted to growl but her back ached more than her irritation. She didn't know how long she could stay huddled up. When her back couldn't take it any more, she yelled out, "How much longer?"

"I'm going to circle the station several times to make sure we weren't followed and then I'll look for a way to get inside the building without you being spotted," Kendall said, in a calm, unconcerned voice.

He handled himself well under stress, keeping his head on straight while panic invaded hers. She had thought she had mastered that bad habit. Now she had to admit defeat. Depressing.

The car rocked her for at least another fifteen minutes, probably only five but definitely seemed every bit of fifteen.

"We are lucky," Kendall sang to the rhythm of the new song. "There's a garage behind the police station. I just saw a police car enter."

Betsy tightened her grasp on the blanket as the car took a sudden drop. It was like she had gotten into an elevator and it had sunk twenty floors in a matter of seconds. The car screeched to a stop and Betsy tugged the blanket off her head. Safe.

She heard Kendall talk to someone. "I know I'm not allowed in here, but under the circumstances—"

She couldn't make out the words of the officer who stopped Kendall. She covered her head again.

"Yes, I know. We think a person's life might be endangered and we know we're being followed. We didn't want anyone to know she was here. She came yesterday and needs to talk to Detective Rex."

More mumbling. Betsy squirmed under the blanket.

"Yes, Mr. Rex." Mumble. "Thank you, sir. Promise we won't stay parked here very long."

Betsy listened to the footsteps go around the car and the door open. She tugged the blanket off her head. "Ah, I thought we'd never make it." After saying that, she looked up at an officer with short, bordering plump, and possessing an air of authority.

"This is Officer Kurt Wakeland. He'll be sneaking us in."

"Our hero!" Betsy said, extending her hand until she saw her fingers and quickly withdrew it.

The officer didn't seem to notice. He marched across the parking garage like he was in the military. It took only minutes for him to sneak her into a back office. He said he'd get Mr. Rex and they would soon be on their way.

Betsy sat at the table and tried to drum her nails on the desk. Pain shot through her hand when the raw tip struck the hard surface. "I hate you for making me destroy my nails." She glared at Kendall.

He laughed. "The price you had to pay when you decided to go under-cover."

"Why couldn't I have worn gloves?"

Kendall stared at her. "Well, um, you might have to take them off. We don't want to give whoever is after us clues."

"Okay then why couldn't I have put on a different color of nail polish? A kind that I'd never wear in a million years."

Kendall laughed again. "It would still look like you, and what male is going to notice the color change?"

Betsy smiled. "You're right. What was I thinking?"

"Another reason is my wife doesn't own nail polish. It'd look bad to go buy some if we're being followed."

"She doesn't own any! Not one little bottle?"

"She's not that type of woman. She's more natural. Simple. Down to earth."

"Does she like being like that?"

"Of course." He leaned further back in his chair.

"Dumb question. Sorry, I've been thinking about taking on a lifestyle more simple, more natural."

"It cuts down on time and effort. My wife feels that if she spends too much time working on her make-up, hair, and clothes she has exhausted energy on herself and not on others."

"What?" Betsy's voice increased in pitch. "Serve others and look like a slob. Spending time on making yourself look beautiful for the world is selfish! I think it's one of the best gifts you can give each other. I shudder when I see someone who pops out of the shower and thinks they look marvelous. They're hurting my eyes!"

Kendall didn't respond and Betsy strolled around the room, muttering over and over, "Selfish? To make the world more beautiful –selfish?"

"It's a theory," Kendall said. "You don't need to get all worked up."

"I'm sorry, but that theory as you call it, really bothers me. What data did she base it on?"

"Huh?"

"What led her to believe that?"

Kendall went to answer, but then Mr. Rex entered. He darted a glance at Betsy. "Have you had any more trouble?"

She nodded.

"I was afraid of that. You're playing with the big boys."

"What?" Betsy shrieked.

"The diamond was smuggled out of Amsterdam. One of the cutters must've stolen it. There has to be some sort of tie between the diamond cutter and your ex-husband. We're working on that right now."

"Does this mean I have to hideout in an apartment with a police officer protecting and irritating me?"

"We don't have the funds for that. Officer Wakefield informed me of what you've been doing. It sounds like you're doing a fine job so far. Continue."

"What?" Kendall asked. His voice shrilled. "We pay taxes which is where your salary comes from. Now you're telling us when we have a crisis, you say good luck?" The tips of his ears reddened.

"We'll work on it from our end, but we simply don't have the resources and you seem to be a natural."

"It's not that hard," Kendall said, obviously pleased with himself.

"So what are you going to be doing?" Betsy asked. How could Kendall be so easily charmed? He was supposed to see through the kiss up.

"We have some men right now trying to discover who's behind this diamond theft."

"Why don't you have any women working on it?" Betsy questioned.

"We do. I just said men as a manner of speech."

"You need to be careful how you phrase things." She sat down.

The officer chewed his gum and handed Betsy paperwork to fill out. "You were right in bringing the diamond to us."

"Can I please have it back?"

"I'm sorry we can't do that right now."

"Why not? It's my diamond."

"It's stolen property."

Betsy rested her hands on her forehead. "I've got a headache. Can I leave?"

"Yes. Take extreme caution and don't be seen until we bust these guys."

"How long is that going to take?"

"Perhaps a week or two. It's hard to say."

"A week or two! I have to stay jammed up in a storage room for that long?"

"I don't want to kid you; it could go even longer. But look on the bright side, at least you're able to keep your life. That's the important thing."

"I'm going to kill Philippe." Betsy looked at the crinkled brow of the officer. "That was a manner of speaking. I didn't mean it. I just meant that I'm real upset at my ex-husband for putting me in such a situation. If I were really going to kill him, I would've done that years ago when he had the affair. I did think about it. But I'm not the killing type. I couldn't kill someone even if my own life was in danger. If you want, I'd be more than happy to take a lie detector test—"

The officer motioned his palms down as if to calm her. "I understand. You don't need to explain further."

"Good," Betsy said. "Let's smuggle me back to prison."

✦

When Jeff woke up Wednesday morning, his son was calling for him. He rushed to the stairs. "I'm down here," he yelled.

Chad wheeled his chair over to the staircase. "What are you doing?"

"I had trouble sleeping."

"What are you doing with Mom's pillow?" Chad gestured to Jeff's hand.

He hadn't realized he had impulsively clutched onto it last night and still hadn't let go. He tossed it to his other hand. "I'm hanging on tight to it, son.

That's what I'm doing."

"Dad, I didn't know you did that?"

"Yeah, I do, especially when I miss her. It helps me feel closer to her."

Chad twisted his fingers in his lap, avoiding eye contact.

Jeff nodded, glancing at the floor. The uncomfortable moment was broken when his son added, "I do that too."

"I thought I saw her pillows downstairs. Which one do you have?"

"It's her pajamas I hold onto." Chad spoke in a soft voice, face blushing. "The ones she wore when she'd hug me good-bye in the mornings."

The muscles in Jeff's neck pulsed.

"Some of those mornings she'd ask for a kiss, I'd roll my eyes and grunt, 'Why do you always want that?' I'd pull away from her and she'd wrestle me. She wouldn't stop the fight until she at least got the top of my head. Sometimes...I'd try to dodge her." Chad's whole body shook from the sobs.

Jeff rushed to his son and wrapped his arms around him tight. "Shhh," he whispered.

"She didn't know I loved her."

"Yes, she did. She did," Jeff's voice sounded hoarse. His own doubts squeezed his heart. His son shouldn't suffer from the same guilt. He had done nothing wrong. Chad had given her a lot of joy. He knew that for a fact. He gripped Chad's shoulders. "I promise you she knew. She spoke often about how happy you made her and how she couldn't ask for a better son."

The boy's shoulders shrugged as waves of tears overtook his thin frame.

Jeff gulped. What could he say to help his son?

"Chad, she loved you. She was sure proud of you. She used to tell me, 'I got myself the best boy. Look at him. Isn't he the most handsome guy you've ever seen?' I'd then joke with her saying, 'What? You don't think I'm the most handsome?' She'd laugh and pat me on the arm, and say, 'Where do you think he got his looks, silly?' Your mother loved you, boy, and she knew you loved her. Remember she did have a lot of brothers. She understood how we men are."

"You really think she knew?" Chad asked.

"Yes. I just had an idea."

"What?" Chad asked.

"Would you like to read your mother's journals? Maybe she wrote about you in them."

"Could I?"

"Yes. You know what's better yet, maybe we should read them together. It'd do us both good. It'll be our therapy sessions."

"Therapy?" Chad squinted his eyes.

"Yes, I've been told that it's not good for either of us to keep things bottled in. We should read the diaries together and discuss them as we go. That'd be a good way for us to get out our feelings."

"Whatever, Dad, get the diaries."

"Should we start with the most recent or an old one?"

"I'll close my eyes and pick. Go get the journals."

Jeff smiled at his son's impatience as the gnawing intensity grew in ¹ ⁱ·ᵘ also. "Before we get started just let me ask about your bedsore. Is it dᴏ⋯ better?"

"A little," Chad said, avoiding his father's eyes.

✧

In the morning, Karen paused from her work. Something was wrong. What?

She typed in a few more figures. Yes, Betsy was missing, but it wasn't that. It had to do with something about herself. Something with how she felt. She completed several more invoices before it came to her. She didn't have a headache. Not even a hint of one. Come to think of it, the tight muscles in her neck had loosened up and she wasn't exhausted. How odd. She felt wonderful!

Of course her stomach growled. This new diet was murder. She constantly struggled with what to eat. She asked Mary about it.

"I've been on a similar diet for years," her co-worker declared. "It sure does make a difference."

"But what do you eat?" Karen asked.

"That does get hard. I eat this really good spinach salad with nuts sprinkled on top. You'd be surprised at how yummy it is. I'll bring some for lunch tomorrow if you want."

"I'll try anything," Karen said. "Thank you."

"No problem. I'll also bring a couple of recipes. I make a real tasty carrot bread. My kids even gulp it up."

Karen realized she looked forward to trying this food. Her stomach growled and she stood to clock out for lunch. She wanted to talk to June anyway. It'd be nice to have someone listen empathetically to her concerns about Betsy. June would listen well. She dialed June's number.

After Karen dumped on June's sympathetic ear for fifteen minutes, her friend asked her how her diet was coming.

"I'm so starved I'm tempted to eat sawdust, but I feel a billion times better. My headaches are almost gone. I haven't had one migraine since I started and my neck tension isn't so painful."

"That's great news. You know it makes sense. After all, you're living the Word of Wisdom found in section 89 of the *Doctrine and Covenants* where the Lord said no alcohol or tobacco." Karen knew about those passages from the missionary lesson.

"There's more to it than no caffeine and smoking," June continued. "Look what it does say to eat—grains, fruits, and vegetables. Basically your new diet."

"Wow. So cool," Karen said.

"The neat thing about our religion is that it's true. Science is finally catching up to what our prophet knew back in the 1800's."

"Now for the other reason I called you, June."

"Yes."

"What is this calling I just got and why did you pick on me? I'm still new to this whole church thing. I can't—"

"Hush, and you can too. You can do anything with God's help. Anything. And for your other question, I didn't call you to be mean. I called you because your name kept popping into my mind. Heavenly Father wants you in this position. I don't know why. But you'll have plenty of help. Betsy, your sister-in-law, was called to do whatever I decide and I put her with you to work jointly in serving the sisters."

"What exactly does that mean?"

"You'll need to visit the sisters and see that we are taking care of their needs. I was going to tell you at our meeting but since Betsy...I'll go ahead over the phone. What I want you and Betsy to do is to pray over the sisters and let it come to your mind who needs a visit. I'll also be adding people to your list. I'd like you to drop off something that might brighten up their day and make their trials lighter."

"But what if I never see Betsy again?"

"Karen, have faith. She hasn't even been missing for a whole day yet. There's hope. Lots of it. I know she's okay. You've got to believe me. Do you?"

"I'm trying. It's just so hard."

"It must be. Why don't you stop by after work and we'll talk about it. I can give you some papers you'll be needing for your calling."

"What am I suppose to do?" Karen asked.

"I'll let that be up to you. Do what the Spirit guides you to do."

"I'm still not sure if I understand what the Spirit is or how I know when it is guiding me?"

"You remember the missionaries talking about pondering over a problem you have and working it out until you have a solution in your mind that you feel good about?"

"Yes, they said that God expects us to do as much work as we can. That this isn't a church where you get something for nothing."

"Exactly. What do you do when you come up with a solution?"

"Pray about it. If the answer is yes, then I'd feel good about it, if no, then I wouldn't know what to do. I'd be left feeling confused."

"You have it down pat."

"But I don't know—"

"I'll help you along and Betsy will be there for you, too. Pray. Ask Heavenly Father for help and direction."

"Are you sure Betsy—?"

"Karen, you need to believe that Heavenly Father's taking care of her. I promise you she's alive and safe."

Karen hung up with mixed emotion. June seemed so positive Betsy was alive and safe. Her optimistic attitude was catching. Karen smiled. June, after all, might be right.

"Ready for lunch?" Amber broke into her thoughts.

"Yeah," Karen said. "I was just dreaming about food. Do you mind if we go somewhere where there's salad?"

"You and Mary are going to make us healthy," Amber joked. "No, I don't mind even though my stomach might."

⬧

Betsy gazed at the white bucket and the golden canisters in the cell room. Might as well get used to the decoration. From the way the cops talked she'd be spending a long time in this room shut up like a rat that had to hide for safety from humankind. Thankfully she'd nibble on drops of food from June, but it was nothing like she would've chosen. Her health would take a major dive from eating white flour, sugar, and fatty foods. She already longed for her diet of herbs and brown rice.

June tapped on her door and carried in a bowl. "I hope you like vegetable soup."

Betsy smiled, pleased. Perhaps she had exaggerated her state of mind. "Thank you! I'd love some. This morning's events really wore me out. I'm starved."

June set the steamy bowl on the plastic container. Her movements were jolted and out of rhythm and her glance darted back and forth.

"June, we need to talk."

She flipped her golden highlighted hair. "What about?"

"Jeff."

Instinctively her jaw tightened and her eyes narrowed. "Yes?"

"I can see that my dating him causes you a lot of pain. Since we're stuck together for a while and I'll be working with you in Relief Society, I've decided that I won't date him."

"Really?" June asked.

Betsy nodded. "Our relationship can't possibly be right if it hurts other people. I never wished that. I just wanted to find a man who is good and kind and who I can make happy. I'm tired of seeking truth by myself. I thought if I could find someone who believes as I do, we could really go far. We could help each other and he could point out details that I didn't see. Wouldn't that be a glorious journey?"

"Truth seeking? You're in to that?"

"Of course. I want to know what is right. I thought Jeff would make a good choice for a team member."

"Cindy always talked about discovering the truth," June muttered.

"I heard she wore loud clothing. I used to also, but now I'm going to try to be moderate in my dress."

"Why?" June asked.

It was then Betsy explained her dilemma with Apostle Paul and how she wanted to conquer the first offensive thing, then build up to the more blood pumping quotes. She also told June about her search for what was right in clothes. "June, when I thought I was no longer allowed to wear beautiful colors, I tell you my heart about leapt out of my chest with grief. I love color. Life is so bland without it and if I had to wear those plain straight jumpers— ahhh. Not that there is anything wrong with them." Betsy's hand waved as she ranted. "It's just so ordinary and I like to be different. I like loud clothes. But you know I'd change if that's what God wanted me to do. When I felt His spirit and joined this church, I knew that no matter how hard things got I'd do what He asked me to do. Now the hard part is trying to figure out what that is."

"You're right," June said. "I struggle with what is right a lot. Many times things are gray. Betsy, I'm sorry I was so rude to you. You do have a good spirit and I feel bad that I misjudged you."

Betsy waved it off. "No matter. You let your emotions and feelings about your sister block your vision. Perfectly understandable. Who knows? I might have done the same thing."

"I didn't say I can accept you dating Jeff. I can't."

"Okay." Betsy leaned over and sipped a spoonful of soup with her hand shaking. "This is good. Is it homemade?"

"Yes. I need to talk to you about your calling. Do you mind if I go get your notebook and review the information with you?"

"No, I don't. I don't know how—"

"I know you can't do your job being locked up here. But I do have an assignment I'd like you to start thinking about."

♦

It had taken Jeff quite awhile to convince Chad to wait until that night to read the journals. They both had to leave soon and it wouldn't be a good idea for either of them to be late. Jeff drove Chad to school to save him embarrassment. He'd park about a half block away to not draw attention. He'd invested in a van, especially equipped with a chair lift. Chad didn't have to go through the torture of being lifted and put in the car or chair. When he got a ride from church leaders or friend's parents, he'd have to endure the embarrassment.

Jeff had sneaked a look out the window when one of Chad's friend's parents dropped him off. The father climbed out of the car and lifted Chad, who stared looking off in the yonder, his chin lifted as though he was too proud to admit the circumstances he was in. Jeff had left the window, struggling to shake the vision of his son's paled face.

But today, after he mentioned the journals, there had been a noticeable change in Chad's spirit. He even went so far as to make Jeff promise he wouldn't sneak a glimpse. Jeff now had something to look forward to, and in two days, he'd be skiing. Light was finding its way back into his life.

He thought fleetingly of Betsy, wanting to call her. But no, it was better this way.

Chapter 16

"Will it bother you if I get a little ice cream and maybe a brownie?" Amber asked at lunch.

"No, not at all," Karen said with a smile. "Feel free."

Her co-worker stood.

Karen bit her lip. A couple of bites of ice cream... She'd been good...just—one bowl. It wouldn't hurt anything. By the time she decided to give into her urges, her friend returned.

"Are you sure this doesn't bother you?"

Karen shook her head.

"I admire your discipline. You have much better control than I could ever dream of having."

"You could if you were a migraine sufferer. Believe me, you'd do anything, even give up sugar, if it meant you could see, and your head wouldn't kill you."

"You may be right. I just hope that I don't ever have to deal with it." Amber shoved a huge bite of ice cream into her mouth.

"It isn't fun." Karen would have to fill her sugar craving with the compliment. She looked away. Betsy probably wasn't even eating.

✧

Betsy strolled the storage room as the walls seemed to press in from every side. She paced faster with her hands over her eyes. She hated being confined. She longed to talk, for freedom, and her spirit needed out. Upstairs June's children raced around screaming and yelling. The noise caused Betsy to be very grateful she'd never had to deal with little children. That'd take a special talent she knew she didn't have, especially since the noise seemed constant. The only break was when June visited her at lunch. Then the house remained still for a couple of hours. June explained it was quiet time.

Betsy sat on her cot, leaned against the wall, and opened her scriptures. It was as good a time as ever to conquer more of Apostle Paul. When June checked on her again, she'd ask for some commentary books.

She flipped to the verses she'd decided to tackle first about women's dress. Pondering those scriptures had been a long, bumpy road, but now she felt satisfied she'd reached the right solution—to wear clothes that feel like you but don't give yourself or other people around you the impression that you're better than they are. Perhaps the reason Lydia dressed expensively was that she enjoyed the attention. Was her friend scornful and vain like the scriptures warned?

Betsy knew she couldn't truly judge Lydia's heart but *from their fruits you will know them*, the Relief Society lesson a couple of weeks ago had taught. Lydia might be the classic example of what wearing costly apparel might do to a person. Enough. She needed to return to her quest.

Betsy flipped the *Bible* open to 1Timothy 2:11-15.

Let the woman learn in silence with all subjection.

But I suffer not a woman to teach, nor to usurp authority over the man, but to be in silence.

For Adam was first formed, then Eve.

And Adam was not deceived, but the woman being deceived was in the transgression.

Notwithstanding she shall be saved in childbearing, if they continue in faith and charity and holiness with sobriety.

Betsy got off her bed again and paced. Steam seemed to fog her mind. Those were the verses that had gotten to her before. How could a prophet of God think women should be silent in meetings? How could they have such low respect for women? Did the church she joined have the same view?

She strolled across the room and sat to examine the footnotes. These verses surely weren't correct.

The only thing she could find to help ease the sting of the verses was the change in Joseph Smith's translation from "Notwithstanding she shall be saved in childbearing" to "Notwithstanding *they* shall be saved in childbearing." That suggested Adam's fall wasn't completely woman's fault. She remembered the missionaries saying this was the case. It was one of those points that helped sway her to believe the Mormon church wasn't full of sexist men. In fact, she faintly remembered them quoting Joseph Smith in the *Articles of Faith*. She turned the pages as she scanned the verses until she found it.

"We believe that men will be punished for their own sins, and not for Adam's transgression."

This proved that sin wasn't going to be laid completely on the head of poor Eve. It was also interesting to note that it was Adam's transgression, not Eve's. The sick feeling in Betsy's stomach lightened. There had to be a reason why Apostle Paul's words made it into a canonized scripture.

She continued to scan, looking up the topical guide references, searching for answers when June walked in.

"Hello," June said, smiling faintly.

"Hi," Betsy said.

"What are you doing?"

"Trying to figure out why Paul said the sexist things he did in Timothy."

"Hmm, you found those verses, huh?" June leaned against the doorframe.

"You know what I'm talking about?" A pump of excitement went through Betsy.

"I do. It put me in a spin for a while."

"So you had problems with it, too?"

"Oh, yes. I think most women do when they read those lines."

"Do you have an explanation?"

"I have, but right now we need to talk about something else."

"You don't understand, I have to know—"

June stepped out of the room and called back to her, "I'll return in a second."

"That was rude," Betsy mumbled. She hurried to the door and strained her ears to hear what was going on. There were voices and people moving. She paced the room when June said from somewhere upstairs, "I must've left the binder in the storage room when I was in there earlier this morning. Could you check?"

Betsy scanned the room for a place to hide. June had betrayed her! She fell to her knees and was halfway under the bed when she heard a scream. Startled, she jerked her head up. "Holy solar system," Betsy said.

"BETSY!" Karen yelled, dropping onto the floor next to her sister-in-law. She hugged her so tight Betsy thought her lungs would burst.

Betsy looked into Karen's wild eyes.

"Why are you in June's storage room?" her sister-in-law asked.

"It's a long story, but to put it simply, the diamond ring Philippe gave me is worth a fortune and a lot of people are after it."

"You're kidding?"

"Does it look like I am?"

Karen frowned. "We thought you were dead or kidnapped or something awful."

"I can see how that would upset your harmony."

"Upset! I've had a hard time thinking of anything else! If only I would've put in an alarm system, you wouldn't have disappeared."

"Oh, dear." Betsy patted Karen's back. "It's nothing like that."

"The other thing I kept worrying about was why you asked to have an alarm system put in the whole house except your apartment."

Betsy laughed as she pushed herself up from the floor. She extended her hand to Karen and they both took a seat on the bed. "That's simple. I thought it'd be easier to come and go if my alarm wasn't hooked up with yours. And when someone else lives in the apartment you wouldn't be forced to give away your code."

"You plan on moving?" Karen's brow furrowed.

"Not anytime soon. I'm not going to stay with you guys forever. I'm not sure yet, but something else is calling me and when I figure it out, I will follow."

Karen shook her head. "There's lots about Betsy that will never change."

"Should it?"

"I didn't say so."

"Why didn't you tell me your reason for the alarm system? I would've understood. Why the secrecy?"

"I had a strong impression something was wrong," Betsy said. "I decided to keep quiet. Now I'm glad I did since I have a better understanding of what I'm involved in. My plan was to have the alarm guys sneak in my apartment and install a silent alarm. I wanted to catch whoever was ransacking it."

"I don't like this, Betsy."

"Me either. I don't know what to do about it. The police are still working on my case."

"Yeah, right. Like they were working on finding you. They could've at least told me you were in hiding."

June knocked on the doorframe and poked her head in. "Just seeing that everything is all right. I know you two ladies have a lot to talk about, so I'll leave you alone. But I'd appreciate it, if you could find some time to work on the first assignment I gave you. We do need to get going on that. I'd volunteer to do it myself, but with this pregnancy and my kids—"

"Don't worry," Karen said. "You can't do it all. We need to get your little one here safely."

Relief washed over June's face. "Thank you."

After she left, they went over the past events and Betsy told her sister-in-law everything she knew about her situation and how it had to remain top secret. "So you see why I couldn't communicate with you? I hate the fact that you and George worried so much. How are Mikey and Sam doing?"

"She's upset that you're not around. Actually she's not stopped complaining because she's traumatized that she didn't even get a speaking part in the play she tried out for, and Sam is still wearing all black and is in la-la land over some girl at school. He won't let me meet her. We played down your whole situation for them so they wouldn't worry."

"I'm glad."

"We said you caught one of your bursts of inspiration and were in such a hurry to find it you left without leaving a note. We also explained that your stuff all over the counter was the result of you hustling to find an address or something in your purse."

"Did they believe it?"

"Not a word."

"How did you explain the kicked-in door?"

"We said we didn't notice it when those kids broke in the house. It probably fell after someone slammed the door shut."

Betsy laughed. "Pretty good."

Karen smiled. "I'm gaining brain cells in my old age."

"You're not old."

Karen shrugged.

"We better get talking about our Relief Society assignment," Betsy said. "June has been very kind in taking me in and I've been a lot of extra work for her. Just the fact she has to come up and down the stairs to talk to me must be exhausting."

"I can't believe you came here," Karen said. "Isn't she upset about you and Jeff?"

"Very, I'd say. But she's trying to handle it as maturely as possible."

"Wow."

"Of course I told her I'd stop seeing Jeff."

"Betsy, you didn't? He's is so perfect for you. You can't give up on the good guys. They're so rare and then you run the risk of marrying another Philippe."

"Don't worry, Karen, my search for love has been adjusted. I won't date anyone that's not LDS. That should help me find someone of quality."

"I hope so. You wouldn't be locked up in a storage room if you used that wisdom years ago or even this past season. Keep that in mind."

"Now for our assignment," Betsy said hastily. "She wants us to pray make a list of people who need help and to do something special for them.

"You summarized it well," Karen said.

"What can we do?"

"I have an idea, if you want to hear it," Karen said.

"Shoot."

"Remember those bears I made at Christmas and took to the hospital?"

Betsy clasped her hands. "That's a wonderful idea."

"I thought we could make wreaths too. It depends on the person and what we think they need."

Betsy nodded. "I don't know why I didn't think of that."

"While you're shut-in, though, why don't you organize my craft supplies? It's a real mess since Christmas and I know that Mikey and Agatha have rummaged through it. I also need you to list which ladies in the ward we need to send these to."

"You're trying to keep me from actually making the wreaths."

Karen sighed. "Face it, Betsy, you're very talented in lots of areas, but crafts isn't one of them."

"Don't you love the walls in my apartment? I painted those."

"I know, and they fit you. I need to go. It's been a long day and I have to cook dinner. I was hoping to make it to a natural food store to find something I can eat."

"Oh, how's your diet coming?"

"I'm hungry."

"You look great. How much weight have you lost?"

"Only five pounds."

"What do you mean *only?* It's only been a couple of days." Betsy batted her eyes.

"From how hungry I feel it should be at least twenty pounds."

"You know you're not supposed to starve yourself to death. That defeats the purpose. You're suppose to gain your health back and lose weight gradually."

"You have never been on this diet."

"But the natural principles are still the same."

"It's hard to eat just vegetables and lettuce. I get so tired of rabbit food. I'd rather go without than cram another carrot down my throat."

"Give it some time. It takes getting used to."

"I hope you're right. But I just don't see a carrot taking the place of a brownie."

"The question is how is this diet making you feel?"

"That's the most frustrating part of this whole thing. It's working. I don't have a constant headache any more, except when I slip up and eat cheese. I haven't had one migraine since I started the diet. It's a miracle. An absolute miracle. And I'll continue to do anything to keep it going, even eat carrots."

Betsy clapped her hands. "I'm so glad."

✧

When Karen prepared to leave, June escorted her. Karen fumbled with the door then opened it before stepping onto the porch and taking a breath. "Thank you for having me over," she said loudly for whoever listened. "Now I'm beginning to understand my calling."

"You're sure welcome."

"I'd like to get working on the craft project. I'll bring over the supplies tomorrow."

"The what—" June said. "Oh, is that what you decided to do?"

"If that's okay with you?"

"Sounds perfect. I'll see you tomorrow. You'll find my craft room great."

Karen waved.

✧

June closed the door and wondered if what Karen just did was a way for her to come back and visit her sister-in-law. That was fine. She sensed Betsy growing restless. Hopefully this whole situation would clear up soon.

The Braxton Hicks or false labor came on strong and she found herself spending more and more time in bed. Other times she was exhausted. It was normal for her to experience the contractions from the beginning of her pregnancy. As long as she laid down and drank plenty of liquids, she should be able to carry the baby almost full term. The only problem seemed to be she wasn't able to tell when she should go to the hospital. She just hoped she didn't brush it aside when it was serious and arrive at the hospital to late to stop labor. In fact, the contractions pressed on her uterus hard now.

"Agatha," she called.

Her daughter ran into the room. "The pains again, Mom?"

June nodded. She was so lucky to have such a responsible daughter. "Do you mind watching the children while I take a nap?"

"But I haven't...no, I don't mind."

"Bill Nye, the Science Guy should be on. You can watch that with them."

"But what about dinner?"

"I'll order pizza."

Several of the kids who had followed Agatha into the room jumped up and down screaming, "Yes. Yes. Yes."

June noted a spark in Agatha's eyes. She had made it up to her daughter a little. "I'm going to go downstairs to rest. I'm hot and it's cooler down there."

"Mom, it's February and it's freezing," Agatha protested.

"Doesn't matter. I'm still really hot. Thank heaven this time I'm having a baby in the winter. Those August babies sure are miserable."

Agatha set to work gathering the kids while June hobbled down the stairs. Her six-month stomach had protruded out to the point where she couldn't see her feet and balance had become a struggle. With her first two babies, she would forget she was middle heavy and would bend down the wrong way and end up rocking on her stomach. She had heard once of a lady who did that and couldn't get on her feet. She had to wait a whole hour until her husband arrived home from work to help her back up. The lady had reassured June the baby was all right. But the whole situation sounded like the pits.

She went to the storage room again. The only other time she had remembered coming down here so often was when they worked on their year supply of food storage. The basement was truly the unvisited part of the house. It was the ugly part, too. When they first moved in, she had worked hard on remodeling the kitchen and the upstairs bedrooms and bathrooms. By the time it came to do the downstairs, she had simply run out of energy and Kendall was too busy with his work to be of much use.

"Yes?" Betsy sang. She was always so cheerful. Just like her sister had been. She didn't want to think of them as similar even in that aspect. Jeff had called her earlier that day wondering if she had seen Betsy. Of course she could say nothing. "I was just hoping," he said. There was something about his manner that bothered June. So sad, so intense. She wouldn't tell Betsy about it. If she did, then she might change her mind about her promise of not seeing him. June didn't feel guilty about that. Since Betsy had volunteered to give up Jeff, obviously it wasn't true love. She wouldn't have made such an offer if it was. Besides, Jeff could love no one else because he loved her sister and there was only room for one true love in a person's life.

"Hi, I've come to talk to you about your questions."

Betsy's blue eyes brightened. "Great!"

"One thing, though."

"Yeah."

"I need to lie down. I don't feel so good. I hope that's not a problem for you."

Betsy shot off the bed. "No problem at all."

June laid down and blew a couple of breaths to lessen the cramping. The contractions ran the full length of her stomach, the pain, long and hard. She closed her eyes and imagined riding a wave. Relax, she told herself as her body's tension lessened. She opened her eyes and turned toward Betsy who studied her.

"Were you using creative imaging?"

"What?"

"What were you just doing?"

"Thinking about riding a wave. I found if I relax, the contractions don't hurt as much."

Betsy smiled. "You know we aren't so different after all. I use that technique all the time."

"You do?"

"Especially in here where I feel like a caged tiger. I don't imagine riding waves, but I picture myself in one of my favorite places."

"What is one of them?"

"France."

"Never been there. I always picture Hawaii."

"I bet a lot of people do that," Betsy said.

June nodded. "From your questions earlier, I got the impression you worry about women's equality and those kinds of issues."

"Exactly. Does Heavenly Father truly believe men are superior? I hate to even ask such a question because it's so far from what my inner-self tells me. Now, obviously we don't practice women being silent in church, so what is Apostle Paul talking about? I remember reading in the commentary by Bruce McConkie about the man being the leader and this is a heavenly order. He also said something about it being the culture."

"I think some background information would be helpful." June closed her eyes, allowing the pain to flow. "The Greek people had a profound influence on the Israelites back in the 300's to about 30 B.C. With their domination came many of the poor views of women. The Greeks blamed women for the evil in the world. Do you remember the story of Pandora?"

"Isn't that where someone stole fire from the gods and Zeus decided to punish them by sending down a woman?"

"Yeah."

"Didn't she supposedly ruin the happiness of man? When actually if you look at the story right, it was the guy who stole the fire and Zeus was really punishing the women by placing them on the same planet as men."

"Now come on," June said. "I like being on the planet with men. It'd be boring without them. It's just some of them I could do without. Same goes for women."

Betsy agreed.

"Anyway, this story became the accepted version of the creation," June continued. "This view was so widely affected it seeped into every aspect of a woman's life. She was legally considered inferior. Some of the writings called women wild beasts who needed marriage to tame them."

"Sounds like the premise of 'The Taming of the Shrew.' I always had a problem with that play. If it was me in that situation, I'd never be tamed."

"Then you'd starve," June said, although she felt the same as Betsy. Betsy was right, they were a lot alike. "Women had one major job in society in the first century, if free, to reproduce, if a slave, to serve. They weren't even allowed to teach their children. That was a job left to the men."

"But many women have natural tendencies to teach and nurture."

June shrugged. "The culture also suppressed women from a social aspect except when they greeted each other at the well. Politics were forbidden and they weren't allowed to intellectualize either."

"Keep them dumb so they won't protest. That philosophy worked well for the slave traders," Betsy said, shaking her head. "I guess control freaks are control freaks no matter what generation."

"The men during the first century in Greece took their superiority so far that they preferred to have relations with other men, which was permitted, but the wives had to remain faithful."

"Of course. What hypocrites."

"I think you're beginning to understand the kind of environment Paul originated from. Another thing that'll make your blood pump, I know it did mine, is they would often kill their girl children because they weren't a blessed male."

"I can't believe some women still have to live like that."

"I can't either," June said. She put her hand on her belly. "I'm very grateful I was born in different circumstances."

"Amen," Betsy said.

"A couple of centuries later, Christ was born. Let me tell you a bit about the situation then. Women were still excluded from public life. They were forced to cover their heads and faces so as not to distract men from their worship."

"What?"

"By this time, they didn't believe as much in the Pandora theory. The operating theory was Eve was evil and God perpetually punished all women for her sins.

"The rabbis took it so far as to separate women from the men in worship. They couldn't be called on to read the scriptures or be taught the Torah. The men would even be warned constantly not to talk too much about women."

"Can you imagine construction workers without catcalling?"

June changed positions on the bed. "The Israelite women did have more clout than a non-Israelite male."

"Glad we scored somewhere."

June laughed again.

"It wasn't all anti-women, though. Jewish people did honor heroic women like Sarah, Rachel, Deborah and Esther. And I'm sure not all men agreed with this predominant view. I like to think there were good men in every generation."

"I'm sure that's true. At least the Israelites recognized goodness in the heroic women. This was getting depressing."

"We're going to get to the exciting part. The part about how Christ was one of the biggest advocates for women. I think some of the views He had were incredible, especially considering the prominent thinking in that time. When you hear the things He did for our benefit, your love will deepen for your greatest advocate, and you'll understand more why some people hated Him so much they killed Him."

"How do you know so much about this?"

"I studied it during the kids' naps. That is, I did before I became Relief Society president."

"Wow. Every day?"

"Almost, except when I took a nap myself. I get really tired when the baby has growth spurts. I've always wanted to be a scriptorian and one-day while I was cleaning the toilet I decided, why not? The house is going to get dirty in a matter of seconds, but what I harvest out of the scriptures will not only benefit me but also my children."

"And others," Betsy said. "I feel strongly that people should follow their talents God gave them. If we don't follow our dream to play the organ or learn to paint, what is the world missing? Think what God wanted to communicate to another person that only that specific person could do?"

"It took me a long time to realize this was true and also the concept that you need to replenish your reservoir before you can benefit others. I heard it explained that it's like when a plane is going to crash. What do the flight attendants tell you to do? Put the oxygen mask on yourself before assisting another person. You have to make sure you are okay before you can effectively help others."

Betsy smiled.

June looked at her and waited for the conversation to continue but it didn't. Betsy just smiled. Finally, June asked, "What?"

"I think we're going to be friends despite ourselves."

June chuckled. "You're right. We have a lot in common and I'd like to be friends. As long as you stay away from Jeff, I can keep my cool."

"I promised I would."

June grinned.

"We're getting side tracked," Betsy said. "You were going to tell me how Christ is an advocate for women. My soul is excited to hear this. Even the promise is telling me that it's true."

"One of the ways we know Christ was an advocate for women is because the New Testament has more references to females than the other canonized scripture. I read a number once. It said out of 1400 or so names mentioned in the Old Testament about 1300 of them were men. Women were mentioned less than ten percent of the time. This isn't the case in the New Testament. You don't have to dig deep to learn about women in Christ's time. More often than not, He would choose to use a woman in his stories of what a model disciple should be like. The apostles were clueless to his message sometimes, being blinded by their first century prejudices."

"I don't remember any verses saying women are of value or anything else that supports what you're saying. Not that I'm disagreeing. I mean I do remember there being a lot of women in the book. That much I agree with. But did Jesus even talk to our sex exclusively? Show us some respect? Honor us?"

June savored the questions before answering. "Betsy, if He would have singled us out as a class, then He would have limited our potential. It's important to understand that Christ wasn't trying to say women are equal to men. He didn't make that difference. Instead, He focused on humankind being righteous or wicked. That is where He made the distinction. Because He was willing to see a woman as an individual with failings and strengths, our sex received fair treatment. Women aren't better than men. We are all human and should be held responsible for our actions. That's truly what it boils down to."

Betsy thought about that insight before concluding, "That's true. He honored us by not limiting us to some set of boundaries. I've always hated those lectures where men are a certain way and women another. I've felt like bursting out of the clone cloak they threw on me."

June nodded. She sucked in her breath as she bent more into a ball.

"I'm sure by now you want more concrete examples than taking my word for it?"

"You read my thought patterns perfectly."

June smiled. "Let me look through the scriptures and I'll give you a textual example." Betsy handed the book to June and she turned pages until she came across the section she was looking for. "Read St. John 4:1-26." The passage was the story about Christ traveling through Samaria. The time of day was around noon and He had grown weary and tired. He approached a Samaritan woman and asked her to draw water for Him. She asked why He would talk to her. Then the Savior proceeded to bear His testimony that He was the Savior. He also prophesied that she was living in an inappropriate relationship with a male. She gasped at his words and believed He was the Savior.

"What's the significance of this story?" Betsy asked, reading the words.

"Some history would help you, I think. The Samaritans and the Israelites were enemies because they disagreed on religious doctrine. Plus, the Samaritans were of mixed decent so the Israelites shunned them. The feud accelerated to such heights the Israelites looked on the Samaritans as pigs. To show how far they took their dislike, anyone traveling from Jerusalem to Galilee would go clear around Sychar, a highly populated Samaritan city. This avoidance would make longer travel time and much inconvenience. Christ, in the story, didn't follow that tradition. It was an extraordinary event that a Jew would talk to a Samaritan and to top it off—"

"He talked to a woman," Betsy added.

"Exactly. Even the Samaritan questioned why He was doing it." June stood up and then sat back on the bed. "Read the verse after where I had you stop."

Betsy cleared her throat and sat up straight on the food storage bucket. "And upon this came his disciples, and marveled that he talked with the woman: yet no man said, What seekest thou? or, Why talkest thou with her?"

Betsy set the *Bible* down next to her and laughed. "If that doesn't beat all. The disciples were shocked and upset that He was talking to a woman but none of them had the courage to openly question Him about it. I call that shocking them into silence."

"It was quite the teaching moment," June said. "Other examples of Christ's affection for women is the fact more women were faithful to Him. For instance, only women stayed at the cross when He was dying. The other disciples fled. Mary, His mother, was the first disciple and she accepted the call graciously and praised God for the salvation that was coming. Elizabeth, mother of John the Baptist, correctly understood the meaning behind her boy leaping in the womb when she saw Mary."

"Whoa! All of this is in the New Testament! I have one more question. Why has the church kept this point of view so obscure?"

"I don't think it has. It hasn't been much of a problem. Joseph Smith and Brigham Young showed great respect for women, and it never became an issue. Of course, come to think of it, every prophet has offered nothing but compliments toward our sex."

"I've felt that way about our bishop. He's always been supportive of me," Betsy said.

June nodded. "Yeah, he's a great guy. Of course, there are those in the church who think we still have a long way to go. I personally feel the church is making progress with this issue."

Betsy slapped the cot. "June, thank you so much for spending the time to share this with me."

"You're welcome," June said, standing. "I need to go check on the kids before they think I have completely deserted them. I've enjoyed our conversation and I hope I have helped you with your questions."

"Yes, you definitely did. I feel much better about the church now. These philosophies ring true to me. I can understand the Apostle Paul was a product of his time and had some things to learn. I've been told a thousand times that the leaders aren't perfect. I believe it. But Christ was said to be perfect, and He was an advocate for fair treatment for everyone. I can full heartily support that."

"I'm glad this helped. I'll look in my books tonight about Paul's statement. I seem to remember reading something that satisfied my feelings toward those verses and hopefully I can share it with you and it'd do the same for you."

"Thank you." Betsy stood and wrapped her arms around June. "You can't possibly know how much this means."

Chapter 17

The ball spun straight for the windshield. Karen cranked the car hard to the right. The back of the vehicle fishtailed and slid on the snowy roads into the embankment.

Sam jogged up to her, eyes wide and face flushed. When Karen had climbed out of the car, he said, "Sorry, Mom."

"Your dad is never going to believe this," she muttered, glancing at the dented bumper. "I just got the car out of the shop."

"I was practicing my hook shot. It was supposed to veer to the left."

"Looks like you need more practice."

Sam shrugged. "Guess so."

"It also seems like you need to find a different car to borrow for your date on Friday. I'll have to take this back to get fixed."

He ran his hand through his short hair. "What am I going to do?"

"Cancel."

His voice took on a squeaky quality. "I can't do that."

"You can have your father chauffeur you."

"Mom!"

"Well, you could. Or you could see if you can work out an arrangement with Betsy."

"Her car's lousy in snow."

"What were you planning for this date anyway?"

Sam's eyes dropped. "Ice blocking."

"What's that?"

"You buy some ice blocks and then find a hill and slide down it."

"So you were planning on going to the mountains?" Karen's voice peeked despite herself.

"That was the plan."

"Why don't you double? Then the other couple could drive. I bet you would have more fun and I'd feel better. You're too young to be single dating."

"Sounds like you have been talking to people at that church of yours."

"Why's that?"

"That's what Tory's mom tells him."

"It's sound advice."

Sam rolled his eyes. "Don't let that church stuff get carried away, Mom. I can handle it."

Karen wrapped her arm around her boy. "I trust you."

She pulled him in for a kiss while his face contorted. He wiped it off. "Yuck."

Karen laughed. "You still act like you did when you were in first grade. Boy did you hate kisses."

"You'd think I could grow out of being kissed."

"Then how would you know that I love you?"

"Mom, I know."

"Well I'm going to make sure you never forget." She stood on her tiptoes to kiss his cold cheek. He pulled away.

"I better call some friends about Friday."

"Yeah, wait a minute, aren't you going to help me get the car to the driveway?"

"It's only dented on the back side. I'm sure you can drive it. But I'll wait here and make sure you can, if that'll make you feel better."

Karen smiled. She loved the protective nature of her son even though from his dress it felt like Satan looming over her. Hopefully it was a harmless phase.

⟡

George arrived home about half an hour after Karen. She watched her husband through the window. He had parked in the garage, but came back out to study her car. His narrow eyebrows crinkled as he examined the dent. He shook his head and smiled faintly.

He's thinking I'm a dippy woman, Karen thought. The fact he had a faint smile meant he was in a good enough mood. She rushed to the front door closet and threw on her coat. She already wore her snow boots. She headed outside and trotted to her husband, grabbing the back of his elbow, smiling. "Hi." She pulled him in for a kiss.

"Wow. This is a change."

She laughed and playfully hit him. "Come on, let's go for a walk."

"You have some explaining to do, huh?"

"Come with me."

"Okay. Let me change my shoes first."

A few minutes later they strolled down the hill glove in glove. Karen whispered everything she'd learned about Betsy's situation. George acted like it was no big deal. But she saw his tension wrinkles relax.

"What do you think?" she asked him.

"I knew everything would be fine. I'm glad we know what happened, though, so maybe you can calm down and get some sleep."

"Don't you realize that right after we prayed all this unfolded?"

"That's technically true but—"

"It's a wonderful example of how God hears and answers us. He listens. Because we prayed, He inspired June to find a way for me to learn that Betsy was okay."

George didn't respond. He kept walking, then he broke the silence with a question. "How did the car get dented?"

"Can't you at least admit that God answered our prayers?"

His jaw tightened.

"Come on, just that."

"Karen, that's enough. I don't appreciate you cramming religion down my throat. I already told you my feelings about it and I will tell you when they change. Until then, I don't want to talk about it."

"That's not fair. Religion is an important aspect of my life and you can't expect me not to talk about that part of me."

"It causes hard feelings and I want there to be peace between us. I don't like constantly arguing with you. We used to rarely fight but since you joined that church, we're butting heads all the time."

"That's not true."

"It is. I don't want to offend you. There have been positive things come out of it also."

"Like what?" Karen asked through a firm lip.

"You haven't been as depressed. You're taking control of your health, and you seem more willing to have faith in things. Those are positive steps."

She nodded, struggling to swallow the lump in her throat. Oh, how she wished her husband would accept God into his life. They could have an eternal marriage, be a forever family and share the same value system. But this seemed an impossible dream, especially when he became so upset at the mere mention of religion.

"To be honest, I didn't take control of my health because of the church, even though they encourage that."

"Then why did you?"

Karen glanced down, wishing he wouldn't look at her. "Because I thought I was going to lose you if I didn't."

George sighed as he brought her in tight. "That's silly. I love you no matter if you get headaches."

She felt the thuds of his heart beating.

✧

Chad was so excited to read the journals that he vetoed dinner. "The journals, Dad. Let's do it now."

Jeff laughed. It was good to see the light back in his son's eyes. He hadn't seen this happiness since before Cindy passed away. Her death had robbed their son of his youth. It seemed so unfair that he was faced with the challenge of having no legs and no mother when other boys worried over zits that splattered across their faces. "I'll get the book. Let's read it in the living room." He knew it'd take about as much time for him to retrieve the journal as it would for Chad to roll his wheelchair into the living room and get it turned around, nestled next to the living room couch. When he came back, Chad was squeezing the chair in.

"Where shall we start?"

"Let the book fall open and whatever is there, we'll read."

Jeff agreed. The book flopped open toward the beginning. Jeff read in a loud clear voice.

Dear Diary,

Today was a marvelous day. I am one of the most blessed people in the world. I got to spend almost the whole day with my son, my little gentleman. He wanted to play catch, so we did. After that, we went grocery shopping. I know that sounds ordinary, but Chad has a way of making it an adventure. We'd run our carts up and down the aisle. I gave him half my list and we raced to see who could fill their orders first. He always wins.

We had planned on watching the World Series as a family tonight, but Jeff never came home. I guess he is busy working on some important deal. I appreciate him working so hard, but I miss him. Some day we will have the time to spend together like I long for.

He could read no more. "What have I done!" His trembling hands covered his face.

"Dad, you're home all the time now, but then you always said you were too busy. Mom would look out the window when she thought I wasn't watching. She really missed you. She'd always say, 'Your father's a good man. He works hard. But he's not perfect. He doesn't know how to have fun. That's why he needs to have you and me in his life so he won't die of over-seriousness.'"

Normally Jeff would've laughed at that expression 'over-seriousness.' He couldn't move, breathe, or think as scissors cut into his conscience.

✧

Betsy had busied herself with studies. Since she was confined to the damp storage room, she might as well make the best of her time. Besides, it kept her mind off the ache in her bones the cold brought. June had gotten her medication for the arthritis. She had spent the late afternoon and evening reading, studying, pondering, then sleeping. She woke, her mind ready to concentrate on the next couple of chapters. She decided to attack the New Testament chronology. Examining the details one author would include and what one wouldn't, showed a lot about the different personalities of the apostles.

The studying progressed well until she read John's rendition of what Christ responded to his mother when Mary said, "They [the guests at the wedding feast] have no wine." Betsy and Christ understood the language of a woman. If you make a statement like that, it means you want help. Betsy had a problem with quite a few men who hadn't caught on to that concept.

It was Jesus' response that disturbed Betsy. "Woman, what have I to do with thee? my hour is not yet come."

It seemed cold and rude. Why would He call His own mother, who had gone through the pains of birth in a lowly cave with the stench of animals, woman? This statement lacked the respect Betsy thought Jesus would pay his mother.

Betsy remembered to check to see if there was a Joseph Smith translation to this phrase even though the translations hadn't helped her much with her questions concerning Apostle Paul. There was a translation and it read. "Woman, what *wilt, thou have me to do for thee?* that will I do; for mine time is not yet come."

She gasped, her hands covering her mouth as she held back emotion. Joseph Smith's version seemed so much clearer. A storm of understanding and joy raged in her heart. Joseph Smith had translated the *Bible* correctly to portray Christ in a more gentle, loving way. The way He was. Perhaps somebody, with his or her own agenda, got their hands on the scrolls of the *Bible* and slanted the material to make it appear that even Christ treated women with disrespect.

June walked into the room, carrying books. "What ya studying now?"

"I'm going over the New Testament as you suggested. I just came to the part where Mary asks Jesus about the wine at the wedding."

"Ah yes, the first public miracle."

Betsy looked at the text. "I haven't gotten to the miracle part yet. I got hung up on the way Jesus spoke to his mother, but when I read the Joseph Smith Translation, it made more sense."

"That story says a lot. From everything I read about the customs of that day the wedding must've surely been for one of Jesus' siblings. The fact that Jesus attended it suggests it is all right to participate in social events."

"I always felt it was," Betsy said. "I feel my soul rejuvenated every time I go to such functions. We shouldn't be recluses. It's against our natures."

"In the verses you were talking about, Mary asked Jesus to use His power. His answer was simple. It wasn't time for that yet. It shows how much Mary knew of her son and His mission."

June slumped on the bed, putting the books next to her. Betsy scooted away to give her more room. "I think it shows a lot about Christ's love. Even though it wasn't time for Him to show His power in miracles publicly yet, He goes ahead and produces 150 gallons of wine."

"Wow," Betsy said. "Thank you again. I love this. I read along, I stumble over something. I ponder it. I think about it, I twist my brain over it and even sometimes gain an insight and then in you walk with incredible truths that set my heart on fire. Thank you, June. Thank you."

She flushed. "The reason I came here is I found a quote that I think will help you with Paul. Joseph Fielding Smith, one of our latter day prophets, commented on it in the book, *Answers to Gospel Questions*. He said, quote: 'Times have changed from what they were in the days of Paul. The counsel that Paul gave in his day were in strict conformity to the law of the times in which he lived.'"

"So the reason he said women couldn't talk in church was because it was the law of the time?"

"That's what a modern day prophet said. You can imagine what kind of trouble the church would've had if it had allowed women to speak. You know a little of the culture, and besides—in the *Articles of Faith* it states that we believe in upholding the law."

"This rings true, too! Oh, June where have you been all my life? You have all the answers."

"No, I don't. You just happen to be asking the same questions I've asked for years."

Betsy smiled. "We're kindred spirits."

♦

Karen and George snuggled in each other's arms as they sat on the couch watching the evening news. The doorbell rang and rang again. The person on the other side of the door kept pressing the button.

George pulled his arm away from Karen. "Who could that be?"

"I don't know," she said. "Maybe we shouldn't answer it. It's late."

"It might have to do with Betsy and the diamond." George went to his closet and reached for his bathrobe. Just then they heard a click of the front doorknob and someone crept in.

The heart beating in Karen's chest threatened to race out of her body. "They came in." She mentally rebuked herself for being too lazy to double check that the front door was locked. She knew she had locked it earlier and felt positive that no one had used it since then. Obviously she was wrong.

A high pitched female voice called out. "OOOwwwhhhoo, anyone home?" The footsteps approached the staircase.

"Who's that?" George's voice had taken on force.

"Lydia."

Karen's shoulders sagged. "What are you doing here at this time of night?" she asked, heading down the stairs.

"I'm sorry to bother you, but I haven't been able to reach Betsy. Do you know where I could find her?"

"We haven't seen her for a couple of days," George said. "We thought maybe she went on some wild adventure with you."

"No. I've been sick from the stroll in the snow the other night and I haven't been anywhere for awhile. So you don't have any idea where Betsy is?"

"None."

"Do you mind if I look in her apartment? Maybe I can find some clues there."

"We have already done that. There's no need for you to worry about anything," George said.

"If you don't mind, I'd like to try anyway."

George took the last step off the staircase and blocked Lydia who had stepped toward it. He got up close to her. "I do mind."

She looked at him and batted her eyes.

"If you don't mind, we're going to bed now."

"Oh," Lydia said. Karen guessed she was trying to think about something, but felt rushed.

George grabbed her elbow and escorted her toward the door. "If we hear anything, we'll be sure to let you know."

She thanked him and left. George locked the door then immediately went to the new alarm system on the wall and punched it on. "I'm glad we decided to do Betsy's rooms too. It seems to be of great interest lately."

Karen nodded. "I wonder why Lydia wanted to go in it."

They went back to watching their program. Karen grew tired and rested her head on her husband's chest and had almost drifted to sleep when she whispered, "Lydia has to be involved. I bet if we follow her she'll lead us to the main people behind this. She's been ill for the past couple of days. Tomorrow she's sure to renew contact."

"Great idea!" George said. "I'll follow her first thing tomorrow."

✧

A noise as loud as a bomb exploding woke Karen with a start. She shot out of bed and clutched her pounding heart. "What is that?" she screamed at her husband over the noise.

"The alarm."

His answer didn't lessen her fear. She raced out of the bedroom screaming, "Who is it? Who is it?"

George rushed to the alarm system and turned it off. "That sucker is loud, isn't it?" he called to Karen.

Clutching her arms to her chest, she asked, "What set it off?"

She heard a couple of beeps as George pressed buttons. "It came from Betsy's apartment."

Karen hustled into her sister-in-law's room, searching the place for a robber or Philippe. She found nothing but the door leading to the outside rocking in the breeze.

"It must've blown in from the wind. I guess we forgot to lock that one too."

Karen looked at the door with uneasiness spreading through her. "No, I don't think so."

George reassured her and they climbed back into bed, this time Karen shivered in her husband's arms. Despite her nerves and active heart, sleep reclaimed her.

Boom. Boom. Boom.

Karen sat up in a start. She looked at her husband who slipped back into his bathrobe. "Good grief, I shouldn't have taken it off."

He turned off the alarm, then headed to the front door and answered the pounding. Karen waited on the stairs, the porta phone close to her chest in case she needed to call the police. She heard talking, then her husband laughed and closed the door.

"What was that?" she called.

"The police. Apparently when we have a false alarm we're supposed to call them and cancel it or they'll send somebody out. They don't like false alarms. They also said they've had a lot of calls about this house lately."

Karen rolled her eyes. "I wonder why." Her hand swung down and the phone hit George's leg. "What is that?" he asked.

"The phone."

"Going to call the police, huh?" He wrapped his arms around her. He whispered in her ear, "Afraid the boogy man was going to get me?" He started tickling her.

She squealed. "Stop that. George, stop that."

He released her and she ran up the stairs with him close behind. He caught her again and the tickling torture began.

✧

Karen awoke with an uneasy feeling fluttering around her stomach, like a restless child forced to sit still on her mother's lap. She knew she should have George follow Lydia. She knew Lydia was somehow mixed up in this whole thing. But sending her husband to the she-wolf unprotected didn't seem wise. Yet, if she mentioned it to George, he'd put on the he-man act and refuse any help and laugh at her efforts. If she were going to be his bodyguard, she'd have to do it cleverly.

She slipped out of her bed to prepare.

◇

Jeff took two days off work. Thursday and Friday. Thursday was the day Cindy had died and he wanted to spend that day with his boy. They needed each other. Friday was his big skiing escape.

Today he let Chad sleep in. Later, they'd get a carrot cake and chocolate ice cream—Cindy's favorite—and they'd have a picnic at her gravestone. That was the best way Jeff could think of to remember her.

◇

Karen held onto George tight. She whispered into his ear, "I don't know about this."

He whispered back, "We already went over it. This is the only thing I can think of doing to stop this whole situation. It's not fair to Betsy; it's not fair to us, and the kids deserve a good night's sleep. We must put an end to this before someone gets hurt."

"But I feel like I'm sending you to a sneaky fox." A tear watered Karen's eyes.

"Don't worry. You know you're the one I love. Karen, I'm faithful to you. I couldn't stand Lydia more than a day."

"How do you stand me?"

"Enough. I'm not going there. Now let me go so we can get this over with."

They kissed again and George patted her on the arm. "This is for the best."

After he left, Karen tugged off her bathrobe, revealing black clothes underneath. Sam would approve. She snatched up the backpack that she had filled earlier and hurried to her car. She waited until George rounded the corner before following him. The plan was he was going to follow Lydia. George had a sense, too, that she was somehow involved especially from the scene late last night. He thought Lydia would lead him to the person in charge of this big operation.

Karen slammed on the brakes in front of June's house. She rang the doorbell. June answered with an apron tied around her protruding stomach and kids climbing around her arms. "Hi, I'm dropping off the craft projects that I promised you." She spoke loud and clear.

"Thank you," June said, reaching for the bag. "Won't you come in?"

"Sorry, I can't. I've got an appointment."

June looked confused but masked it. "All right. Are you still coming over to help with the projects after work?"

"Yes, you'll see me."

Karen hurried into the car and called her work on the cell. "Something's come up and I'll be late. I'll stay later tonight to make up for it."

She rushed to the hotel where she knew Lydia was staying. If Lydia were anything like her normal self, nothing would happen until eleven at the earliest. Karen glanced at the car clock and hoped today would be different. She was too tired to stay late at work.

She drove by the hotel and saw her husband parked several yards away. He had stationed himself in a parking lot across the street and could see all the comings and goings. There was no question that he'd see her. He never noticed anything he didn't want to and he wouldn't be expecting her.

Karen circled the hotel and parked a couple of blocks away from her husband. From there she couldn't see the hotel, but she could see him and she'd know when the whole operation went down.

She flipped on a light rock radio station to help pass the time. It was like the cliché went—always the calmest before the storm.

Chapter 18

George's car crawled out of the parking lot. Karen laughed at her husband's efforts at being sneaky. She snapped a picture of the hotel for reference, in case she was asked questions. He followed Lydia through town and out toward Springville, the Art City.

Karen looked at the old buildings and small farmhouses and wondered what type of people lived in this little community. George suddenly stopped on Main street. Karen kept driving to avoid being obvious and parked a block away from Him. She grabbed her binoculars and peered into the mirror. This continued for about three minutes then George stepped from the car.

He's making his move; Karen thought, and realized the position she had chosen was wrong to witness the action. She waited for the light to turn red so she could flip around. No one would notice her. If someone was watching Lydia, they might spot George, but they wouldn't think that another person would be following him. She drove into the passing lane and stayed there until she was close to the street George had gone down. She watched him turn the corner. Hurriedly, she parked then slapped her husband's baseball cap on, pulling her hair underneath, and slipped on his big snow parka. He never wore it, claiming he was too cool for a coat. She doubted he'd recognize it even if she held it up to him and said it was his.

She rushed behind the buildings where she had last seen her husband. Then she spotted him. Another man much bigger held him in a chokehold. She heard him say, "Lydia, I just wanted to see you alone." Gasp. "That's all. I don't know what...this is about..."

The man pulled tighter on his throat and George gagged. Karen remained frozen, then jumped into action. She pulled out her camera and began clicking, then hid around the corner of the building.

"Let him go," Lydia said. "He knows nothing."

The man flinched. "How can you be sure?"

"He's one of my old boyfriends. We go way back. Don't we?" She dragged her long fingernail across George's chest. When she asked him the question, her big eyes peered into his.

Karen grumbled.

"Let him go, Mark," Lydia said.

"But—"

"Let him go. He can't do anything. I'd like to talk with him a few minutes alone. I'll meet up with you."

"But—"

"Now!" She snapped her fingers.

He kicked the snow and left.

Karen stared at her husband and then at the man that could be the key to everything. He might lead her to the information she needed to free Betsy. She had to make a choice.

✧

After Chad pushed around his uneaten cereal for five minutes, Jeff asked him to come sit by him in the living room.

Chad rolled his wheelchair over to the Lazy-Boy Jeff sat in. "Yeah, Dad?"

"I want you to know that I love you and I'm proud of you. The past year hasn't been easy, but you handled it like a man. You make me and your Father in Heaven proud."

Chad looked at him through teary eyes. "Thanks Dad. I love you too."

Jeff ruffled his son's hair.

"Dad?"

"Yeah?"

"You're doing a good job taking care of me. Don't forget that. You've done the best you can."

✧

George looked into Lydia's face. Somehow the sweetness he'd once seen had faded. Her skin appeared tense, darkened, but her beauty still apparent. The deep brown eyes had always had a way of penetrating his heart. The red full lips, inviting.

"Lydia," he whispered.

"Why are you here, George?"

He stared at her and swallowed. How could he respond? "How do you truly feel about me?"

Her whole face lit up at the question as she tilted her head in his direction. "I knew you'd see things my way." Her voice had taken on a deep sexy tone. She smiled as she neared him.

George's heart immediately pounded as he stood unflinching, wondering what he should do. She drew closer to him and then pressed her head on his chest. The silk of her hair tickled his chin. Sweet smells of strawberry scented hair brushed by him. Memories returned to him of her soft touch. "Lydia."

She gazed into his eyes. "You want me back, don't you? I knew in a matter of time you'd come around. I'm glad you can recognize true class." She turned fast and then grabbed his head, tugging hard, she kissed him.

As their lips touched, George instantly pushed her way. "Lydia, don't."

"What? You can't tell me that you haven't longed to kiss me ever since I came back. I saw your look across the room. The magic still exits."

"I'm married."

"Yeah, to a nut case." She laughed. Wrapping her fingers in his shirt, she said, "Karen doesn't matter. She would never have to know."

George swallowed a lump. "Whether she has problems or is perfect, I love her and I'm going to make her happy."

Lydia tipped her chin toward him. "Yeah, right. Enough of the heroics. I bet you get tired of having to walk on egg shells fearing she'll have another one of her episodes." She circled her finger in the air in a cuckoo gesture. "And now she joined that Mormon church. I don't see you joining. I bet that's another sore spot."

"Lydia, I'm not talking—"

"I'm not saying that Karen is all that bad. Don't get me wrong. She finally got a stylish hair cut, I noticed. I must have had a lot of influence over that. She tries hard, but can't seem to be the real woman you need."

"Lydia!"

"I'm not saying you should leave her. That'd make the whole family thing messy. You'd have to deal with lawyers, divorce agreements, the kids—it's emotional hell. Believe me. I just survived one. But what I'm suggesting is that you come over every so often to get the pressure off, it'd be a-get-away. You'd have someone to listen to you and to be there for you. We could call it a selfish retreat. Something that would offer you joy and peace."

George's shirt began to move from the beating of his heart. Boom. Boom. Boom. Rapid. The sound echoed in his ears.

She smiled up at him, her brown eyes searching.

"Good-bye," he said loud and clear, shoving his hands into his coat pocket and turning to leave.

"You can't go just like that," Lydia shouted.

"Watch me." He refused to look back.

"George, you're giving up everything," she called after him.

◇

Once they had dished up the carrot cake and chocolate ice cream on their plates and had taken a couple of bites, Chad said, "Dad?"

"Yeah."

"Why did Mom like carrot cake with chocolate ice cream?"

Jeff shrugged. "I don't know."

"It tastes awful," Chad said softly.

Jeff laughed. "Did you hear that Cindy? Your boy agrees with me."

Jeff poked his finger in the cake and got a big dab on the tip, then he reached out and smeared the piece on the granite headstone, close to the pile of daisies they had rested against it.

His son smiled.

"Do you want the honors of doing the ice cream?" Jeff asked.

Chad nodded.

◇

The knotting in her stomach increased. She glanced at him then the mystery person in black disappeared out of sight. She could stay and fight off Lydia, but Lydia could always return. She clenched her fingers into a fist and walked away. If she couldn't trust her husband at this point, their relationship wasn't worth a thing.

She jogged behind a barren bush and watched the man get into a car. She grabbed the binoculars stored in her coat pocket. "Got it," Karen whispered. "Betsy, I'm going to save you."

✧

When June came into her room with the box full of stuff for her to do, relief wasn't the right word to explain how Betsy felt. Being locked up with only books to read wore on her sanity. The feeling of living had somehow escaped out of her in the room filled with gray walls and white buckets full of millet and rye. Karen had left a note.

> *Growing bored yet? I bet being locked up like that is worse than physical torture for you. I sent you something to do. Please get busy making bows for the bears and cut out the fabric for the shirts and dresses. I included the patterns. Hang on in there. I'm working on getting you out.*

"Thank you," Betsy said, then bringing the stale piece of paper to her lips, she kissed it. "Karen's an angel. Still doesn't trust me to touch her crafts, but she's an angel. I'm going to make bows that she'll be proud of. Some she'll actually use. I'm going to exercise restraint on my creativity."

She pulled out the royal blue ribbon first and dug for the orange and purple, but caught herself in time. The plain boring choice would be to use white. She sighed. She couldn't be plain and boring the whole time. She'd alternate from making Karen happy to allowing herself fulfillment.

✧

Karen called the detective working on Betsy's case and demanded that he look up the license plate number. The policeman muttered excuses. Karen snapped. "Look, I'm tired of you guys not doing anything. My sister-in-law's life is in danger and I think it's important to find out who's behind it."

"I understand your concern but following someone doesn't give me enough evidence to—"

"He's one of the key players. Can't you guys investigate him?"

"I don't see that this will—"

"Just try this for me, okay?"

"All right. I'll look into it."

Karen hung up.

Later that day, she sat with the list of Relief Society sisters' names. She needed to choose who'd be getting the bear. June had told her to study it out in her mind. She had and had chosen Sister Stanfield, the person Betsy had often referred to as the blue-haired-lady. Her husband was first counselor in the bishopric and Betsy had talked about how cold his wife was the first day she was introduced as an official saint.

Karen tossed her pencil against the table. Why her? She seemed to have it all. A decent house, a husband who took orders, grown kids who came to visit every once in awhile. She knew this because Sister Stanfield would always stand up with a sort of scrawl on her face and say, "This is so and so, my son or my daughter. They're here to visit."

Perhaps she chose the wrong person. She knelt and prayed. When she stood, she felt nothing. Not good, not bad.

✧

June lay on her bed resting. Betsy had been in the basement a little over a week and the church calling was a lot more demanding than she had expected. The phone calls and problems were draining. So was the pregnancy. She was approaching the very tired stage.

The phone rang again and she looked at it, pondering if she should ignore it. Finally her conscience seized her and she answered.

"June, how's your day?" It was her husband.

"Exhausting."

"You need to take it easy."

"Easy for you to say. You're not the Relief Society president and you don't have to be home all day with the kids, not to mention the mouse in the basement."

"Come on." Kendall laughed. "The mouse isn't much trouble. We're glad to keep her out of the cold."

"It's just an added pressure and worry. I stay up nights wondering if I am putting my kids in jeopardy by—"

"Shhh, that's enough. You're doing what is right. The Lord will bless you for it. You're pushing yourself too hard. There's nothing wrong with taking a vacation every now and then. It even says in the *Doctrine and Covenants* that you shouldn't run faster than you have strength."

"You're right. If you don't mind, I'm going to take a nap while this house is quiet."

"Take the phone off the hook."

"I can't do that. What if someone needs me?"

"At least turn the ringer off. You can catch the messages after you wake. The most important thing right now is to take care of yourself."

"Okay."

The doorbell rang.

"June, don't get that."

"I better, then I'm going to bed."

"Promise?"

"Yes."

✧

June saw Karen shuffle her feet and bounce up and down in protest against the cold. Her friend had rung the doorbell three times before June answered."

"I'm sorry I rang the door so many times. It's freezing."

"No problem."

"How's the mouse today?"

"Quiet. I think that package you dropped off did her tons of good."

"Great. I have information that'd probably help you both. Why don't we go downstairs and talk about it?"

June looked toward her bedroom and nodded. "That's fine." She hobbled down the stairs as the baby in her womb dropped a tiny fraction. It was too early for that kind of thing, but her muscles were fatigued.

Betsy pounced on them at the door, reminding June of the way Tigger jumped on top of his frustrated friends. She smiled. "I cut out all the patterns you wanted and have the bows done. Did you bring the bears so we can get started?"

"No. I'll take the stuff you worked on today and finish the bears tonight. I want to make the first delivery tomorrow."

"You already have someone in mind?" June asked.

"Yes, I do. When I prayed, I really didn't get any inspiration, but I'm going to go ahead and give Sister Stanfield the bear. I feel like I should."

"Sounds like your prayers were answered to me," June said.

"You really think so?"

"Yes. The Lord doesn't always strike us with lightning. Sometimes He will, but most of the time it's not so clear. We may never know why we should do things that we feel we should. I bet you'll experience that more than once with this new calling."

Karen smiled. "I almost forgot the news. This morning George and I decided to see if there was anything we could do to help you out, Betsy. We know that being stuck in a storage room has to be really hard for you."

"NO!" Betsy yelled. "I don't want you involved. It's not safe. I've put enough people at risk."

"Well we found that out."

"What!" Betsy shrieked.

"SHHHH!" June and Karen said, glaring at Betsy.

She cupped her hands over her mouth. "Ohhh."

The conversation fell into an immediate halt as footsteps thundered on the floor above. Everyone's neck cranked toward the noise as if they watched fireworks.

The steps seemed too heavy to be her children's, June realized, as a river of fear surged through her senses. The mouse had sprung its trap.

The noise neared, then sounded on the staircase. Betsy and Karen clung to each others sleeves as June stepped toward the door. Suddenly the door swung open in a rapid slap, missing June by centimeters.

"There you are!" Lydia screamed, pointing an accusatory finger at Betsy. Her dark eyes burrowed. "You've put us way behind."

"How'd you get in here?" Karen asked, voice quivering.

Lydia sneered. "I'm no dummy. Where's the ring?"

June crept away from Lydia as Betsy inched toward her.

"I don't have time for that. Where's the ring?"

"Why would you—?" Betsy stammered before Lydia pulled a small gun from her purse.

"The ring. Now! Don't think I won't shoot."

"You're in on this with Philippe!" Betsy gasped, her fingers flying to her mouth.

Lydia laughed hard. "You're so observant."

"Why would he...with...you...I don't—"

Lydia's eyes widened as a wicked smile crossed her face. "Betsy, you were such an easy target. You thought Philippe was in love with you and wanted to marry you again."

Karen gasped.

"What are you talking about? He gave me the ring."

"Because I told him to. The Feds were hot on our trail. You served as the perfect diversion. They had no knowledge of your rote in the plot. You'd keep the ring safe until we returned to get it. Isn't that right, my love?" She turned toward the doorframe and signaled to someone.

Philippe slipped into the room on cue and winked at Betsy. "You had us confused for a while, but we knew if we stuck to Karen we would find you again."

"Is it true you're in this with Lydia?" Betsy asked.

Philippe kissed Lydia on her cheek. "Yes, she's my wife."

Shattering glass turned everyone's attention to the back window where men dressed in black jumped over the windowsill.

"My window," June muttered.

The swat leader pointed a Colt M-16 rifle at Philippe and said, "Put your hands up."

The place turned chaotic as armed FBI agents filled the storage area, military guns pointed at Lydia and Philippe.

Lydia swore.

Karen smiled from her position smashed against the storage containers. "You might have followed me, but I had the FBI track you."

Lydia spat at Karen. Karen leaned farther back.

The police slapped cuffs on the criminals. Once the room emptied, June, Karen, and Betsy looked at each other.

"Unbelievable," Betsy said. "Lydia caught up in all this? Truth seeker, Lydia? How could she be swallowed into so many lies?"

Karen spoke. "Lydia, was never a real truth seeker. She just said those things because she knew that's what you wanted to hear. It was the manipulation tool she used to get closer to you. It was pretty good, too. It worked."

"But I loved her. Why did she betray me like that?"

"It says more about her than anyone," June added. "She's the one who isn't trustworthy. You opened up to her and she used you."

Betsy began to cry. "I want to close down and not let anyone hurt me again. I don't ever want to feel this way again."

"If you don't feel the pain, you'll never feel the joy. That's what life is all about." Karen said.

Betsy sniffed. "I guess you're right. But it still won't be easy to open my heart. I don't know if love is worth it." She looked up at June and watched.

The ladies exchanged awkward glances. Karen broke the silence. "The good news is Betsy doesn't have to stay locked up."

"If this group would've been successful in selling the ring, the police said that there's no telling what they could've done," Karen continued. "Betsy, they said they need to thank you for keeping the ring out of the crooks hands."

Betsy bowed low. "They're most welcome."

Chapter 19

The room was crisp and had a bite to it early Friday morning. Jeff edged down farther into his blanket. A huge hole inside swallowed up his peace. He had spent an hour on his knees, begging the Lord to forgive him and to tell his wife he was sorry.

The dull ache returned. He longed to share his problems with Betsy. She'd comfort him and point out the positive attributes he seemed unable to find for himself. She might even make him laugh. But he couldn't call her, he wouldn't do that to Chad. It tortured his son. It was a sacrifice he'd make for his boy's sake. He had put his own interests first for too long.

The phone rang, forcing him out of bed. "Yeah?"

"Jeff, this is Bishop Hawthorne. Are you ready to hit the slopes?"

"Will be."

"Good. I wanted to make sure everything was a go."

"I heard the snow's perfect."

"An extra foot fell last night."

"Sounds like a powder rush to me. I'll be over to your house right after I drop off Chad."

Jeff hung up the phone. The wake-up call worked like coffee or perhaps even better. He was totally ready for the day. He strolled into the kitchen and took muscle relaxants to help with his lower back pain. The drug used to make him drowsy, but he had taken them too long for that. He set the bottle on the kitchen counter and grabbed Chad's medicine, also putting it on the counter.

When he called Chad to the 'breakfast of champions', or in other words, Wheaties, he noticed puffy eyes, darkening under the eyelids. A heavy silence filled the room.

"Have a good night?" he questioned his son.

"It was all right."

"It doesn't look like it. I can tell you mine wasn't. Something about hearing your mom's voice in the journals resurfaced the pain."

Chad looked at his father. "You had a problem because of that?"

"Yes. Not that I necessarily think it's a bad thing. I've been reading getting over grief books, they say you have to go through the pain before you get any peace in your soul. The big hole inside that feels like an empty crater that won't go away until we feel the loss."

"But it hurts," Chad whispered.

Jeff reached out to his son and hugged him. "I know."

"I want my mom," Jeff thought he heard his son say but wasn't sure.

Chad pulled away. "Dad, can I stay home today? I don't feel good. My head is pounding. And my sores hurt."

"That should be okay. Do you need me to stay home with you?"

"No. I'll be fine."

"Are you sure? I don't think you'll be able to reach me today."

"Yes, I'm sure. I'm just going to get some rest."

"Don't forget to take your medicine." Jeff stood and kissed him on the head.

He ruffled his son's hair. "I'm going to be headin'. Tell you what, I'll wear my pager, so give me a buzz if you need anything."

Chad didn't respond.

He left, putting his ski gear in the car. He'd change over at Bishop Hawthorne's house. It would drive Chad deeper into a depression if it was in his face that he couldn't go skiing. A little guilt about leaving his ill son pricked him, but then he rationalized that he needed a break and Chad didn't seem that bad.

◊

Friday. Valentines Day. Karen smiled. She had the best gift for her man. She bent over and kissed George until he woke up.

He blinked. "What's going on?"

"I want to give you your Valentine's gift."

"Can't it wait?" George asked.

"No, so wake up."

George obeyed, pulling himself into a sitting position.

Karen leaned across the bed, reaching for the card on the coffee table. She handed it to George.

"You woke me up to give me a card?" he asked with a smile.

"Open it."

He did, and in it he read:

> *George,*
>
> *I love you. I love you so much. I love the way you so lovingly take care of me. I love the way you so confidently run a successful business. I love the way you shovel snow. But most importantly, I love you for who you are. You are such a good, kind man and I am so privileged to have you in my life.*
>
> *Please forgive me for trying to force my religion on you. I promise I'll no longer try to change you. I will from this day forth love you for who you are.*
>
> *Happy Valentines.*

George put the card on the mattress and kissed her.

◊

Jeff and Bishop Hawthorne chatted about sports until they arrived at the hill. Then Jeff set to work renting equipment as Bishop Hawthorne bought the lift tickets. The day was overcast with a couple patches of sun breaking through. As Jeff slipped his foot in the ski boot, the feeling of the old days returned. He and his dad used to ski a lot. Every New Year's Day and the day after Christmas their ma would approve. Then he and his dad would sneak away on a couple of hills that were off limits. Jeff had liked the way his dad made time for him. Was he doing the same for his son?

"This is going to be a great day," he said, approaching the bishop.

The bishop smiled. "I'm glad we got you out of that office. You know Jeff, you really have to learn to take it easy. You can't take the pressures of the whole world. It's not good."

"Right now I'm not taking on the pressures of the world. I'm just committed to beat you down the hill." He was off, racing to the lift, his colleague gaining on him.

✧

Chad pulled himself into his bed. The drugs he had taken caused him to be extra tired. That was all right. He wanted to get away. Sleep was a nice thing. He pulled the blankets up and then rolled onto his right side to look at the picture on his nightstand. He and his mom had their heads touching as they looked into the camera. Big smiles on their faces. It had been at one of his scout meetings. She'd never missed being there. Always called Grandma and told her how her son had earned this and that. She had talked about him getting his eagle and now and now...he didn't know if that would ever happen. All he wanted was sleep. Sleep forever.

✧

Half an hour after Karen returned from lunch, the front receptionist asked her to come into her office. Karen typed in a few words before leaving. On the way to the front, she noticed piles of roses lining the wall.

"Chris, where did all these roses come from?"

"You tell me. They arrived along with this card for you and this small box also."

Karen opened the envelope with a smile. She laughed. "I can't believe this," she muttered.

The card read:

> *Here's a hundred roses to*
> *match the hundred reasons*
> *I love you.*
>
> *George*
>
> P.S. The diamond bracelet is a mere
> token of how very precious our relation-
> ship is to me.

Karen smiled as her face grew red. She opened the small box. Her hands shook as Chris helped her put on the golden bracelet studded with diamonds.

✧

Chad woke about three in the afternoon, overcome with pain in his right hip. He reached down to pull the sheets away from the open sore. He looked on his hip and saw brownish-black goop oozing out. He rolled onto his back to relieve the pressure, but that took all the energy he had. His head felt heavy and his stomach growled. After spending fifteen minutes, thinking about getting himself more drugs, his body granted mercy and let him sleep.

♦

Jeff skied up to Bishop Hawthorne, spraying snow over him. He laughed as the bishop wiped the flakes away. "That was great. Oh, it's been such a long time since I've been skiing. I need to come here more often."

"Let's do it every month."

"Deal." They scooted closer to the chair lift. "This will have to be the last run. I need to get back to my son. He wasn't feeling very well this morning and he didn't answer the phone when I called at lunch."

"You better watch out then. The last run is where I put my all into it. You're going to be eating my snow dust."

"We'll have to see about that."

Jeff jumped off the lift before his skis hit the chair mound. Time to prove that he still had what it took. As he rounded the corner, he tucked his poles up under his arm and bent his knees picking up speed. He felt the bishop right behind him. This race would be down to the last second. The sun had started to sink and the slushy snow turned to ice, but if you flew over it, it didn't matter.

His eyes and skin burned as wind whipped against him. His coat blew like a flag in a windy rainstorm, flapping loud and rapid. He bent lower when he hit the unseen jump. He panicked as he took air and allowed his skis to cross. When he came down, he hit a steep part of the hill, tripped and fell forward, landing on a pile of rocks. His lungs throbbed. It took several seconds before he regained his breathing.

Bishop Hawthorne skied up to him, "Jeff, are you okay?"

"My ribs...huuurrt. I think I bruised them."

The bishop offered to get Ski Patrol, but Jeff refused. "I'm fine. Let's go home."

♦

When Jeff stumbled in the front door and heard the silence of the room, he knew something more was wrong than his bruised ribs. He dashed into Chad's dark room and found the boy hot with fever and too weak to move. He called an ambulance as his stomach grew weak. As he waited, brushing the hair off his boy's forehead, he chewed himself out. How could he have left when his boy needed him home?

He rushed in the other room to alleviate the unsettled feeling that penetrated his stomach. This was his fault. The ambulance finally arrived. He hurried to the men who were coming to the door. "My boy. My boy. This way."

They checked his vital signs, muttering medical terms to each other, and then hurried him into the ambulance. Jeff climbed in too. How could he have done this?

At the hospital, he was left with his guilt and the phone to pass the time as the doctor examined Chad. He had called June and she said she was on her way. He looked down at his hands that trembled in his lap and closed his eyes. He couldn't lose his son too. That would be too much.

$\diamond$

Betsy drove as June knotted her hands. "I can't believe this. God wouldn't take his son. Would He? He couldn't take him."

"Let's not worry about that now," Betsy suggested.

June nodded, her chin quivering as she watched the road. "I want to be there and see for myself that he's all right. Please, oh, please."

Betsy echoed her prayer. Chad had always been her favorite pupil. He had a talent for keeping her on her toes. The boy was a great example of what a soul could accomplish even amidst a lot of trials. He had even managed to maintain his popularity. That was truly rare because children loved to pick on people who were different from themselves.

At last the car rolled up to the hospital, and they hurried into the emergency waiting room. Betsy hadn't given one thought to seeing Jeff again until she saw his dejected gray face and tears brimming. When he stood, she threw her arms around him. He trembled underneath her touch. She grabbed hold of his hand and didn't let go. She didn't care if June was there, Jeff needed her. Her grip still remained on Jeff when the doctor came out and informed the group that one of Chad's bedsores had turned infectious. It could be life threatening. When the news hit Jeff, he held onto Betsy so tight she thought all the blood had drained out of her hand.

She threw her arms around the stunned man. He stood straight as though not noticing her. "Can we see him?"

The doctor nodded. "He needs sleep, so make it short."

The group slipped into the hospital room. Chad lay perfectly still.

Jeff raced to his son. Chad's eyelids fluttered before opening. "Dad," he whispered.

"I'm sorry! This was all my fault."

Chad struggled to talk. "No!" he forced out. "You were the best Dad. I love you."

"Chad, don't leave me!"

"I miss Mom."

"I know you do, and some day you'll be with her again. But now you need to live. Hang in there, buddy." Jeff patted his son's hand as he spoke. "I want you to grow-up, to marry a beautiful girl who loves you like your mom loves me. I want you to watch your babies come into the world and someday see your grandchildren and great grandchildren."

Chad nodded as he fell asleep.

$\diamond$

June's shoulders had more knots in them then a kid's old shoelace. She stretched slowly, feeling the tension. Taking a deep breath, she unlocked Jeff's front door. She had promised her brother-in-law that she'd pick up some clothes, a razor, and a toothbrush. Jeff wanted to spend every moment with his son in case...

June fought tears again. Chad couldn't die. The door slammed shut behind her. She turned on the hall light to see Jeff's ski equipment strewn across the hallway. The objects seemed to scream of Jeff's fears and of her sister's death.

Swallowing the gagging lump in her throat, June made her way through the obstacle course only to be greeted by Chad's empty wheelchair and unmade bed. "Oh, my," June whispered.

She raced up the stairs and opened the top drawer of the chest to find an array of Cindy's jewelry. "He never emptied her drawers," she gasped as her body began to tremble.

She needed to get out of here. She tugged open drawer after drawer until she found a pile of jeans. She threw the top two pairs on the bed then opened the closet. A slight relief dashed through her when she saw she had picked his side and not Cindy's. It took only moments to collect the other toiletries. Her shoes clicked down the staircase like a trotting horse.

Once in the car, she realized she hadn't picked-up a suitcase. She'd find one at her house, she decided, pressing on the gas. She couldn't go back.

◊

Betsy spent the night on her knees praying. "Please, Father. Please don't do this to Jeff. Please. He's lost so much."

◊

Jeff listened to the soft breathing and the loud groans through the night. The doctors were giving Chad a blood transfusion. They seemed hopeful that Chad would pull through.

Bishop Hawthorne had been by to give a priesthood blessing. In it he said, Heavenly Father's will would be done. And the spirit would take away the fear.

Jeff hung onto the words.

◊

By nine in the morning, both Betsy and June had arrived.

"Here's a chocolate donut," Betsy said as a greeting. "You'll be needing your strength."

Jeff took it automatically. His hair was a tousled mess, and heavy black lines ran down his face.

"How's...?" Betsy asked, faintly nodding toward the silent bed.

"He slept all night." His voice sounded like he suffered an acute case of laryngitis.

Betsy nodded and leaned against the sink on the far wall.

The room continued in silence for the next thirty minutes until June gasped, "His eyes are opening."

Everyone gathered around the bed to see that they were in fact open, although a bit droopy.

Chad spoke. "Mom!" His eyes looked far off. His face had brightened to a sharp glow. "Mom! I love you." He smiled off to where ever he looked and nodded. "She says she loves you, Dad. Do whatever it takes to be happy. She will understand. She just wants you happy." Chad closed his eyes.

Jeff leaned back into the chair.

The rest of the day loved ones gathered around his bed listening to Chad's faint groans. Prayers were offered.

Finally the nurse asked everyone to leave.

✧

Jeff stayed awake most of the next night, listening. "Please," he choked as he stroked his son's hair. "Please not my son. Please don't take him too. How can I go on?"

✧

The next morning went much the same. In the early afternoon Chad's breathing grew fainter. Everyone stared at the bed. Several minutes ticked. His lips paled as he struggled to breathe. Everyone waited for another hoarse gasp. Instead, silence penetrated the room until Betsy flung herself over the skeletal body. She wailed, "No! Not him. Not now."

The others stared in shocked disbelief. Betsy sobbed and the nurses hustled into the room in time to catch Jeff, who passed out.

✧

June wrapped her arms around Jeff the day after the funeral. He sobbed uncontrollably.

She bit her lip and stood, going into the kitchen. She popped a few pills in her hand and filled a glass with water, then shuffled back into the living room. "Take these."

Jeff did without protest. After he swallowed, he broke into another grieving fit. "He died...He died." He rocked in violent jerks. "I can't go on. I can't."

"Shhh," June said.

"I can't go on," Jeff choked.

"Yes, you can," June whispered, wondering how he could.

The sedative put him to sleep in thirty minutes. She pulled a blanket over him and then prayed at the foot of his couch.

She awoke in the dark, early hours, head pounding. She slipped into the kitchen to grab an aspirin. Chad's last words came back to her. He had said Cindy wanted Jeff to do whatever it took to be happy. Did that mean letting Betsy... No, it couldn't. But what if that was the only way Jeff could find the courage to go on?

✧

The next few days were a jumbled up mess for June. She was filled with grief and obsessive worry for Jeff. The shock had been too much for him and the doctors had ordered sedatives, but that couldn't last forever. How could he go on without either his wife or son? She knew what she had to do. She hoped she could find the strength.

She pulled up to the Ashforth's house and went to the door to ask for Betsy. Sam nodded, giving her an awkward glance as though he didn't know what to say.

It took Betsy five minutes to come downstairs. Her hair had an unwashed ratty look, her eyes, huge apple puffs, and she covered her nose with a tissue. She took one look at June and burst into tears. "How could God take him?" she asked between sobs.

June pulled Betsy into a hug. "He knew you loved him," June said at last.

"I did. Oh I did." She broke into tears again. "Now what is to be done? Chad is finally happy. He's with his mom again, but what will Jeff do?"

"That's what I came to talk to you about."

"What do you mean?" Betsy asked.

"I mean I was wrong to ask you to stay away from Jeff. The Lord was bringing you into his life to help when this tragedy happened. I interfered because of my own selfish feelings."

"I understand how—" Betsy protested.

June held out her hand. "That's enough. I was wrong. I can admit that. I believe that was Cindy communicating through Chad that she wants you two together."

"I wouldn't go as far as to say—"

"You heard what Cindy said through Chad. I heard him and it's okay. You two belong together. I was pulling you apart. Jeff's guilt and Chad were pulling you two apart."

"No. I can't let you take all the blame. I came between us too. Truthfully, I don't know if we were meant to be together. We haven't had enough time."

"What's holding you back?"

Betsy straightened and blinked. "What?"

"Karen told me that ever since your second divorce you've been very aloof when it comes to relationships."

"Do you blame me? Two divorces are quite enough for one person. Two more than one should have to live through."

"But you can't be happy, I mean really happy, if you don't risk."

"You don't have to make the same dumb mistakes either. And are you saying that I can't find joy without a man?"

"No, I'm not saying that. I'm suggesting that you have the chance to be with someone who could be your soul mate. You have the chance to have that extra splash of love and you want to give it away because you're afraid to love again? Afraid to get hurt? How can you live with yourself?"

"I don't understand this, June. You didn't want me near your brother-in-law. You wanted him to be true to your sister."

"I know. But he's so devastated. I don't know how he's going to make it without your loving support. What Chad said just before...it was then I knew that my sister's wish wasn't mine. The Lord must have some sort of system that I don't understand. I do know Him well enough to know that He loves us and if we make it to heaven we will be happy. We can't make it alone and I'd appreciate it if you'd help my brother-in-law. I do have to agree with Jeff, you remind me a lot of Cindy. That's why I have faith you two will be perfect for each other. "He needs your passion, your enthusiasm, and you need his stability and good heart."

Betsy smiled. "I do find those qualities annoying at times."

June laughed. "So did my sister, but he kept her balanced like he'll do for you."

"All right, you've convinced me. I'll go to him. I wanted to anyway, but I promised you... The poor man must be in so much pain, he can hardly stand it. I'd love to help him in any way I can."

✧

Death always has a way of teaching, Karen thought, and she wasn't going to let that sweet little boy die for nothing. His passing felt like a slap in her face. "You could die any time," it yelled. "Anyone can. Tomorrow, watch out, I might take you or George or Mikey or Sam."

Karen rocked in her chair. She had to make the most of what she had because one never knew—it sounded cliché, but it was true. For Chad's sake, so his death wouldn't be in vain, she'd learn the lesson. Instead of growing irritated at her husband for not wearing his coat while shoveling the snow, she'd enjoy it. Surely when he was gone, she'd miss it. The same philosophy she'd apply to her children and friends.

Mikey. She was losing her to a pretend world. It was time to stop denying it and take her to a psychologist and see how serious the situation was before it grew too late.

She sighed. She couldn't save Chad, but she'd honor his memory by letting his life and death change her for positive. Bring her closer to Heavenly Father.

Several days after Chad's passing, she worked on the peach teddy bear like a woman possessed. Somehow she knew the bear had to be delivered today. She looked over the pouty face and the peach ribbon she glued around the body. The bear was quickly being clothed in a twenties low swing dress with accentuating long pearls. Karen laughed at it. It was cute. Really cute. But what was she doing taking it to Sister Stanfield? It looked nothing like that controlling old woman who dripped with bitterness.

Once she finished the outfit, she glanced at the clock. Eight-thirty in the evening. If she hurried, she probably wouldn't be too late. She knelt and prayed again. "Heavenly Father, I feel dumb bringing this to Sister Stanfield. Please let me be doing the right thing."

Once she climbed out of her kneeling position, she headed for Sister Stanfield's house, a house with dark blue side paneling. The hands on the clock were inching closer and closer to nine. Maybe she should come tomorrow at a better hour. What would one day matter?

Her stomach knotted and she sighed. Might as well look stupid and intrusive. She offered another silent prayer and walked carefully up the icy walkway. The doorbell echoed through the house. She shuffled her feet. Nothing. She rang the bell again. She listened for noise. She held her breath and counted to ten and was about to leave when the door opened.

"Yes?" Sister Stanfield asked, her face screwed up like an extra dry raisin.

"Sister Stanfield, I brought this bear over for you." She held it out in her arms.

"What did you say, child?"

"I brought over a stuffed bear for you."

"Why would you do that?" She puckered her lips.

"I don't know. I just thought maybe—"

Sister Stanfield flipped on the outside light and Karen held up the bear.

A loud helpless gasp flew from of the old lady's lips. "Oh, my goodness," she said, her hands reaching out, touching the fabric carefully, fingers trembling. "Come in," she said, eyes tearing up. "Come in."

Karen stepped into the hallway where stacks of newspapers lined the front entry and so did countless breakable knick-knacks. The walls were covered with wildflowers.

She motioned her into the living room and gathered up newspapers and magazines to make a spot for Karen to sit.

"I'll be just a second. Let me get you a cup of hot chocolate."

Karen began to protest, to tell her she couldn't eat sugar but decided against it. As dishes clanged in the kitchen, she sat observing the inner working of this person she knew so little about.

Five minutes passed before a hot cup with steam floating off the top was done. Sister Stanfield handed the cup to Karen. She set it on the coffee table.

"How did you know?" Sister Stanfield questioned.

"Know what?"

"You got the date right. The color. The style. How did you know?"

Karen blinked. "I'm sorry, but I don't understand."

"Thirty years ago my daughter died in a train wreck. Her beau thought he could outrun the train in his car. He was with it enough for him to escape, but my Molly froze. She didn't realize..."

Sister Stanfield started to cry. "I'm sorry, my child. After all these years it still feels the same as it did when the police knocked on the door. All the same."

"Tonight was the night she died. I was just praying to Heavenly Father, a bit angry as to why He took my joy away from me. I was asking Him if He hated me. Then the doorbell rang. This was His way of answering my prayers." She broke into tears again. "Molly's favorite color was peach. She would collect all kinds of stuffed animals, but she liked bears best. My Molly must've helped you pick the colors. Thank you."

✧

When Karen arrived home, she ran to George. She couldn't wait to tell him about Sister Stanfied. Her new calling promised to be full of these types of experiences. Her life had taken a complete turn since she joined the church. She called out to her husband, "The most marvelous thing happened to me. It was a miracle."

"I thought you stopped trying to convert me."

"Oh, I have, but I had the most wonderful experience. I have to tell you. I don't expect you to join the church after hearing it. I think I learned my lesson on that one. I just want you to listen."

"Listen? I think I can handle that."

Karen smiled. "Good." The feeling of overwhelming love for him flooded through her. She had searched for a way they could make their relationship work and the answer was there all the time. She needed to love him the way he was. If he wanted to change great, but she would take him as is. That wasn't a problem because she had married a good man and she knew deep in her heart that his goodness would lead him to accept the truth. She'd just have to wait for his time. Until then, she was very lucky to have him at all.

✧

Betsy decided to toss out all the formalities of society and rushed straight into Jeff's house. "Jeff, Jeff?" she called.

Seconds later he staggered into the room. "Betsy?" he questioned. His hair was unwashed, his face sagged with weariness, and his clothes smelled.

He had a far off look. "The doctor called. It appears Chad took my muscle relaxant medication instead of his. That's why he was so tired. He...he slept on his bedsore all day. The bedsore infection killed him."

His skin had turned ghastly white. "I killed my son."

"Nonsense!" Betsy yelled. "You can't blame this on yourself. God wanted him home. The medicine just made the journey easier."

"That's what the doctor said." Jeff avoided eye contact.

"The doctor talked about God?"

"No, he said Chad probably would've died anyway."

"See."

"But if only I would've taken him to the doctor—"

Betsy held up her finger. "No!" she said loudly, "I won't let you take the 'if only' trip. They are too dangerous and will destroy your soul! You loved your son and he knew that. He's happy now. All he wanted was to be with his mom. Now he has his wish. And knowing Chad, he's telling Cindy you are sorry for everything you did wrong and she's crying, forgiving you. They're up there anxiously awaiting your return, but you have to prove yourself. You still have more distance to travel in this life. That's why I am here."

"Why?" he asked, blinking.

"I've come for you," she said, straightening her sleeve.

"What do you mean?"

"What I mean is you need me and so here I am. You better get used to it because I'm not planning on going anywhere. You've had enough sadness in your life and I'm here to supply the joy. I'm going to help you with the pain but I'm also going to make you laugh."

"Betsy, I'm sorry, but I can't handle this right now."

"Baloney. First off, look at this house. How are you ever going to feel well if you live in a pigsty? You're going to get sick and that's the last thing you need."

"It's fine—"

"Nonsense. The Lord still has things for you to do on this Earth and I'm going to see that you accomplish them. Now roll up your sleeves and get to work."

"I don't know."

"I thought I said that was enough. Now move this couch for me. I need you to pick up the big items so I can vacuum."

A few hours later Betsy placed her approval stamp on the house. "Now this feels much better."

He nodded. "You're right."

"Jeff, I'm here for you. You don't have to face this life alone and I won't let you. You have so much to give."

He looked at her long and hard. "Thank you. You've given me back a little hope. I didn't know how I could go on. I haven't really seen much reason."

"I know." Betsy patted his knee. "That's why you're going to marry me and then we're going to go on tons of missions."

"What?"

"Really. The change will do you wonders. I've found the only way to deal with our problems is through service. Your problems are so big, in order to get you through all of them, it will be a twenty-four-hour job for God. He and I are teaming up to get you through this."

Jeff pondered for a long while, then grabbed Betsy's shoulders, pulling her closer he whispered, "Cindy always said love is more precious than diamonds." He bent and kissed her hard.

Betsy's head swam. She thought about pushing him away, then decided that she should stop her search for love because she had found it right here in Jeff's arms.

Biography

Lisa J. Peck loves to write and thinks the perfect way to die would be sitting at her computer putting the finishing touches on her last words. The only thing she likes better than writing is being a wife and a mother to her six kids. Her oldest child is eight, and no, there are no twins. She loves exploring the big world with them.

She graduated from Brigham Young University in English. She is the author of *Dangerous Memories, Life with the Kids, Lovin' for a Lifetime,* and the movie, *Only Once.* She is also one of the authors for *The Choose the Right Series.*

Lisa welcomes comments and can be reached at 2241 Larsen Parkway, Provo, UT 84606, or send email at *Pup7777@aol.com.*